I0594520

FINDING HOPE'S RIDGE

SILVER MCKENZIE

HOPE'S RIDGE BOOK #1

CONTENTS

Once you choose hope, anything is possible.

CHRISTOPHER REEVE

1

*A*sha drew in a lungful of early morning mountain air as she walked the half mile from her two-bedroom cottage to her pride and joy, *Irresistables*. Her stomach fluttered as her thoughts raced ahead. As much as she loved the small food truck she ran her business from, on Wednesday, she'd be signing the lease on new premises. Irresistables would continue in name but as a cafe in a prime location on the corner of Main Street and Lake Drive with uninterrupted views of the lake.

As she rounded the corner of Lake Drive, the rising sun shone a light on the rippling waters of Lake Hopeful. A smile formed on her lips as a wisp of vapor rose from the town's main attraction. Its treelined shores and sandy beaches made it the perfect summer vacation destination, which thousands of people attested to each year. This year Asha wouldn't be running out of coffee and cakes as the line wound its way from the food truck to the lake; this year, people would be sitting at chairs and tables, being waited on and hopefully loving her expanded menu and new premises.

Asha rubbed her hands together, her gloves not quite cutting out the morning chill, and ran through her to-do list in her head. She'd prepared her muffin mixes the day before, so they were ready to bake. She'd received a new order of coffee yesterday, and the coffee machine was ready to switch on and start brewing. She glanced at her watch. It was a little after six, which, based on her customers' usual Saturday routine, gave her an hour before she needed to be ready to serve.

Asha reached the food truck, her earlier excitement over her impending move fading as she admired the colorful van. She realized she would miss it. Jenna, her best friend, had done a fantastic job with the signage and painting, and the four tables out the front were attractive and inviting. *Four tables*. She'd have thirty tables to fill soon.

She unlocked the door and, humming to herself, began her morning preparations. She knew there were people in town, including her parents, who thought she should do more with her life than serve coffee and cake from a food truck, but at twenty-eight, she was happy and content. She interacted with many of the townsfolk daily, and she constantly experimented with the muffins and brownies she made available to her customers. Her dream had been to expand the business and the menu, and that was precisely what she'd be doing the minute she signed the lease on Wednesday.

"Ash?"

Asha's thoughts were interrupted as she deposited a tray of raspberry and white chocolate muffins into the oven. Not expecting anyone this early, she was yet to open the service window. She unlatched it and grinned as it rolled upwards, and she locked eyes with her sister.

"You're early. Taking the first class?"

Steph nodded. "Bohdi's asked me to open the studio and take the hot yoga. I was hoping to grab a cup of coffee before I go."

Asha raised an eyebrow. "Coffee? I thought that was against all your yogi ideals. That you had to," she did her best to imitate Steph's voice, "stay clean and cleansed on the inside and out."

Steph shrugged. "I've hardly slept, and I need something if I'm to get through the morning." She handed Asha a mug she'd brought from home.

"At least you're looking after the environment, even if you're not looking after yourself."

Steph laughed. "Says the town's dealer. Coffee is an addictive substance, you know."

Asha grinned as she used a tamper to pack the portafilter full of the beans she'd ground earlier. "How come you couldn't sleep?"

Her sister's face clouded over. "The nightmares have returned."

Asha stopped what she was doing and stared at Steph. "Since when?"

"A few days. Don't worry; it happens from time to time. I think anytime I'm stressed, my subconscious takes me back there."

"Okay, so what are you stressed about? If we can work that out, then the nightmares might go away."

"Possibly. It's Mary. She was offered a job in San Francisco. She accepted it yesterday and is moving on Monday."

"Monday? But surely she has to give you more notice than that?"

Steph nodded. "She does, and she'll pay her share of the rent until the end of the month unless I can get someone in earlier."

"That's not so bad then."

"Ash, it took me four months to find Mary. I was eating

3

soup for two meals a day to make ends meet. I can't afford the rent on my own. You know that."

"You can always move in with me. There's room for both of us in the cottage."

Steph shook her head. "No, it's your space. I love you to bits, but I don't want to share with you. We both like our independence and living together changes our dynamic."

"Well, it's an option if you decide you can't afford to stay in your house, okay."

"Thanks."

Asha continued making Steph's coffee. "But in the meantime, with the nightmares, can you make an appointment with Dan?"

"Probably, but I want to see if I can deal with it myself this time. I should be able to move on."

Asha gave her sister a sympathetic smile. "You suffered a trauma, Steph. Dealing with it will take time, and asking for help is completely normal. Speaking to a psychologist isn't a sign of weakness."

"I know, but I don't want to be offered medication either. I'll be fine. Now, when do you sign the lease on the cafe?"

Asha knew Steph well enough to know that the topic was closed. She'd make sure she checked in on her over the next few days. "Wednesday. Are you free for a drink afterward? I'll need to celebrate."

"Should be. Jenna might be free too."

Asha looked up as she finished pouring the coffee into Steph's cup. "Jenna? She's in town?"

"Will be. I bumped into her mom yesterday."

Asha frowned as she finished making Steph's coffee. It was unusual for Jenna to come back to town without contacting her first. They usually spoke at least once a week and exchanged messages daily. But Asha had been so caught up in her dealings with the bank and other suppliers for Irresistables' new premises she realized it had been close to two weeks since they'd spoken. Her phone pinged with a message as she passed the coffee through the window to Steph. She smiled as she glanced at the screen.

Arriving midmorning. Make sure you have your party shoes ready for tonight. Time to celebrate Irresistables' big move. Love u, can't wait to see u. xxx

"Jenna?"

Asha nodded. "Sounds like we're going out tonight. Come with us if you're free."

Steph shook her head. "No, tonight I plan to meditate, then have a long hot bath before hopefully having a proper night's sleep. Now, I'd better run. Tell Jenna I said hi, and if she's still here, I'll see her on Wednesday for that celebratory drink."

Asha's smile faded as she watched Steph place her coffee in the cup holder she'd designed especially for her bike, before pedaling in the direction of Heat Wave, her workplace. It was close to a year since the accident, yet Steph's nightmares continued to plague her. She said yoga calmed her mind and helped her find peace with what happened, but the fact she was still using her bike as transport suggested she had not healed.

Zane was aware of his twin stealing glances at him as he stared out of the passenger window, oblivious to the scenery that zipped past as the white Jeep wound its way around the narrow mountain road, signaling they were halfway to Hope's Ridge. He didn't want to deal with any more of Jenna's questions, but he knew that was asking far too much of his outspoken sister.

"You haven't said anything for close to an hour," Jenna said.

"So?"

"So, talk to me. Tell me something."

Zane sighed and turned to look at her. He knew Jenna well enough to know she wasn't asking him to talk about just anything. "I think I've told you everything there is to know already. It's why I'm in the car with you now, remember? It's why a truck will be turning up next week with all my belongings, proving what Dad said all along, that I'd never make it in the city, that *they'd eat me alive*."

"You don't believe that, do you?"

Zane shrugged. "It's pretty much the truth. I couldn't handle the pace, and now I'm returning home with my tail between my legs."

"That's so not true," Jenna objected.

But it was. The last three months had unraveled Zane. Sure, he'd survived ten years in the city, not giving his father's words much thought, but now they were as clear in his head as the day they'd been said. *You don't have the strength of character, son. You should stay here, become involved in the business. One day it'll be yours to take over.*

Zane had pushed his father's lack of confidence in him aside and pursued his dream. He'd loved his job, was in a relationship with a girl he'd seriously thought was *the one*, and spent plenty of time with friends. Life had changed overnight, and he wasn't sure he'd ever fully recover. He'd never work in finance or banking again. He hoped that at some stage, he'd be able to close his eyes and relax, rather than close his eyes and re-live that day.

"How about we talk about you instead of me." Zane grinned. "After all, I'm pretty sure that's your favorite topic."

Jenna raised an eyebrow. "Should I be offended?"

"Only if you choose to be. Distract me. Tell me about this new guy you've been seeing."

Zane only half listened as Jenna launched into a detailed account of Brad, a realtor she'd met two weeks earlier and had decided she was in love with. He'd give it to her, his sister lived life with a passion and never did anything by halves. His phone pinged with a text as Jenna continued her monologue. He glanced at the screen.

Heard you'll be back in town this weekend. Let's grab a beer. I have a business opportunity you might be interested in. Will be good to see you. Matt.

"How would Matt Law know I'll be back in town?" Zane looked at Jenna. He'd made her swear not to tell anyone. He wanted to slip back into Hope's Ridge, ideally unnoticed, and surface when he was ready.

"Not from me," Jenna said. "I haven't told anyone what you're doing. Probably Mom or Dad. They're pretty excited about you returning. Dad, in particular."

Zane groaned. "I know. He'll hassle me to work at the mill. I've already told him it's not part of my plan, but he's assured me he can change my mind. That it's my inheritance, so I should learn the business now."

"What did Matt want?"

"A drink. Said he had a business opportunity I might be interested in."

"Mm."

"What's the mm, for?"

"Nothing, but be a bit wary. He has a reputation for being arrogant and out for himself."

Zane laughed. "He's always been arrogant, but underneath he's a good guy. Well, he was in high school. He gets his business mind and entrepreneurial spirit from his dad. Do you remember him?"

"Everyone remembers Walt Law," Jenna said. "I'd hardly

forget all of those protests we had to attend every time Walt decided the town needed modernizing and tried to build something new. I'm not surprised he moved out of Hope's Ridge. He rarely got any of his projects through."

"It's interesting isn't it," Zane said. "The things he did achieve have made a huge difference to the town. Made it more attractive to visitors, which it needs. The mill's one big employer, but it does need tourism to be sustainable. Think of how tired the main street was before Walt coordinated the upgrade of the sidewalks and roads and then convinced the shop owners to spend money on their store frontage, signage, and fit outs. At the time, he modernized the place."

"That was fifteen years ago," Jenna said. "Last time I was here, I thought that the whole town looked pretty tired. It probably needs another overhaul to make it modern and appealing."

Zane laughed. "Without Walt around, I can't see that happening."

"Will you catch up with Matt?"

Zane hesitated for a moment. He had planned to slip back into Hope's Ridge, fish, run and keep to himself as best he could. A drink with Matt, no doubt at Traders, would immediately let everyone know he was back in town. But then again, if Matt knew he was coming then, many others would too. The town grapevine worked quickly. And really, what did it matter anyway? He didn't have to talk about what had happened in the city. It was no one's business but his. "I guess it wouldn't hurt. Be interesting to see what his business idea is. He knows I work, I mean worked, in finance, so if it's anything to do with that, then I won't be interested."

Jenna laughed as the Jeep sped past the fading *Welcome to Hope's Ridge* sign. "A finance position in Hope's Ridge? I doubt it. Now," she turned toward the lake. "Let's grab a coffee and some fresh air before we see the folks. I'm not sure I can face them without either."

"Sounds good." Zane smiled. He and Jenna were complete opposites on most things, but when it came to their parents, they were definitely on the same page. As kindhearted as their parents were, they were also hard work.

Asha saw the white Jeep pull into a parking space seconds before Jenna honked to get her attention. She smiled and waved as her friend climbed out of the driver's seat. It was great to see her. While they usually made their plans ahead of time, this surprise visit was welcome. She'd hoped to celebrate Irresistables' new beginnings, and to be able to do that with Jenna would be perfect.

Asha pushed open the door of the food truck and stepped down so that she could hug Jenna. She strode toward her friend, stopping abruptly as the passenger door of Jenna's car opened. The smile slipped from her face. What was *he* doing here? She had no time for further thought as Jenna reached her and threw her arms around her.

"Hey, hon! Surprise."

Asha hugged her friend back, her eyes on Zane as he walked toward them. His dark hair was tousled as if he'd just got out of bed, and his eyes were fixed firmly on the ground. In the ten years since graduation, she'd managed to avoid Zane Larsen on most occasions. She'd bumped into him a handful of times when he was home from the city to visit his parents. Other than saying hello, she never engaged in conversation with him. She had no interest in knowing anything about him.

"Hey, Ash." He chewed on his bottom lip as he met her gaze, his smile not reaching his eyes.

Asha stared at him for a moment before forcing a smile to her lips. "Hi, Zane. Back to see your parents?" That was the most she'd said to him in ten years.

"Kind of."

Asha nodded. She didn't need him to elaborate; she didn't need or want to know anything more about him.

"We thought we'd stop for coffee before we see them. Maybe a muffin, too," Jenna said.

"You've come to the right place." Asha moved into the food truck to prepare the coffee. Without asking, she knew Jenna would have a latte, but had no idea what Zane would want. "How do you take yours, Zane?"

"Cappuccino, thanks. I'll be back in a minute. Just going to check out the lake." He stuffed his hands in his pockets and turned to walk toward the lake edge. Asha looked away, cursing herself that she'd noticed the snug fit of his jeans and how good he looked.

She lowered her eyes and, with a slight tremor in her hands, began preparing their drinks. She'd been on edge the moment he'd stepped from the car. Why did he still have this effect on her? Why, ten years later, was she still so angry with him that she'd have a physical reaction?

"How long are you here for?" She focused on Jenna.

"I'll head home tomorrow."

Asha raised an eyebrow. "You've always said it isn't worth coming this far for one night."

Jenna glanced toward Zane, who had reached the lake's edge and was skimming a rock. "It's not usually, but I'm the one who suggested Zane come home, and it turned out the only way of getting him here was for me to drive him."

"Is everything okay?"

Jenna sighed. "No, but Zane will kill me if I talk about his business. Now, more importantly, what time are you free? I heard a rumor there's a bottle or two with our names on them at Traders."

Asha laughed. "Sounds good. I usually close up at about two on a Saturday. I have a few errands to run and can meet you anytime from four."

"Four it is." Jenna reached for the two coffee cups Asha held out to her. "Can you put a couple of muffins in a bag for me too." She glanced over to where Zane was skimming rocks into the lake. "I think we'll both need some sustenance before we see the folks. Anything with chocolate is good."

Asha used the tongs to take two chocolate-orange muffins from the tray and placed them in a bag. Normally she'd be curious about what was going on with Jenna, especially turning up for twenty-four hours and needing sustenance before facing her parents. It wasn't like her, but it was related to Zane, which was why she had no interest in finding out more. Hopefully, he'd been dumped and was nursing a broken heart. He deserved to know the pain of rejection.

Jenna pulled a twenty from her pocket and held it out to Asha.

"Don't be silly. Save that for drinks tonight. This can be on me. It's great to see you, Jen."

Jenna's green eyes twinkled as she smiled. "See you at four." She turned, sipping her coffee as she made her way across to Zane.

Zane gratefully accepted the coffee Jenna held out to him. It was a chilly morning, and he needed something to warm him. The cool reception Asha had given him hadn't gone unnoticed. He sighed. He wasn't sure he'd ever understand women. He and Asha had gone out together once. The night had ended with Asha storming away from the high school gym in the middle of the prom, refusing to speak to him or give him an explanation. She'd told Jenna she wasn't well, which was no excuse for the way she behaved and still not a reason he believed. But that was ten years ago. Why on earth was she still holding a grudge? He could hardly apologize when he still didn't know what he'd done wrong.

"Ash and I are catching up for drinks this afternoon if you want to join us." Jenna's words broke into his thoughts.

He gave a wry laugh. "Did she suggest that?"

"No, but she'll be cool with it. She's celebrating the expansion of her business, so the more the merrier."

Zane fell silent. Jenna didn't see how much Asha hated him. Other than leaving him feeling a little uneasy anytime he visited Hope's Ridge, in case he bumped into her, it hadn't mattered while he was living in the city. But now, with him moving back to the Ridge, things might get uncomfortable. He'd need to make sure he stayed clear of her. "No, I won't come, but thanks for the invite. I'll probably give Matt a call, arrange to have a drink with him and see what he wants."

Jenna stared at him for a moment before averting her eyes back to the lake and its mountain range backdrop. "I sometimes forget how beautiful it is here. You'll probably love living here again."

Zane snorted. "Says the woman who rushed out of here the day after graduation and has never looked back."

Jenna laughed. "Got me. Although, I wasn't running from Hope's Ridge; I was running from the mill. Dad had it all planned. I would get a business degree and come back to do the accounts and other administrative tasks." She fell silent for a moment. "You know I can't remember him ever asking me whether that was what I wanted to do. He decided that was the role that I'd be good for, or, more likely, the role he needed filling."

"We must have been such disappointments to him. You becoming a graphic designer and me a banker. I hope he realizes that nothing's changed. I'm not working at the mill, ever."

Zane found the same words racing through his mind half an hour later when he and Jenna sat opposite their parents in the cozy kitchen they'd grown up in, sipping the peppermint tea their mother had insisted they needed.

"Let me get this straight," Roy, their father said. "You've thrown away everything you worked for in the city and have returned here permanently."

Jenna spluttered on her tea. "He hasn't thrown away everything, Dad. He needs a change. Zane's been through a stressful time and coming back here will hopefully help him relax."

"Relax? You need to keep busy. That's how you deal with stressful times. No point dwelling on the things you can't change. What could be so stressful anyway, you're twenty-eight for goodness sake. It's not like you have a wife and a family to provide for. You're a single man in the prime of your life. It's this ridiculous millennial thing, isn't it? Can't handle pressure or hard work."

"Roy." The warning tone was clear in their mother's voice.

"It's okay, Mom," Zane said. He turned his attention to her, doing his best to ignore his father. "Jenna's right. I need a change, and I hope coming home will offer me that."

His mother reached across and squeezed his hand. "It must have been frightening what you went through."

A lump caught in Zane's throat. He hadn't realized his mother knew what had happened. He glanced at Jenna, who gave a small shake of her head. If she hadn't told her, who had?

"Walter Law," Roy said by way of explanation. "He heard what happened at First National and called me to see if you were affected." His cheeks colored. "Embarrassing it was. Here's Walt ringing me to check on your well-being, and we don't know anything about it."

Zane stared at his father. They knew what had happened and they'd never rung to ask if he was okay?

"Your father thought it best we leave you in peace. He figured you'd talk to us when you were ready." Janet smiled. "And the fact that you've moved home is a sure sign that deep down you know where to go in times of trouble and when you need to heal."

Roy snorted. "More likely, he knows where to go when he wants a paycheck." He stood, picked up his empty tea mug, and placed it in the sink. "I need to go to the mill for a couple of hours and work through some paperwork." He looked to Zane. "Why don't you come with me? Might as well get a head start on things."

"Head start?"

Roy rolled his eyes. "Let me guess, hard work for a millennial is either non-existent or only possible during regular working hours." He threw up his hands. "Fine, I'll run you through everything on Monday morning. We don't work regular hours either. You'll need to be in the office by seven."

"Dad, we haven't discussed me working for you."

"No need to son, the mill's in your blood. It'll be yours one day, so getting as much hands-on experience now will set you up for the future." He held his hands up, not allowing Zane to speak, let alone object. "I'd better go. We can discuss the finer details on Monday."

Zane's heart sank as his father left the room. For all his

14

jibes and eye-rolling, his father's eyes had been full of pride as he spoke of the mill being in Zane's blood. He sighed. He'd let his father down when he'd left for the city ten years earlier, and here he was about to let him down again.

Asha locked up Irresistables a little after two and decided to walk the long way home, via Main Street. This change in route had become the norm over the last few weeks. It was an opportunity to look in on the new premises, peer through the windows and go over the plans in her head. She had a notebook at home full of her ideas and added to it each afternoon after walking past the currently closed Sandstone Cafe.

She followed the lake path from the food truck the half mile to Main Street. Excitement fluttered through her, as it had done each day since having confirmation from the realtor that a five-year lease was acceptable to the owner. She'd ensured there was a clause to allow her to extend the lease beyond the five years. The last thing she wanted was to pour her heart and soul into the premises only to lose it a few years later. On the one hand, five years sounded like a long time, but realistically she knew the time would fly past.

She allowed herself to think ahead briefly. Where would she be in five years in other parts of her life? Would she be in a relationship? Married? Kids? She shook her head; unless a hoard of new men moved into town, the likelihood of finding a relationship in Hope's Ridge was slim. The summer brought with it plenty of vacationers and plenty of opportunities for a fling, but that was all. The reality was, if she hooked up with any of those guys and wanted something long term, she would probably have to move. She pushed the thoughts from her mind. A relationship was not her priority at the moment; the expansion of her business was. And anyway, after the last relationship she wasn't sure she wanted to go there again.

She veered off the walking track as the quaint, glass fronted, sandstone building came into view. Previously run as The Sandstone Cafe, the premises had sat empty for the past month. It had been a massive shock to the town to discover the cafe's owner was wanted for tax evasion. Auditors from the IRS had arrived, and the cafe closed the next day. What was a shock for the town, had provided a fantastic opportunity for Asha. She'd gone in to see Andy Farley, the town's realtor, the day she heard of its closure. It had taken him three weeks to contact the owner, who'd been hiking in the Himalayas, but he finally had, and the owner had immediately agreed to lease the premises. Andy said it would take him a week to finalize the new paperwork, so a meeting had been arranged for Wednesday.

Asha stared in through the windows. Andy had arranged for cleaners to attend the property after it shut down. All food and perishables had been removed, a thorough clean had been performed, and the chairs were neatly stacked upside down on the tables. It looked like Asha could move straight in and start operating, not that that was her plan. She would receive the keys on Wednesday and then put her stamp on it. Make it Irresistables. She was expecting her signage to arrive on Monday, along with two large chalkboards she planned to use as menu boards. It was a shame Jenna was leaving the next day, or she would have asked her to help design the boards and write up the menus. Jenna's eye for detail was amazing.

"Dreaming about your new venture?"

Asha pulled back from the window, her face heating as she realized people probably noticed her gluing her face to the windows each afternoon. She turned to face one of the town's oldest citizens, ninety-six-year-old Charlie Li. She smiled. "Caught me, Mr. Li. How are you?"

He rubbed his hands together. "Looking forward to a large slice of apple pie, I am. I hope you'll be putting it on the menu? And call me Charlie; you make me feel old." His eyes twinkled as he spoke. He was quite a character.

Asha smiled. At ninety-six, it was probably safe to declare him old. "I think I'd be run out of town if I didn't have pie on the menu. How about you come in on my opening day and have a piece on the house?"

Charlie shook his head. "Don't you go giving all your profits away. A prime location like this can't be cheap. I'm so glad that it's gone to you. Those rumors about developers were worrying me."

"Developers?"

Charlie nodded. "Didn't you hear? They were talking about it at Traders a couple of weeks ago. Talk of knocking the old place down, turning it into lake view apartments." He smiled. "You'll be pleased to know that the townspeople are happy that you've signed the lease, and that's not going to happen. There'll be a line out the door on opening day; you mark my words. Now, I'd better get moving. Promised the neighbors I'd drop in for a chat this afternoon, and, at the rate I shuffle along, it'll take me another hour or two to walk the last two hundred yards home." He laughed as he continued past Asha and turned the corner onto Lake Drive, where he'd lived in a beautifully renovated cottage for the last fifty years.

Developers? How come this was the first Asha had heard about this? She hadn't signed the lease yet. Her heart sank. This was her dream, her future. She couldn't imagine what she'd do if this fell through. She hurried down Main Street toward Hope Realty. She needed to speak to Andy immediately.

She was outside the door before she had an opportunity to give it much more thought, a benefit of living in a small town. The closed sign was already up. It was Saturday, and he closed at two. She took her phone from her bag and found his number. It went straight to voice mail. Knowing Andy, he was in the middle of the lake, a fishing rod in one hand and a beer in the other. She didn't bother leaving a message, instead sent him a text message. *Checking we're still on for signing the lease Wednesday?*

She stared at her phone, willing a text to appear, but it didn't. Surely, he would have been in touch if there was any likelihood of it falling through? She'd known him since grade school, considered him a friend. He knew how much this meant to her. She took a deep breath willing her heart rate to calm. She was reasonably sure she had nothing to worry about. She just wished she hadn't bumped into Charlie and had a seed of doubt planted in her mind. She wanted to enjoy the afternoon celebrating with Jenna, not speculating on whether the cafe was going to go ahead. Dread replaced her excitement. She gave her head a shake and continued down the street toward home. Other than an old man spreading what most likely was gossip, she had no reason to believe the deal would fall through. Andy would have told her. She was fairly sure she had nothing to worry about.

2

_Z_ane let himself out of the back door at the same time Jenna left for her catchup with Asha. He'd been home for only an hour, and already the weight pressing on his chest was suffocating. Why had he let Jenna talk him into coming back to Hope's Ridge? Having to listen to his father's opinion on everything and suffer through his disappointment again at Zane's reluctance to join the family business was more than he needed right now. One thing he knew for sure, he couldn't stay with them. He needed to find his own place as soon as possible. He'd make an appointment with the one and only realtor in town on Monday and hope something was available now.

He walked along his parents' road, its familiarity taking him back to memories from his school days. Most of the houses lining the street looked like they'd barely been touched in the last ten years. One had been repainted, and a second story added, but the rest were looking tired. As he reached the intersection leading into town, he turned left and crossed over to the narrow track that led through a wooded area, eventually arriving at the lake's edge. He started to jog, knowing the rhythmic thud of his Nikes on the dirt would soothe him. He'd always been a runner, but since the incident, he'd increased the frequency and lengths of his runs. Some days he'd run three or four times.

He followed the lake's edge along the well-worn path that meandered around the lake for at least two miles. There and back would give him a bit of a run, at least. He had the track to himself, which wasn't a huge surprise. He'd seen a couple of boats out on the lake, no doubt Saturday fishermen trying their luck. He was looking forward to doing that himself. He wondered if his father still had the old boat and whether he'd be allowed to use it? He smiled to himself. Probably not once he told him he wasn't planning to work at the mill. He passed the white and gray Lake House, a detached house that sat on the shores of Lake Hopeful, and continued to increase his speed, knowing the end of the track was around the next bend. He wondered, as he often did, who owned the Lake House. He'd heard a company in the city owned it, but no one had ever lived in it as far back as he could recall. The gardens and house were maintained beautifully by a local gardener, which seemed like a waste when no one was there to enjoy it. His lungs were burning as he pushed harder and faster. He rounded the corner and cried out as he tried to side-step a woman holding what looked like a downward dog pose. He came to a stop and turned back to see whether she was okay. She was pushing herself up to a standing position.

"I'm so sorry." His breath was labored. "I wasn't expecting to bump into anyone."

"Neither was I." She turned to face him, pushing her blonde hair from her eyes. It was Steph Jones, Asha's older sister.

"Steph! What were you doing?"

Steph flushed. "Just some yoga poses. I come up here

occasionally to get away from everyone. It's so peaceful, and I've rarely seen anyone else this far up the track."

Zane turned and looked out at the lake. A light breeze caused a gentle ripple on its surface. The only sounds around them came from birds. He sighed. "You're right about it being peaceful."

"Everything okay?"

The concern in Steph's gentle voice had Zane turning to face her. "Sorry, I've got a few things on my mind. Not sure returning to Hope's Ridge was the best plan."

Steph raised an eyebrow. "You've come back to live?"

Zane nodded. "In theory, although an hour under the same roof as my father has me thinking otherwise."

Steph laughed. "I understand that. There's no way I could live with my family again, not even Asha, as much as I love her. Sharing with a friend or a stranger is much easier. There's something about family. They seem to think that because you're related, they have a right to give you unsolicited opinions whenever they feel like it. It creates a layer of stress I'm not up for."

Zane smiled. "Sounds like we have something in common. Is Andy Farley still the realtor in town? I thought I'd have a chat with him on Monday morning."

"Yep, he's still in charge. Are you looking to buy or rent?"

"Rent. My father might drive me out of Hope's Ridge, so I don't want to be tied to a mortgage. I don't need anything big, and I don't have much furniture. I was sharing with someone in the city, but she took half of the furniture when she left." *And half of his heart.* "Hopefully, Andy will have something furnished or partly furnished available."

Steph nodded. She looked as if she was deep in thought.

"Don't know of someone renting out their place by any chance?"

"Possibly, but it would be a roommate share, not a whole place to yourself."

"That'd work for me. Depending on who it is, of course."

"It's me," Steph said. "My roommate's moving to San Francisco on Monday, and I definitely can't afford the rent on my own. You're welcome to come and have a look at the house if you're interested."

A weight lifted from Zane. "You'd seriously consider letting me move in? You hardly know me."

Steph shrugged. "I've known Jenna most of my life. She practically lived at our house when she and Asha were teenagers." She raised an eyebrow. "If you're as messy as I remember her being, then maybe I'll retract the offer."

Zane laughed. "I'm practically OCD neat. You don't need to worry about mess. I can cook too. The only thing is I'm not working yet. I can afford the rent, that's no problem, it's just that I might be around the house quite a bit."

Steph smiled. "Why don't you come and take a look. The house is perfect for sharing. We both have our own areas and bathrooms. To be honest, unless we choose to spend time together, other than bumping into each other in the kitchen, we won't be aware the other exists."

Zane couldn't believe his luck. What Steph was describing sounded perfect.

"I'll head home now," Steph said. "You're welcome to come back with me, or you can meet me at the house after your run."

"How about I meet you in an hour," Zane said. "That gives you some time to think about whether you'd want to share with me, and gives me a chance to run back and have a quick shower before I come over."

"Okay. It's number four Emerald Bay Drive. Do you know where that is?"

"One of my friends from school lived at number twenty.

We used to complain that it was about as far from my folk's place as you can get." He grinned. "I definitely won't be complaining now. But Steph, do you think Asha will be okay with this?"

"Asha? Why would she care?"

"She's hated me ever since prom."

Steph frowned. "That was ten years ago. She's never mentioned it since. She never said what happened. You didn't do anything against her will, did you?"

"Of course not! We were friends, and we went as friends. Or so I thought. We danced a bit, and I excused myself to go to the bathroom. When I came back, she'd gone home without any explanation. I drove back to your folk's place to see if she was okay, and your mom said she was unwell, and I should go back and enjoy the night. When I tried to speak to her at school on the Monday, she refused to have anything to do with me. It was weird. She's been cold ever since."

"Look, I wouldn't worry about it. If she has a problem with it, she doesn't need to come over. I usually see her at Irresistables or down at the lake for a walk anyway."

"As long as you're sure?"

Steph nodded. "I am. I'll see you in about an hour."

Zane smiled and watched as she disappeared around the corner on the lake trail heading back toward town. He was pretty sure this was one of those meant-to-be situations. What was the likelihood of running into someone, quite literally, who had a place available to rent? Perhaps living in Hope's Ridge was a possibility after all.

Asha changed into her favorite pair of indigo jeans, a loose-fitting white shirt, and her beloved heeled, black leather boots. She threaded a belt of the same color through her jeans and did a quick check of her outfit in the mirror. She looked good. Casual but nice, the perfect combination for a night out at Traders. Jenna would probably be overdressed, but that was Jenna. She dressed up for everything. Even for a night in on the couch, you'd find Jenna in full makeup and a designer outfit. Asha smiled. It was so good to see her friend, but she wished she was visiting for longer. She moved into the small bathroom and took her makeup bag from the bathroom vanity. Mascara and lip gloss were her go-to's. She preferred a natural look and blessed with flawless skin, for now, she could get away without anything else. She imagined that might change as she got older, or she'd be like Steph and embrace her natural beauty. Steph refused to wear any makeup declaring it unnatural and unhealthy.

Asha reached down and stroked Max, her one-year-old Birman, who was rubbing around her legs. "None of that white fur of yours on my jeans, thanks, Maxy. Steph's always telling me I'm covered in your fluff." Max meowed, and Asha smiled.

Her smile turned to a frown as she thought back to her conversation with Steph earlier that morning. She hoped she was okay. Physically, Steph had recovered from the accident, but mentally and emotionally, she hadn't. It was true that at times of stress, the nightmares came flooding back, often taking Steph to a dark place. If the stress was purely over Mary leaving and her needing to find a new roommate, Asha could only hope she found someone quickly.

She wondered if Steph had posted anything on the town's community Facebook page. She knew the answer to that before she considered asking her. Steph's outlook on technology was similar to her feelings on makeup. She refused to have a cell phone, let alone a computer. Asha figured she was probably the only thirty-two-year-old in

24

America to be so tech-phobic. It was annoying when Asha needed to speak to her. Often Steph would let the home phone run out of charge so Asha would have to turn up at her house to have a conversation. She'd put an ad on the Facebook page herself tomorrow and see if she could help Steph find a roommate quickly.

She glanced at her watch. It was almost four. It would only take her five minutes to walk to Traders. She slipped her mascara and lip-gloss into her bag, gave Max one last stroke, and headed to the front door.

Zane walked back to his parent's house more cheerful than he had been in weeks. Bumping into Steph was meant to be. He'd spent the last twenty minutes being given a tour of her house and couldn't believe his luck. Not only was it a perfect layout for sharing, but Steph had created an oasis. From the moment you stepped through the front gate, the yard welcomed you. Bald cypress trees gave the house privacy, and the features Steph had added brought to it a tranquility he hadn't expected. The water features, buddha statues, and incense burning on the front veranda immediately made him realize Steph's interest in yoga was more than the physical. From things she'd said, he realized she was quite spiritual. She had a meditation area out the back next to a small pond surrounded by a rockery featuring a variety of plants. He'd sucked in a breath when he'd seen it, so blown away by the little touches she'd added. She had several carvings around the house too, which immediately drew his interest. He hadn't done any carving since he'd met Lucy. She'd turned her nose up at what she considered "old stuff." She loved clean, modern lines. He smiled, thinking of her reaction if he brought her to Steph's home. Its rustic charm would be lost on her. His wood carving tools and bench would be arriving with the rest of his belongings later in the week. He wondered if Steph would mind him setting up an area to work in. There was plenty of room in the garage as Steph said she didn't have a car and, until he bought himself a new one, he didn't either. Even then, the garage was more than big enough for both the pickup he'd probably get and his carving equipment.

He let himself in through the front door, his phone pinging with a text as he did. It was Matt Law suggesting they meet at Traders at nine. That would suit him fine. He could have dinner with his parents and then make his escape. Wafts of roast lamb filtered down the hallway, causing his stomach to rumble. Other than the muffin he'd had with Jenna earlier, he hadn't eaten all day. He was starving. He grinned. Fresh air and the prospect of moving into Steph's had brought back his appetite, something he'd been missing the last few months.

"Hey, hon," his mother poked her head out from the kitchen. "Why don't you wash up and then come and have a drink with your dad? He's back from the mill and is enjoying a beer out the back around the fire pit. He's in an excellent mood. I'm sure he'd love for the two of you to chat."

"Sure, Mom." Zane headed into the half bath to clean up. Unfortunately, he was pretty sure his dad's excellent mood wouldn't last.

Less than ten minutes later, he was proven right. Roy Larsen's face went from relaxed and happy to bright red within a matter of seconds.

"What do you mean you're not working at the mill? Isn't that why you came back?"

"No, Dad, it's not."

Roy leaped to his feet and began pacing near the fire. "Then, why are you back?"

"I needed a change. You always said the city would eat me up and spit me out, and I guess it has. I'm looking for a quieter, less stressful life."

"You'd get that at the mill," Roy practically shouted at him.

Zane stared at his father. If he needed any convincing that he'd made the right decision, this was it. This was exactly how he'd treated Zane throughout his childhood. Telling him what he should do and getting angry anytime Zane decided to take another approach. His father wanted to control him as he controlled Zane's mother, but he wouldn't let it happen. "Dad, the mill's not where I want to work. I told you that years ago. I don't think you and me working together is a good idea. I have different ideas than you, and we'd end up arguing the whole time."

"No, we wouldn't. You'd follow the rules and the processes that my father put in place sixty years ago, and the mill would continue to provide the town's livelihood."

"Processes from sixty years ago would need updating," Zane said. He held up his hands before his father objected. "Which is exactly why I should stay away. In this day and age, automation could help to make the business run more effectively and be more profitable."

Roy shook his head. "Of course, you think you're better than me, don't you?"

"What? Of course, I don't. I'm saying that if I were involved, I'd want to make changes. I'm assuming you wouldn't let me, and I'd find working there utterly demoralizing."

Roy continued shaking his head. "Unbelievable. How did I end up with two such ungrateful children? Work my fingers to the bone I do, and for what? So you and Jenna can throw it in my face and say it's a waste of time."

"I never said that." Zane tried to keep his voice level. "You've done an amazing job and given Jenna and me opportunities we're incredibly grateful for. But, both of us have our own dreams, and they don't involve working in the mill."

"What happens if I die tomorrow?" Roy asked. "The place has been left to you to run."

Zane stared at his father. "That's not what I want to do, Dad."

"You'd sell it? A business that's been in the family for three generations?"

"That's not something I've given any thought to. I have no idea whether I'd sell it or not. If I didn't, I guess I could hire a manager to run it. And Dad, you shouldn't be leaving it to me. It should go to Mom, and if she's no longer alive, then split between Jenna and me."

Roy stared at Zane as if he were mad. "You're my heir. You're the one I choose to run it."

"I'm sorry, Dad, it's never going to happen."

They were interrupted by the slam of the fly screen and the back door opening. "Dinner's ready," his mother called.

Zane stood ready to go inside.

"Zane's not staying," Roy announced.

"What?" His mother voiced the question before he could.

Roy turned to Zane. "Get your bags and go. We're obviously not good enough for you, so don't take advantage of us."

"No, Roy. Please don't do this," his mother pleaded. "I've gone to a lot of trouble for tonight's dinner."

Roy continued to stare at Zane. "You heard me. Go."

Zane's stomach churned as he realized his father was serious. He knew he'd be upset but hadn't imagined he'd throw him out. Thank goodness he'd already arranged to move into Steph's. He couldn't do that until Monday, so for now, he'd have to hope that one of the rooms above Traders was available to rent for the next couple of nights. He turned away from his father and walked toward his mother. A lump filled his throat when he saw her pale face and tear-filled eyes. He stopped and hugged her. "Don't worry, I'll be fine. I'll pop in and see you during the week, okay?"

His mother nodded. "Whatever's happened, I'm sure we can fix it. Your father will come around."

Zane turned back and stared at his father, who was poking the fire with a stick, his face dark as thunder. "I'm not sure he will this time, Mom." He hugged her again before heading into the house to collect his bags.

Traders was already busy when Asha pushed open the saloon doors. Music blared from the old-fashioned jukebox, and the local band, Zeebars, was setting up in the corner in preparation for their Saturday night set.

"Hey, Asha." Mark Boulder gave her a wave from the pool table, before slapping his forehead as his opponent sunk the eight ball.

Asha smiled and waved back. She'd known Mark since pre-school. A lot of the kids they'd grown up with had moved away, but there was still a handful that loved Hope's Ridge like she did and had chosen to stay. It surprised her sometimes that Steph had. Steph liked to keep to herself and would probably have found anonymity easier to find in a big city than in a small town. Still, she wasn't suggesting that to her sister. She'd miss her terribly if she moved away.

Her phone pinged as she spotted Jenna sitting at the bar chatting to Isaak, the owner of Traders. She slipped it from her bag as she wound her way through the crowded tables toward the empty stool next to Jenna. She stopped as she saw the text was from Andy. Her heart rate increased as she opened the message. *Yes, I should have everything ready for signing by end of Tuesday. I'll bring the paperwork to you around ten on Wednesday. Saves you having to close up, and you can shout me a cup of coffee to celebrate!*

Relief flooded through Asha. Charlie had his wires crossed, thank goodness. She typed a quick reply before slipping her phone back in her bag and joining Jenna. Her friend turned to hug her.

"You're looking happy."

Asha smiled. "I am. I had a slight heart attack this afternoon when someone mentioned The Sandstone Cafe might not be mine after all. Andy's confirmed the papers will be ready to sign on Wednesday morning."

"That sounds like the perfect excuse for champagne." Jenna turned to Isaak. "A bottle of your finest thanks."

Isaak laughed. "Our finest isn't as fine as your city tastes, but it'll still do the trick." He set about organizing an ice bucket and two glasses.

Once their glasses were full, Jenna turned to Asha and raised hers. "To my entrepreneurial friend and all the success you deserve expanding your business."

They clinked glasses and sipped their sparkling wine.

"Will you keep the name?" Jenna asked.

"I was planning to," Asha said. "Irresistables has built up quite a reputation over the years, and people coming for the summer will know it's me."

Jenna laughed. "Ash, other than the bakery, you'll be the only cafe in town. Whether they know it's you or not probably doesn't matter. In summer, you'll be overrun. Competition isn't a problem. But I agree, it is a great name."

"Good, because I've already ordered new signage."

Jenna raised her glass again. "To Irresistables."

Asha took another sip of her drink, the tension of the afternoon leaving her body. Charlie's comments had shaken her. "How did you go with your mom and dad? They'd be happy to see you."

"I only stayed for a short time. Dad was already winding Zane up, so I took off. I'll spend some time with Mom in the morning, but if Zane drops his bombshell on them, I'll probably take off early."

Tension returned to Asha's shoulders at the mention of Zane. Why did he have such an effect on her? Other people had done things to her in the past that had upset her, and she'd forgiven them. Why couldn't she put what he'd done behind her? She wished she could change the subject, but her friend looked concerned, and it certainly wasn't Jenna's fault he was such a jerk. "Bombshell? What's happened?"

Jenna sighed. "The usual. Dad assumed Zane's return to town means he's *come to his senses*," she perfectly mimicked her father, "and will be taking his place at the mill."

"Zane's back permanently?"

Jenna nodded. "Possibly. He needed a change. Some stuff went down in the city, which has left him a bit messed up. But, working for Dad isn't something he's planning to do. I'm not sure when he plans to tell him, that's all."

Asha digested this news. *Zane was moving back to Hope's Ridge.* She swallowed. Avoiding him when he was in town for a few days was bad enough, but a permanent move? "What do you think he'll do if he's not going to work at the mill?"

"Honestly, he needs to chill and get his head together for a few months. I'm hoping that's what he does. He's got plenty saved so can afford to do that. But, knowing Zane, he won't want to sit still. I'm hoping he'll take up carving again.

He's so talented and could turn that into a business if he wanted to."

Asha remembered some of the carvings Zane did in high school. He'd produced a stunning eagle which he'd presented to the school principal at their final graduation. A symbol of freedom, which he believed every student had now that they were flying the symbolic nest. The intricate detail on the carving had been incredible. Her eyes shifted to the other end of the bar, where another of Zane's carvings was grafted to the polished wooden bar top. It was of a spotted owl. One of North America's endangered birds that were occasionally seen in Hope's Ridge. "He likes birds." Asha nodded toward the carving.

"He does. Birds and squirrels for some reason."

"Squirrels?"

"Yep, any animal from the family Sciuridae is too cute to bypass apparently."

Thinking of Zane calling anything cute made Asha smile. He was so masculine and strong but appeared to have a softer side. She brushed away the thought. She had her best friend beside her for one night, so they should make the most of it.

"Tell me what's happening with you," Asha said. "How's work, and how's that guy you said you were dating? Was it Brad?"

Jenna's face lit up at the mention of Brad.

Their drinks were empty by the time she'd given Asha the full run down. "I think he could be the one," she said as she refilled their glasses.

"Really? After two dates, you know that?"

Jenna nodded, her eyes dreamy as she thought of her boyfriend. "He's different from any guy I've been with. He loves to hang out and chat. I can be myself with him. It's not about my job or whether I'm wearing sexy clothes. He says he's as happy to hang out in sweats and watch Netflix as he is to sit in expensive restaurants."

"But, your first two dates were in expensive restaurants."

"They were, but he wants to just hang on the weekend next time. I would have seen him yesterday if the Zane situation hadn't escalated."

"Escalated?"

Jenna nodded. "I can't say anything, Ash. Sorry. Let's just say he's been through a hard time, and I found him at a pretty low point. That was on Wednesday. I took Thursday and Friday off work to help him pack and clean the apartment, and here we are today. He needed a change of scenery."

Asha nodded, wondering what on earth could have happened for Jenna to act so quickly.

"Anyway, let's start talking about the menu for Irresistables. What have you got planned?"

Asha's thoughts quickly moved away from Zane back to her life and the most exciting, yet in some ways, daunting, thing that was about to happen.

Zane glanced at the clock on the bedside table. It was almost nine. He'd gone straight from his parents' house to Traders. He'd seen Jenna and Asha at the bar but hadn't spoken to them. Instead, he'd found Isaak serving and arranged to rent a room for the next two nights. His appetite had faded following the confrontation with his father, but he'd still gone ahead and ordered a burger from the kitchen and had it delivered to his room. He figured he'd be having a few beers with Matt later, and he was probably better off not doing that on an empty stomach.

He sighed as he stared at the roof; it's dark wooden

beams crisscrossing in places. The room was basic but clean, which was all he needed. He could hear the music and laughter from below and assumed that trying to sleep any time before the bar closed at two would be pointless. His heart ached for his mother. He knew how upset she'd be tonight, and he also knew how disappointed his father was. He wanted to shake him sometimes. He'd never said he would work at the mill; for years, he'd made it clear he never would. So why did his father get it in his head that a move home meant he'd changed his mind? It was frustrating that they couldn't relax and enjoy a friendly relationship without Roy making assumptions. He wondered how and why his mother put up with him. It did leave him in the situation of needing to find a job. Banking and finance weren't an option in Hope's Ridge, not that he planned to continue in that field anyway. The nearest bank was in Drayson's Landing, thirty minutes away.

The mill was the biggest employer in the area, which was annoying. He could probably pick up work in the summer easily enough with one of the small operators which suddenly appeared, renting out water sports equipment or taking vacationers on hikes and tours of the area. He'd enjoy running tours. The problem was he'd still need employment for the other nine months of the year.

Zane pulled himself up off the bed. It was nine, and Matt might have arrived. He'd said he had a business proposition, maybe that would give him employment for the short term. He grinned as he changed his shirt. If he found a place to live and a job, all within hours of being home, he'd know Jenna was right, that Hope's Ridge was where he was meant to be.

Zane entered the bar, his eyes scouring the tables for any signs of Matt. He would be easy to spot. As the linebacker for the school's football team, he'd been nicknamed *the walking wall.* When they'd met two years earlier, other than a slightly receding hairline, Matt had looked as frightening as he had in their senior year.

Matt hadn't arrived, but Jenna caught his eye as he scanned the room. She waved him over. He hesitated momentarily. He wasn't sure Asha would be as welcoming as his sister. But Jenna's insistent waving had him move in their direction.

"Join us for a drink." Jenna held up a bottle of champagne.

Zane shook his head and smiled. "No, I can't. I'm meeting a friend." He turned to Asha, annoyed to feel butterflies flitting in his stomach. Why did he still react so strongly around her? "Having a good night?"

Asha's sea-green eyes met his. When she'd spoken to him that morning, they'd been hard, accusing. But now they had a softness in them, an understanding. Heat spread across the back of his neck and onto his face. He'd kill Jenna if she'd told Asha why he'd moved back.

"We are, thanks."

"Are you meeting Matt?" Jenna asked.

Zane nodded. "After what happened with Dad, I need a few drinks tonight, so it's worked out perfectly."

"You told Dad?" Jenna asked.

He nodded. "He didn't take it well. He kicked me out."

Jenna's hand flew to her mouth. "He didn't."

Zane grinned. "Sure did. Mom almost had a heart attack. It's fine. I'm staying here for the next two nights, and then it looks like I've found a place to move in to on Monday."

"Really? Where?"

"Zane!"

Zane's attention shifted as a strong hand clapped him on the back. He turned to face Matt Law, who immediately threw an arm around him.

"Great to see you," Matt said. "It's been ages."

Zane laughed. A hug from Matt was like being tackled. He was still built like a truck. He turned back to Jenna and Asha. "I assume you guys all know each other?"

"Course we do," Matt said. "Although I haven't seen you in ages, Jenna. How are you?" He eyed her appreciatively. "You're looking exceptionally well."

"Okay, bro." Zane clapped Matt on the back. "She's my sister, don't forget."

Matt smiled. "Just appreciating that she looks after herself. Nothing more." He smiled at Asha. "Hey, Ash, nice to see you."

"You too, Matt."

Zane steered Matt away from the two girls to a table on the opposite side of the room.

Matt was laughing. "If Jenna wasn't your sister, I'd be asking her out."

"Well, she is. So, don't! Now, let me buy you a drink. Beer?"

Matt nodded. "Sounds good. I'll get the next round."

Eight rounds and five hours later, Zane stumbled up the stairs to his room. He wasn't sure why anyone badmouthed Matt Law. He was a great guy. They'd had a lot of laughs reminiscing about high school before getting on to talking business. Matt's eyes had lit up as he described a proposed new development and what it would do for the town. It reminded Zane a little of the stories he'd heard growing up of Walter Law. While a lot of Walter's ideas were rejected through town opposition, the developments he did get approved had been successful. One of the key differences between Matt and his father was that Matt's vision was in keeping with the look and feel of Hope's Ridge. He wasn't looking to radically modernize it or change its look. He was looking to replicate the stunning sandstone charm at the lake end of Main Street with a new restaurant and apartment precinct, and he wanted Zane to project manage the entire process. If he accepted the job, not only would Zane be earning a decent income, he'd be working flexible hours and not have to think about finding a job for at least twelve months. He was meeting up again with Matt on Monday morning. After the fifth beer, the details had begun to blur, as had most of the people in the bar. He'd definitely need reminding.

As his head hit the pillow, a huge smile spread across his face. If anyone had told him returning to Hope's Ridge would turn out like this, he'd have assumed it was too good to be true.

3

*A*sha tentatively opened one eye, then the other. She groaned. Her head pounded, and her mouth was dry and sour. She should have said no to Jenna before she ordered a second bottle. They didn't finish it, but she couldn't remember the last time she'd drunk so much. Probably when Jenna last visited if she was realistic. As much as she loved her friend, she was now glad, rather than disappointed that Jenna was leaving that afternoon. She glanced at the clock. It was close to eleven. They'd stayed at Traders until it closed at two and walked home. She'd seen Jenna home before continuing the short distance to her house. She closed her eyes and groaned again as she remembered the Larsen's front light coming on and Jenna's father calling out to them as they arrived, singing at the front gate. She wondered how many others in the town had witnessed their spectacularly drunk arrival home. If anyone else had, she'd hear about it quickly enough when she opened up Irresistables the next morning.

She dragged herself out of bed. She needed coffee and a shower, preferably in that order, and then she'd think about her plans for the day. She immediately thought of Steph.

She'd planned to post on the town's Facebook page about Steph needing a roommate. She considered this as she turned on the coffee machine to prepare her drink. Steph might not want any random stranger applying. Although, knowing Steph, she'd prefer a random stranger over someone she knew. Maybe she'd better ask her first whether she wanted an ad placed. She nodded, having made her first decision for the day. She'd get dressed, eat something if she could stomach it, and then head around to Steph's place. It would give her a chance to check on her. See how she'd slept and whether there was anything she could do.

An hour later, Asha knocked on Steph's front door. It was open, and although Steph always said to come on in, Asha still knocked. It wasn't only Steph's space; it was Mary's too. Although not for much longer.

"Hey, sis, what are you doing here?" Steph appeared in the doorway; her floaty yoga pants a contrast to her fitted long sleeve shirt. Her blonde hair hung loosely around her shoulders, and her eyes were bright. She always looked a picture of health. Asha could only imagine the contrast they made this morning.

"Wanted to see how you are. Talk to you about the roommate situation."

Steph raised an eyebrow. "News travels fast. Come in, and I'll make us some herbal tea and explain. I hoped it wouldn't be an issue for you."

An issue for her?

She followed her sister through to the kitchen, inhaling delicious aromas of sandalwood and vanilla. Steph's house was always so lovely to visit. As much as Asha joked about the lack of technology and Steph's spiritual roots, she couldn't deny that a sense of calm settled over her the moment she stepped through the front door.

"Looking at you this morning, I think peppermint tea

might be the way to go. It's perfect for hangovers."

Asha gave a wry smile. "That obvious?"

Steph nodded. "I would have expected no less with Jenna in town. Did you have a good night?"

"We did. It was a good way to unwind. I had a bit of a scare in the afternoon, so I needed something to calm my nerves." She went on to tell Steph about her conversation with Charlie and his suggestion that someone else wanted the Sandstone Cafe.

"Surely Andy would have said something if that was the case? Probably Charlie trying to stir up trouble. At ninety-six, you'd think he'd be finished gossiping, but apparently, it's what keeps him entertained, and from the sounds of it, he's now making things up."

Asha laughed. "Appears so. Andy's bringing the paperwork over on Wednesday, so there's nothing to worry about. It was the thought of losing it. My stress levels went through the roof for a few hours. It made me realize how much I want this."

Steph poured boiling water into the tea pot and added fresh mint tea leaves to the infuser. "If it's meant to be, it'll happen. You've done everything possible, and from the sounds of it, it'll all come together on Wednesday."

Asha smiled. Steph was always so philosophical about things, whereas she was impatient and would do anything to be able to sign the lease right now. "Speaking of stress levels, how are yours? Did you sleep better last night?"

Steph nodded. "Slept like a baby. No nightmares, nothing. Thank goodness."

"That's great, and part of the reason I came to speak to you. I was thinking I could put a notice on the Facebook community noticeboard that you're looking for a roommate. It's the fastest way to spread it around town."

Steph added the teapot and two cups to a tray. "Let's take

this out the back. The sun's on the table at the moment, so it should be nice and warm."

"So?" Asha said as they sat down at the outdoor table, and Steph poured the tea. "Did you want me to do the Facebook thing for you?"

Steph shook her head. She looked up and passed Asha her cup. "No need. Mary's collecting the last of her belongings in the morning, and I have a new roommate moving in in the afternoon."

Asha's mouth dropped open. "That's fantastic. Who is it?"

Steph picked up her cup and took a sip. "Zane Larsen."

Asha's cup clattered onto the table. "What? How did that happen? He only got here yesterday. When did you speak to him?"

"I bumped into him down at the lake. He's moved back, possibly for good, and doesn't want to stay with his parents. He came, looked at the house, and loved it. I think it'll work out okay. Do you have a problem with him? He was concerned that you might not like the idea of him moving in here."

"Really?" Curiosity replaced Asha's anger. "What did he say?"

"Said something happened between the two of you at the prom and that you left all of a sudden and never spoke to him again. Mom told him you were sick, but he never understood what happened. He seemed to genuinely have no idea."

Asha's mouth dropped open. "*No idea*! He knew exactly why I left. I was a bet. That was the only reason he asked me, and I wasn't hanging around after I found that out."

"What do you mean a bet?"

"He excused himself to go to the bathroom, and two of his friends came over to me. They asked if I was enjoying the night and had a little chat. Nothing unusual, but then one of them said there'd be some cash in it for me if I didn't go past second base with Zane. His friend then laughed and said he'd make it worth my while if I went to third base. I was mortified. I had no idea why they were talking to me like this. I'd never been on a date before with Zane. He was Jenna's brother, and she'd always said he was off limits. She said she couldn't bear it if Zane and I got together and then broke up. She didn't want to have to choose between us if that happened."

"Okay, so these idiot guys were being smart. What did Zane say when he came back?"

"I haven't finished. I asked them why they were being so rude. Then the truth came out. There was a bet between most of the football team as to how far Zane would get with me. I'd been identified as a Hope's Ridge virgin and was *ripe for the picking*. Zane had guaranteed the team he'd be rounding fourth base with me later that night. It was worth a few hundred dollars for Zane if that had happened."

Steph sucked in a breath. "Oh, Ash, I'm so sorry. I had no idea. Why didn't you tell me this when it happened?"

Tightness gripped Asha's ribs. "I was too embarrassed. I didn't tell anyone. I couldn't tell Jenna. He was her brother. So I decided to block out the whole night and never speak to him again. It's worked pretty well up until now."

"I can't believe Zane lied to me yesterday. His words suggested he has no idea why you're angry with him."

"Maybe it wasn't a big deal to him," Asha said. "And he probably didn't know that I knew what was going on. I should have confronted him right then, but I was seventeen and was crushed. I wanted the whole thing to disappear. He left town soon after graduation, and I never heard anything about it again. The fact that I left the prom early meant there were no rumors about what he and I did or didn't do. They all moved on to making someone else's life hell."

"I'll tell him he can't move in," Steph said. "There's no way I want someone like that living here."

An immense wave of love flooded through Asha. She reached across and squeezed Steph's hand. "Thank you, but you know what, maybe it's time I moved on. He's Jenna's brother, and he didn't do anything that night to hurt me."

"Because you didn't give him the chance."

"I know, but still, if he'll be living in town, I should probably leave it in the past and move on. You always tell me to live in the moment. To let go of regrets and the things I can't do anything about. This might be a good opportunity to take that approach."

"I do say that, don't I."

Asha nodded.

"It's easy to say it when it's things that don't affect you," Steph said. "I'm not sure I can let him move in without addressing this. It's painted him in a whole different light for me. The guy I met yesterday was lovely. I don't know the detail, but it sounds like something happened in the city that turned his life upside down and made him move back here."

"Jenna said the same, but wouldn't elaborate. I know his girlfriend left him, but that's all I got out of her. I think there was something bigger than that, something that's affected him." Asha sighed. "Something a lot bigger than my prom night experience, I expect. Let him move in. You can always kick him out if there are problems, and it solves your roommate situation."

"Only if you're sure?"

"I am." As the words came out of her mouth, Asha knew how hollow they sounded. She'd acted quite mature only minutes earlier, saying she needed to leave the past behind and live in the moment. The reality was, she wasn't sure she'd ever forgive Zane for the way he treated her. The day he'd asked her to the prom, he'd seemed nervous and excited, like he wanted to go with her. She would never have believed he was capable of setting her up. But he had. She'd had a crush on Zane since she was twelve. She would never have admitted it to Jenna or acted on it. Her friendship with Jenna meant too much. But when he'd asked her out, she'd allowed herself a glimmer of hope, a glimmer of what might be. Within hours of leaving the house with Zane, those hopes were crushed. She hadn't dated until that night, so her introduction to men and dating was not a happy one. It had taken her two years before she'd agreed to go on a date with another man. She was strong, independent, and she wasn't going to allow someone else to make her feel the way Zane had. But she was older now. She'd told Steph to let him move in, so she'd need to do her best to make peace with all of this. He was ten years older, hopefully, a lot more mature, and wouldn't be given an opportunity to make her feel worthless again.

After saying goodbye to a hungover Jenna on Sunday, Zane spent the afternoon out on the lake. He hired a boat and fishing gear and spent a few hours on the west side in the shaded pocket of a group of willow trees. As a kid, he'd always targeted this area for bluegills. He'd caught two in what had been his favorite spot, lining up the tree that leaned so far sideways it was almost in the water and the church spire on the lakeshore. He was sure there was a hole down here that the fish loved to hide in. He and his friend Chippy had dived down as deep as they could to check when they were kids. They'd found a hole but never had enough breath to see how deep it was. He smiled at the memory. Now he could use a fish finder to tell him the depth and search for the fish, but he had no plans to do that. Old school fishing was his preference. He was here for his mental health, not the actual fish. He'd thrown back the two he'd caught.

He'd been relieved that Sunday night was a lot quieter at Traders, and the noise ended by midnight. He'd had a couple of beers with dinner and chatted with Isaak, but that was it for the night. The bar no longer resembled the heaving party land of the night before. Friday and Saturday were big nights in Hope's Ridge, but it was nice to see the quieter side of the town on a Sunday. Families came in for their evening meal, and Zane could see why. The Sunday roast on offer was mouthwatering. He'd certainly gone back for seconds.

Now, he packed his bag and dressed in a fresh white shirt and navy jeans. One thing he would enjoy about being back in Hope's Ridge was losing the suits he'd worn to work every day for the last ten years. Casual was his preference.

He zipped his toiletries into his larger bag and took a quick look around the room. He had everything. Isaak said he could store his bags in the storeroom and collect them in the afternoon when he was ready to move them to Steph's. It was a perfect arrangement. His meeting with Matt should only last a few hours so, by the time that was finished, he'd be ready to move into his new home.

Matt was on a conference call when Zane entered his office right on ten as planned. He waved Zane into a seat, and five minutes later ended the call and turned to him.

"Sorry about that. I needed to confirm a few details and make sure the sale had gone through. No point starting any work if the vendor changes his mind at the last minute."

"Was it all okay?"

"Sure was. I'm now the proud owner of the four blocks I mentioned on Lake Drive." He fist-pumped the air. "Even my dad will have to admit this is an achievement. I've jumped through so many hoops to make this happen. It's going to be amazing."

Zane grinned, immediately caught up in Matt's energy and excitement. It was hard not to like this guy. He worked hard, had the town's interests at heart, and was attempting to make a real difference to Hope's Ridge. Zane hoped some of the older residents in town would embrace this as progress rather than resist it.

"Now, let me walk you through the plans. I know we spoke about them on Saturday night, but considering the state I woke up in on Sunday, I'm not expecting you to remember much, other than drinking less beer next time might be a good plan."

Zane laughed. "I remember bits, but I need a refresher and want to see the plans."

The next hour was spent poring over the plans and discussing Matt's vision for the development.

"So, nothing that's already there will be demolished?"

"Nope, that's the beauty in this as far as getting objections from the town. Three of the blocks are vacant, and to be honest, have been a mess for years. The other is the sandstone building that everyone raves about. We'll use the same brick for the new development. It will be an amazing corner. It's right across from the lake and has spectacular views. I want to put a sunset bar on top of this building." He pointed to the building on the plans. "We're so lucky it's a flat roof already as it won't need too much work. The highest cost is creating access from the premises below."

Zane laughed. "Not sure that'll appeal to too many of the town residents. Can't see them paying for the sunset when they can sit down at the lake and watch it."

Matt grinned. "A handful perhaps, but they're not my target. Sure, I want to improve the town, but ultimately my development aims to bring in the tourists. I'm looking to bring some money into the town, and I need places for them to spend it once they're here. I've put in applications to buy the four properties on the other side of the four blocks I've already acquired."

"But they've got houses on them."

"They have, which makes it more difficult. The owners would have to agree to sell. I'm making generous offers, so hopefully, they will. If they don't, I have a backup plan."

Matt went on to tell Zane about the plan for a luxury eco-resort he was submitting to council. "It'd be lakefront, but it's out of town, around Crook's Bend. In theory, no one will object as you can't see the building from here. The bluff will block it from view, and the land it's on was earmarked for development years ago. It's one my dad managed to get through planning. He didn't bother building on it as he got so fed up with town that he ended up leaving. So, if I can't buy up the properties on Lake Drive, we'll build there instead."

Zane stared at the plans Matt had spread all over the conference table. It was a huge undertaking. Zane wasn't sure he could handle so many different projects at once.

Matt must have sensed his hesitancy. "Don't worry; I'm not expecting you to work on all of these. For now, I want your help with the development of the Lake Drive precinct and the financial management of all the projects. It's your finance background that I need. It's the one area I struggle with." He blushed. "Math was never my strong point, and while I do my best to run the budgets and forward project, I'm often second-guessing myself. I hope I'm doing a good job, but I want you to look through the budgets and deliver a report in plain English showing where we're at, what's problematic, whether we'll have enough cash, and so on. That stuff takes me hours to work out, so I need an expert."

"That I can definitely do," Zane said.

"On top of that, I'd love you to manage some of the fit-outs and construction if you're up for it? We're not at that stage yet; the plans will take quite a while to finalize. But when we are, I'll walk you through what needs to be done and then leave you to engage with the contractors to make it happen. You and I can chat daily, so if there are any questions or problems, we can work them out. I'm stretched too thin and need another me." He grinned. "You're the other me."

Zane laughed. "Not sure anyone will mistake me for you, I might need to get into the gym, but I'm excited to work with you. This is so different from what I've done in the past, and it'll help tourism in the town. It's a win-win for everyone."

"It is, although I guarantee we'll still get some objectors. I'll schedule a town meeting so the residents can come and ask questions. Hopefully, we can put everyone's minds at ease." His expression turned thoughtful. "It is something to consider before you accept the job. Developers are often hated. It takes time to turn people's views around, and sometimes it's impossible. I would understand if you have concerns."

Zane thought for a moment. There was nothing Matt was planning that looked underhanded or purely for his own interest. Of course, he would profit from it, but so would the town. It would bring in more tourists and give a section of the town a lift. He would expect his father to object to anything he was involved in, so he wasn't going to give him a second thought. If he wasn't working at the mill, he wouldn't be good enough. He couldn't see any other reason holding him back. He held out his hand. "I would love to work for you, Matt. Absolutely love to."

Asha was pretty sure someone in charge of the universe was messing with her. It was Tuesday night, and she could honestly say the last two days felt like two months. Every minute of each day dragged. She knew that once the lease was signed, time would pick up again and probably speed by so fast she wouldn't be able to keep up with it, but right now, it was doing her head in.

She'd finished dinner, her house was immaculate, her washing up-to-date and put away, and she had nothing else to do. Any other night like this, she'd be amazed that it was possible to be so organized and would curl up on the couch with Max to watch something on Netflix. She looked around the living room for Max. Usually, he'd be curled up somewhere at this time of night. It was still early. It was around nine that he suddenly woke up for the day and went crazy, running up the curtains and wanting to play. She found him snuggled against a pillow on the couch. She picked him up and cuddled him in her arms like a baby. She smiled as she was instantly rewarded with a deep purr.

"This day's dragging forever, Maxy boy. Tomorrow night I'll bring you some fresh fish to celebrate."

Max rubbed against Asha's hand, insisting that she stroke him under the chin. Her phone rang as she obeyed the cat. She glanced down to where she'd put it. It was her parents requesting FaceTime. They had been away for six weeks, which was the longest period in her life she hadn't seen them. She accepted the call.

"Asha, baby, how are you?"

She couldn't help but smile when her mom's smiling face appeared on the screen, so close up, she could practically see up her nostrils.

"I'm great, Mom. You might need to move the phone back a bit so I can see Dad, too, assuming he's with you?"

The screen went out of focus while her mother repositioned it. Suddenly her dad, in a vivid yellow and white Hawaiian shirt, appeared. "Hey, hon, how are you?"

"Great, Dad, how's the trip? Where are you?"

"We're in Phuket. He patted his stomach, which was considerably larger than when they'd left six weeks earlier. "Oh, my goodness, the food is amazing."

"As is the beer," her mother added, rolling her eyes. "I don't think I'll ever get your dad out of here. He's in love."

"With you too." Her dad laughed, throwing an arm around her mother's shoulder.

"Beer first, curry second, me third. Is that the order?"

"Of course not, the curry's winning at the moment."

Asha smiled as her mother slapped her father's arm playfully. It was so lovely to see them relaxed and happy.

"Tell Steph I've been practicing yoga every day," her mother said. "She'll be shocked."

"She sure will! Why don't you tell her yourself? I assume you plan to call her too?"

"Not tonight, love, we wanted to speak to you. How's everything coming along with the cafe?"

"I sign the papers in the morning. The new menu boards and signage arrived yesterday, and I have tradespeople hired for Thursday and Friday to do a few things for me. I'm hoping to open sometime next week if all goes to plan. That might be a bit premature, but certainly by the week after."

"What about staff?" her father asked. "You can't run a cafe of that size by yourself."

"I've got two part-time staff starting as soon as it opens.

They'll job share and when it gets busy, they'll either increase their hours, or we'll need to get someone else. I don't want to overcapitalize."

"We wanted you to know how proud of you we are, Asha."

A lump immediately formed in Asha's throat. Her father rarely said things like that. The moment she chose not to go to college, she'd known she'd let him down; that he expected greater things of her. Cooking and running a business hadn't seemed enough in his eyes. Something must have changed.

"The food truck was a good start, but this provides you with a real career. It's an amazing opportunity."

"It is, love," her mother added. "We're so thrilled for you. As soon as we get home, we'll be coming in for lunch."

Her father laughed. "Any chance you'll have red curry on the menu?"

Asha joined in his laughter. "Unlikely, but I won't say no. Who knows, Irresistables might become a lot more adventurous as we move forward."

"Okay, hon, we'd better go. Tell Steph we spoke, and we'll call her another night. She makes it hard only having that landline. If you can get her to move into the twenty-first century while we're away, it would be appreciated."

"I'll mention it." Asha blew them both kisses before ending the call. She turned her attention back to Max. "How's that for a surprise, Maxy boy? Dad ringing to say well done rather than tell me to do something more meaningful with my life. That's a turnaround I didn't expect."

Max purred louder and pushed his head into Asha's hand, demanding more affection. She laughed. "I've always known where I stand with you, Maxy, that's for sure. Parents, not so much, but you, my friend, are an open book. Let's hope this new venture keeps them off my back and makes them proud." Asha's thoughts remained with her parents as she gave in to Max's demands. She'd always had a good relationship with them, but the disappointment that she hadn't done more with her life was still there. She'd done her best to dismiss it in the past, but it hadn't been easy. She smiled. As of ten o'clock tomorrow morning, she'd never have to think about it again. She couldn't wait.

Zane shivered as he pulled the back door of Steph's house shut. It was three in the morning, and he'd been tossing and turning since a nightmare brought him out of his sleep two hours earlier. He'd had a few nights reprieve from the nightmares. The nightly interruption had been absent since he'd arrived in Hope's Ridge, and he'd chosen not to give it too much thought. He'd hoped the change of scenery had been enough to rid his subconscious of the terror he'd experienced, but it appeared it hadn't. He sighed as he pulled a blanket around him and sat down in Steph's meditation area. He hoped the energy she'd spoken about earlier might still be floating around to help him.

He'd been taken aback when he'd arrived on Monday afternoon, excited after the meeting with Matt and equally excited to be moving in, to find Steph stony-faced and a lot less friendly than she had been on the weekend.

"What's the matter?" he'd asked. "Have I done something wrong?"

"You did something wrong ten years ago."

"What?"

"The prom. I found out why Asha resents you."

He'd been shocked when Steph explained what had happened. That he'd supposedly said he would make it to fourth base with her.

"I never said any of that." He did his best to reassure Steph. "I liked Ash. I always had. When we were about fourteen, Jenna made me swear I would never go near her. That I'd only ever treat her like a friend. She said if I was with Asha and then we broke up, it would either ruin her relationship with Asha or with me. It was a no-win situation for Jenna, and she didn't want to risk it. That was fine with me. At fourteen, I still wasn't all that interested in girls. But, by the time I was sixteen, Asha was definitely on my radar, but I had to respect Jenna's wishes. So, I was shocked when Jenna told me to ask her to the prom. She said Asha wanted to go but didn't have a date and I'd be perfect for her. I asked Jenna outright whether this still meant I couldn't like Asha in that way. She thought about it for a moment and said if I had genuine feelings for her, then I could act on them, but if I wasn't a hundred percent committed, then I was to be a friend only."

"So, what happened? How did Asha end up hearing about a bet?"

Zane had shaken his head. "I have no idea. The guys might have had that bet, but I didn't. I had no plans other than having a good time at the prom. If Asha had let me kiss her, that would have been amazing, but fourth base on a first date?" He blushed at the thought.

"Well, that's why she froze you out from that night on. She believes she was used in a bet, and that's all she meant to you. The fact she was so hurt about it makes me think she probably had feelings for you."

"I'll see her later in the week," Zane said. "Clear it up." Nausea had filled his stomach. No wonder she'd been so cold toward him and still was. Ten years later, he wouldn't expect her to forgive him; he certainly wouldn't. He'd like to punch those guys, supposedly his friends, for putting her through what they did.

Zane took a deep breath and blew it out, watching his breath turn white in the cool night air. The stars were out, and the big dipper was bright. He continued to watch the sky, hoping he'd see a shooting star or a satellite cross over.

He pulled the blanket around him as the temperature seemed to drop further.

"Zane?"

He started at the sound of Steph's gentle voice.

"You okay?"

He turned where she stood at the back door. "I'm fine. Couldn't sleep. Sorry if I woke you."

"You didn't. I couldn't sleep either. I'm about to make some chamomile tea; would you like some?"

"I'd love one, thank you." Zane smiled as Steph went back inside. His mother had always sworn by chamomile tea when she'd been kept awake late at night. He didn't believe it worked for him, but right now, anything warm would be appreciated.

A few minutes later, the back door closed, and Steph walked over, carrying two mugs. She passed him one and sat down. She didn't say anything at first, just warmed her hands on the cup, eventually taking a small sip.

Zane watched her as her eyes moved to the night sky. She looked like she'd done this many times.

"Do you sit out here often at night?"

Steph's eyes moved back to connect with his, and she gave a wry smile. "That sounded like a bad pick up line."

Zane laughed.

"But, in answer to your question, yes, more often than I'd like to admit."

"I thought your yoga and meditation would have you sleeping like a baby."

"It should, but not always. What about you? Why are you roaming around in the middle of the night?"

Zane averted his gaze back to the stars. He'd planned to leave his problems in the city, certainly not discuss them with anyone in Hope's Ridge.

"You don't have to tell me," Steph added. "I hate talking about my nightmares, so I don't blame you if you want to keep whatever's going on to yourself."

Zane's head snapped back to look at Steph. "You have nightmares?"

She nodded. "I was involved in an accident last year. It left me pretty badly shaken, and I haven't been able to get past it. The nightmares come and go, and anytime I feel stressed, they appear more frequently."

"And you're stressed now?"

She shook her head. "Not in theory. I was stressed when Mary announced she was moving out, and the dreams returned that night. I was fine on the weekend after I knew you were moving in and Monday night too. But tonight, they've come back."

"A new stress?"

Steph shrugged. "Nothing significant. A few changes at the studio with work and teaching but nothing that I'd expect to create stress or anxiety. Sometimes it's a feeling. Like I know something's about to go wrong, but I don't know what it is." She smiled. "You'll probably think I'm crazy, but if something goes wrong tomorrow, you'll know I sensed it."

"That's amazing," Zane said. "Like ESP?"

"Intuition, I think. I'm not sure. Might just be left over from last week's stress. Hopefully, that's all it is. Did you want to talk about why you're sitting out here with me at three in the morning?"

Zane sighed. "No."

Steph sipped her tea. "I'm here anytime you do."

"Thanks." They sat in silence for a few minutes when Zane unexpectedly started talking.

"Three months ago, there was a holdup at work." He closed his eyes, willing the memories to stay away, but instead relived every second. "I'd come into the branch for a meeting. Normally I worked out of head office, so I didn't see much of the frontline action. Anyway, I was being processed through the security area into the back office when three people in black masks with guns entered the building. They fired straight away, shooting the security guard in the leg and then disarming him. One of the guys stood over him with a gun pointed at his head."

Steph sucked in a breath, her hand covering her mouth.

"They meant business. One of them came over to where I was and got me in a headlock. Told the teller to let us through and to get ready to open the vaults." He shook his head. "To be honest, as soon as he said that, I almost wet my pants. They were amateurs. Any professional knows staff don't have access to the vaults. They'll get what's in the tills, but that's it. Money is moved from the tills every hour and locked away until it's transported from the bank later in the day. If they'd done their research, they would have known this."

"What happened?"

Zane closed his eyes, willing his eyes to stay dry. A lump caught in his throat. "He repeated his demand. The teller tried to explain that it wasn't possible and that she didn't have authority. He didn't let her finish what she was saying. He shot her and called out for the manager."

Steph gasped. "Was she okay?"

Zane nodded. "Luckily, it was only a flesh wound. She crumpled to the floor immediately. Fainted from the shock. Whether she meant to or not, it was the best thing she could have done. I thought he'd killed her." He wiped a tear from his cheek. "She was okay, but in my nightmares, she dies. I think the gunman thought he killed her too as he left her alone. The manager came forward, said they could have anything they wanted. He explained the vault had an entry lock with a timer on it. This meant that even if he opened it immediately, it wouldn't unlock for ten minutes. In the meantime, he asked the gunman if they wanted the tills emptied." Zane gave a wry laugh. "He was telling them how to rob the bank. The other one, not standing over the guard, put the customers into a group on the floor with his gun pointed at them. They were terrified."

Steph was listening in silence.

"As the tills were emptied, the manager told them that the police would probably arrive any minute, that he didn't think there was time for the vault. One of the gunmen went crazy. He wouldn't listen when the manager tried to explain that entering the bank with weapons was detected by the bank's security systems, automatically triggering the 911 response. That it was nothing he or his staff had done. We could hear sirens as he finished talking. The guy shoved me into the wall and told the other two to grab the moneybags and get out of there. I'd hardly breathed the entire time. I was helpless. I couldn't help myself or anyone else. When he told the others to go, I was relieved. It was about to end. I was wrong. The guy who'd been holding me opened fire. He laughed like a maniac as he emptied his magazine. He shot two customers, luckily only in the arm and leg. He was either a bad shot or hadn't intended to hurt anyone seriously, but we weren't to know that. They left two minutes before the police stormed the building."

"Were they caught?"

"Two of the three were. The third is probably in a remote country far away by now, but I think it's not knowing where he is that keeps me on edge."

"You think he'd come after you?"

"No, he wouldn't have a clue who I am, and I certainly didn't do anything to mess up their plans. It's more that he and people like him are still out there. You can be doing your routine day job, and something like that happens. It happens more and more often, being in the wrong place at the wrong time. I think that's what scares me. I was looking over my shoulder every time I went anywhere. My girlfriend, Lucy, left me. She tried to help me at first, but I think she decided I was a basket case." He smiled. "In hindsight, I don't blame her. I'd hope I wouldn't have done the same, but I might have. I wasn't open to help."

"Until now. You let Jenna bring you home."

"Jenna didn't give me a choice. She came over last Wednesday, unannounced. Let herself in and found me in a fetal position behind the couch. She stood over me and told me she wasn't leaving until I got up and followed her."

Steph stared at Zane. "But she brought you here and left you. Isn't she worried you'll be back in the same position in a week's time? Maybe she should have found you some external help."

Zane laughed. "Don't worry, Jenna doesn't do things by halves. She's ringing me three times a day and has threatened that if I don't pick up, she'll move back here and be in my face every second of the day. In addition to her checkups, she's insisting I see a psychologist. Daniel something or other. My first appointment's on Friday."

"Daniel Varrs," Steph said. "Dan to the locals. I see him now and again. He's quite good. He moved here a couple of years ago, so there's no reason you'd know him."

Zane raised an eyebrow. "Yet you're out here in the middle of the night talking to me, running from your nightmares. Are you sure he's good?"

"He made me realize the accident wasn't my fault. That was a good starting place."

"Did you want to talk about what happened?"

Steph shook her head and checked her watch. "Not tonight. It's nearly four. We should both probably try and get some sleep."

Zane got to his feet. The tea had warmed him through, and he was tired. Unburdening himself to Steph had been unexpected. He stopped and faced her as they entered the house. "Thank you. It means a lot that you listened to me tonight. Other than Jenna, I haven't spoken about what happened. And even with her not in that kind of detail."

Steph pulled him into a hug. "I'm glad you felt comfortable enough to share what you're going through. I'm here anytime you need to talk, okay."

He hugged her back. "You've got no idea how nice it is to feel like I've made a friend."

Steph pulled away and smiled. "I do know. I feel the same way."

Asha opened the roller door of Irresistables at six on Wednesday morning. She was half an hour earlier than usual, but she'd hardly slept; excitement and anticipation pulsed through her veins all night. In the end, she'd pulled herself out of bed and driven over to the food truck for an early morning start. In four hours, she'd be signing the lease, and a new chapter in her life would begin. She'd been baking since four and had six dozen muffins with another two trays in the oven ready for the morning trade. She usually sold out of her baked goods and hoped this would be the case today. If not, the nursing home always appreciated an impromptu afternoon tea. Sometimes she'd bake a couple of dozen extra to have an excuse to drop in on the residents, but today she might not need any excuses, it was quite likely she'd have plenty left over.

First customers trickled in around six-forty-five, and by seven-thirty, she was run off her feet. The seven-thirty to eight o'clock crowd was always the busiest. It would then settle down until midmorning when there would be more coffee and muffin orders and then continue steadily until after lunch. She'd asked Orla to come in a few minutes before ten to look after business for her while she met with Andy to sign the lease and go through the conditions. She was immensely grateful to Orla, who had helped her out on many occasions, and she was one of the women who'd be working part-time at the new premises.

Time slowed down at nine, and the hour until ten o'clock dragged. Orla arrived at five to ten, giving Asha a few minutes to tidy herself. As she ran a brush through her hair, she wasn't sure why she was bothering. She'd known Andy most of her life and saw him regularly when he collected his coffee. He wouldn't be expecting her to look any different than she usually did.

At five past ten, his car drove up. Asha was sitting at one of the tables, nervously tapping her foot, waiting for him. Orla looked over and gave her a thumbs up as Andy got out of his car. He stuffed his hands in his coat pockets as he made his way over to her table and sat down. His smile didn't reach his eyes. Asha's heart raced. Where were his files? The paperwork? She took a deep breath. She needed to act professionally. "Would you like coffee?"

"I would," Andy hesitated. "But we need to talk first."

Asha's heart sank. Something had happened.

"There's been a development with the premises I didn't anticipate."

Asha waited for him to continue.

"I had the exclusive contract to lease the building, but I didn't have the contract to sell it. Jacob's Realty in Tall Oaks did. I had a phone call yesterday from Martin Jacob advising that he was given instructions by the owner to sell the property, and the deal had been closed."

"It's been sold?"

Andy nodded. "I didn't call you because I couldn't believe it, to be honest. I couldn't get the owner on the phone until about an hour ago. He confirmed that an offer had been made through Jacob's, and he'd accepted it. He owned the three lots next to the cafe too apparently, and all four have been sold. He thanked me for my business and hung up. I received an email minutes later confirming everything he said and terminating my contract." He reached into his pocket and took out a folded piece of paper and handed it to Asha.

With a shaking hand, she took it from him and read it. The property had been sold, and there was nothing Andy, or she could do about it.

"Did you ask who bought it? Whether there's an opportunity to lease it from the new owner? They might have bought it as an investment and require a tenant."

"I did ask. Matt Law bought the four lots. He's planning a redevelopment from what I understand. I contacted the council after I got off the phone, and he's already been talking to them about redevelopment." He took another sheet of paper from his pocket. "Matt and his project manager are listed as contacts here. I guess you could call him and ask if they'd consider leasing it to you, but from what I understand, Matt has a clear vision of what he intends to build. I'm not sure that he'll be looking for tenants; staff perhaps, but not business owners."

Asha took the piece of paper from him, her mind barely registering what Andy was saying. She was supposed to be signing her lease. She was supposed to be moving on with the next stage of her career. How had this happened? Her eyes focused on the paper. Matt Law was listed as the owner and property developer. Directly under his name was the name of the project manager. Asha's fists clenched as she was confronted with the name of the one man she'd been willing to forgive. Zane Larsen.

4

_Z_ane was amazed to wake and see it was after ten. At Steph's suggestion, he'd gone back to bed, not expecting to fall asleep, but he had. He stretched and grinned. Unburdening himself to Steph, plus the chamomile tea must have helped. He was meeting Matt at one to discuss his employment contract and to be briefed on the project. His hours would officially start on Thursday. He pulled himself up out of bed and slipped on his running shorts. He had time to run to the far end of the lake trail before coming home to shower, eat, and prepare for his meeting.

He moved quietly through the house in case Steph had also managed to get back to sleep. He smiled as the front door opened, and she appeared in her yoga clothes.

"Thought you might still be asleep."

She raised an eyebrow. "It's after ten. I've taught two classes already. I'll be heading back in a couple of hours."

Zane laughed. "Guess I'm the lazy one then. Thanks for last night. The tea worked a treat. I feel better than I have in ages. It's amazing the difference sleep makes."

Steph gave a wry smile. "I wouldn't know. But yoga helps too. Although I didn't get back to sleep, the energy in the studio gives me a shot of something good. Not to say I won't need a nap between my afternoon and evening sessions."

"Do you find it annoying going to and fro all day?"

"Nope. I love it. We get different people at different times of the day. It's only Wednesday that we do the middle of the day classes. Usually, it's early morning through until ten or eleven and then back again at five. No one who works can come during the day, which in a town this size, is a bit limiting. I have a few of the seniors up from the retirement home for the midday classes today. Gives them an outing and some exercise."

"The seniors are doing hot yoga?"

Steph laughed. "No, I tailor a program more suitable for them. Mind you, a few would be fine with the hot classes and do come to some of them at other time slots."

A vehicle screeched to a halt outside, causing Steph to cross over to the window in the living room to see who was in such a hurry. Asha's small blue van was parked half up on the curb. Her sister flung open the driver's door and jumped out, her face set in a hard line.

Steph turned to Zane. "It's Asha. She looks furious. She might not be as forgiving about the prom situation as I thought."

Zane's stomach churned. He'd planned to apologize to Asha but had hoped to initiate the visit rather than be on the defensive. He took a deep breath as Steph went to let her sister in.

"Where is he?"

The anger in Asha's voice was unmissable.

"I'll kill him."

"Calm down, Ash. You said you were going to put it all behind you. You can't confront anyone in this mood."

64

There was no reply, just heavy footsteps crashing through the house.

"I'm in here," he called from the living room. He wasn't sure whether to go out and meet her head on or let her find him.

She slammed into the room, her face dark, her eyes flashing, with Steph a step behind her. "How could you?"

He held up his hands. "Look, I'm so sorry. I planned to come and find you in the next couple of days and explain what happened. I didn't know anything about it, truly Asha. I would never have done that to you."

Asha opened her mouth, then closed it again. Confusion crossed her face. "You've already done it to me and apologizing in a couple of days won't help."

"Honestly, if I'd had any idea, I would have done things differently."

"You still can."

"I can certainly explain to you what happened from my point of view. Those guys lied to you. I had no idea until Steph told me what you experienced."

Asha spun around and faced Steph. "You knew too? How could you? Why didn't you warn me?"

Steph looked as confused as Zane was beginning to feel. She tried to take her sister's arm, but Asha pulled away.

"I mean it, Steph, how could you. You know what this meant to me."

"Ash," Steph's voice was gentle. "What are you talking about? Zane's referring to prom. He didn't do anything wrong that night, but he hasn't had a chance to come and talk to you about it yet."

"What?"

"She's right, Ash, what the guys told you was all lies. I had no idea about any bet. I asked you to the prom because I wanted to go with you."

"I'm not talking about the prom." Asha's voice verged on hysteria. "I couldn't care less about the prom. I'm talking about my cafe."

Zane ran his hand through his hair. "Okay, now I'm confused. I know nothing at all about your cafe. You'll need to fill me in."

"The cafe?" Steph said. "Weren't you signing the lease this morning."

Asha closed her eyes momentarily as if trying to calm herself down. "There is no lease to sign because this low life," her eyes flashed open and drilled into Zane, "has made sure that any chance of my opening my own business won't happen."

"What? Ash, there's been some kind of mistake. I have no idea what you're talking about."

"Really?" She pulled a piece of paper from her pocket and thrust it at him. "So, this isn't your name on this document?"

He opened it and stared at a council query form. It had Matt's name and listed Zane's as project manager. He suppressed a smile. He knew Matt worked quickly, but he hadn't expected to see his name listed on documents. He wasn't officially employed yet.

"What is it?" Steph asked, moving closer to Zane to look at the paper. He passed it to her.

"It's a council query form that, by the looks of it, Matt's submitted. He's bought some lots up on Lake Drive that he plans to develop. Don't worry, what he's planning is amazing. The development fits in with the sandstone look and feel of the existing buildings up that end of town. It'll give the town a lift. There will be public meetings to answer any questions and present the planning applications before they're officially submitted to council."

"Oh, no." Steph passed the paper back to Zane before turning to Asha. "And the development includes the cafe?"

Asha nodded, her anger subsiding, and her eyes filling with tears.

"I still have no idea what's going on," Zane said. "Ash, why are you so angry with me? Matt only offered me the position in the last couple of days. It's a perfect job for me with my finance background and allows me to learn some project management skills. I can't imagine too many other jobs will throw themselves at me in Hope's Ridge."

Steph put a protective arm around Asha before addressing Zane. "Ash was supposed to sign a five-year lease this morning on the Sandstone Cafe. It was her big opportunity to move from the food truck into proper premises. There was never any mention of the cafe being sold."

Zane's heart sank. "I had no idea." He was silent for a moment digesting the information. "Ash, I'm so sorry. I don't even know if Matt would have known."

"Matt definitely knew." Asha's voice trembled. "I told him of my plans a few weeks ago when the building became vacant." She shook her head. "I probably tipped him off that it was available."

"He would have found out regardless," Steph said. "The whole tax evasion thing was a huge scandal; everyone in the town knew within hours of the IRS getting involved. You know what this town's like for sharing news, particularly bad news."

Asha sighed. "Yes, you're right, he probably would have found out regardless."

"He's planning to keep the cafe," Zane said. "He plans to make improvements, change opening times and menus, but he isn't getting rid of it. Perhaps you should talk to him, see if there's an opportunity to work together."

"I don't want to work with Matt Law," Asha said. "This was supposed to be my business. My dream." She took a deep breath. "Sorry for barging in and accusing you. I can see you knew nothing about my plans for the cafe." She gave Steph a quick hug. "Sorry. It's such a disappointment. I'd better get back to work. I stormed out after Andy delivered the news and drove straight here. Poor Orla has no idea where I went."

Steph put her arm back around Asha's shoulders. "Come on, I'll walk you out. I'll come over and see you after my afternoon classes."

"You don't have to do that."

"Of course I do. I'll bring some wine and cook dinner for you. We'll come up with another solution. Don't worry, Ash, this feels awful, I know, but something more amazing will happen. It's how the universe works."

A lump lodged in Zane's throat as he listened to the exchange between the sisters. Asha wiped her eyes, and in contradiction to the strong words she spouted, Steph looked like she might cry at any minute.

He sat down on the couch and took his head in his hands. Things were finally looking up and now this.

Moments later, Steph reappeared. "It's not your fault. You didn't know anything about it. At least it wasn't you who'd bought the property and planned to develop it. That would have made Ash beyond mad."

"It might have been better if it was me," Zane said. "Then I could lease the building to Ash, and we'd both win. She'd get her cafe, and I'd get a tenant." He stood. "You know, there's no reason that couldn't still happen. Leave it with me. I'm meeting with Matt at one. I'll put it to him as a suggestion. It would mean he could have the cafe up and running immediately, and we could look at renovating later."

"Do you think he'd go for it?"

"He's a good guy, Steph. He says he wants to have the town on board for this project, so this would certainly be a way to show that. It would be amazing PR for him. I gather the town considers him to be a shark like his dad, but from what I've seen, he's not. He's passionate about Hope's Ridge and wants to make a difference to the town."

Steph smiled. "It would be amazing if you could talk him around."

"I'm not sure it will be a case of needing to talk him around. Without doing the figures, it would make good business sense to have part of the project operating and earning an income while the other areas are developed. Like I said earlier, the plans for the Sandstone Cafe aren't too big. The biggest renovation will be building access to the roof for a bar giving beautiful views of the lake. Anyway, leave it with me. I'll chat with him at one and see what we can do. Don't say anything to Asha. I don't want to get her hopes up."

Steph nodded.

"Okay, I'll see if I can still get to the end of the lake trail and back before I need to get ready to meet Matt. I'll call you straight after the meeting and let you know how it goes. Can you write your mobile down for me somewhere, I realized yesterday I don't have it?"

Steph shook her head. "No mobile. Don't believe in technology."

"You don't believe in it?" Zane laughed. "Okay, that's a new one. In that case, I'll drop in and see if you're home. If you're not, and it's good news, I'll find Asha and let her know."

"Thanks, Zane." Steph smiled. "You're a good guy."

Zane laughed again. "Not sure Asha would agree with you there. That's the second horrible thing she assumes I've done to her. I still need to clear up the prom issue. Not that that's a high priority for her right now."

"It's not, but you still need to do it," Steph said.

Zane mock saluted her. "Will do, captain. Now, I'm off for my run."

Asha stopped one street back from Irresistables, needing to compose herself before she faced Orla or any customers. She turned the van off and leaned her head forward onto the steering wheel, her body convulsing with sobs. She was bitterly disappointed. She should be celebrating today, not hiding in her vehicle, crying her eyes out. Her anger had dissolved as she saw Zane's reaction. He'd been genuinely horrified that she thought he'd known what impact Matt's business would have on her plans. She was angry at Matt. Steph was right; he would have known that the cafe had become vacant, and he was a businessman. If he'd had the money to buy the other three lots, then it probably wasn't about ruining her plans. They probably weren't worth considering.

She sat up as she realized this was what hurt the most. She'd been excited about sharing her plans with Matt when he'd come in for coffee the afternoon after she'd contacted Andy and asked him to draw up a lease. Matt had seemed interested and enthusiastic for her. Never at any stage had he mentioned his interest in the property or plans to buy it. Even if he hadn't known at that stage, he should have been to see her the moment the sale went through. They'd known each other for years. It was common courtesy, if nothing else.

Asha took a deep breath, found some tissues in the glove compartment, and wiped her eyes. She needed to be more like

Steph. To think positively, to believe another opportunity would turn up. She still had the food truck, and right now, she should be there, appreciating that she was still a business owner and did quite well. She took another deep breath. She would get on with things. She wouldn't let this disappointment get her down. She restarted the car and continued to Lake Drive. Every positive thought she'd mustered disappeared the moment the food truck came into view. Matt Law stood in front of the serving window holding his hand out for the cup Orla was passing him. She pulled to a stop and took a deep breath. She honestly thought she might kill him.

She pushed open the van door and willed herself to stay calm. He might be here to apologize and to offer her a lease on the premises. She strode purposefully toward him.

"Morning, Ash." He smiled as she neared. "Your raspberry muffins are to die for. I couldn't help myself; ate the whole thing while Orla got my coffee ready."

"Glad you enjoyed it." Asha stared at him and waited. Come on. Where's the explanation, the apology?

"Got a busy day ahead?" he asked.

Asha shook her head. "Not as busy as I thought it would be."

"Well, I have." He grinned and raised the coffee in a gesture of thanks. "Better get on. Have a great day, and I'll see you again tomorrow for another muffin. Can't believe how good they are." He turned and began walking toward his car.

Fury rose within Asha. That was it? No mention of the cafe?

"Matt, wait?"

Asha moved toward him as he turned expectantly to face her.

"Problem?"

71

"Why didn't you tell me you'd planned to buy the Sandstone Cafe?"

He frowned. "I don't usually discuss my development plans with anyone until they're finalized."

"But I told you I was planning to lease the premises for my own business."

"And if the owner hadn't agreed to sell, then that probably would be exactly what would have happened, and I would be disappointed to have missed out."

"You don't think you owe me an apology?"

"An apology? Asha, it's business. I've been in discussions, planning the development of the other three lots on that corner for months. The cafe coming onto the market was a huge bonus. It means what I am planning won't just be good, it'll be fantastic."

Asha shook her head. "You don't care, do you?"

"Would you be apologizing to me if the sale had fallen through? Of course not. You'd be pleased that it all worked out in your favor. Exactly as I'm pleased for myself and the town. It will bring more tourists. The shops will all benefit, as will the rental operators. I won't be able to supply everything to the vacationers; they'll get the benefit of the overflow as will you."

"If your plans are approved," Asha said.

Matt's eyes narrowed. "What's that supposed to mean? Are you planning to lodge objections?"

"Maybe."

"On what grounds? Sour grapes?" He laughed. "I don't think the council will pay too much attention to that line of attack. Grow up, Ash. If you want to succeed in the business world, you roll with the punches. One door closes, you make another one open. Playing the victim won't help you."

Asha clenched her fists. How she'd love to wipe the smile off his arrogant face. "I'm not playing the victim. I told you about my plans for the cafe weeks ago. If the situation were reversed, I would have come to you and let you know that I had plans for the premises. I wouldn't have let you be blindsided the morning you went to sign the lease."

Matt shrugged. "Not my problem. Andy should have been in touch with you earlier. Now, I need to get to work. I have a meeting with my project manager this afternoon to prepare for."

Asha watched as he got in his black BMW. She was furious. How hard would it have been to admit he could have handled the situation better? She picked up a rock and hurled it at the departing car, a satisfied smile playing on her lips at the dull thud as the rock bounced off the trunk. Matt's stoplights came on. He reversed back and opened his window. His eyes were black with fury.

"You'll regret that, Asha. You'll really regret it."

Asha laughed. Throwing a rock at a car wasn't something she'd ever thought she'd do. But right now, it was the only thing to have raised her spirits all morning.

After showering and making a sandwich, Zane walked into town to Matt's office. He realized he hadn't mentioned to Matt that he didn't have transport. He imagined he was going to need it as a lot of the town's suppliers were based in Drayson's Landing and some further away in Tall Oaks. He'd sold his car when he'd moved in with Lucy. He hadn't needed it as it was easier to catch the train into his office, and their apartment only had one car space. As Lucy did need a car, it made sense that his was sold, and they shared hers on the weekends. He had planned to buy one, so that might become a priority.

Matt stood outside his office, examining the back section

of his Roadster. The BMW was rather flashy for Hope's Ridge, not that Zane would tell him that.

"Everything okay?" Zane asked, moving closer. He whistled as he saw the large dent and scraped paintwork on the trunk. It looked like something had hit the car. "Jeepers, what happened?"

"Combination of a rock and a disgruntled resident," Matt said. "It turns out not everyone's in favor of our development."

"You're kidding. Someone threw a rock at your car?"

Matt nodded. "Yep, someone who can't control their anger. I'll get it fixed next week. Will probably cost a packet."

"Insurance?"

"Not sure if they cover crazy rock-throwing incidents."

"It's willful damage," Zane said. "You should call the police. They'll make them pay, even if insurance won't."

Matt shook his head. "She was angry. I understand her point of view, but I don't agree with it. I might be better off waiting until the town hears about the development plans before I get the car fixed. There might be more dents in it by then." He grinned. "Come on, let's chat business. I'm stoked to have you on board, by the way."

"Me too." Zane followed him into the building. "I've been thinking about the development since we spoke on Monday and wondered if you'd considered getting the Sandstone Cafe up and running straight away?"

"After it's renovated?"

Zane followed Matt through to his office and sat down at a small meeting table. "I was thinking, maybe before. That we might work on the rest of the development first and do the cafe last. That way, it can be open to the public immediately and provide them with something they like while the other development takes place. It isn't a bad place to hold meetings to answer the town's questions too, put on some free food and coffee. That usually buys people's votes pretty quickly."

"Use it as a way to butter up the town?"

"If it's needed. It might make them feel more included, part of the development, and be more supportive of it. Once the other lots are finished, we can then decide what happens with the cafe. It would also give you an income stream immediately rather than having to wait until everything's complete."

Matt nodded. "It's not a bad idea. I haven't confirmed my exact plans for the cafe. It wasn't in the original development plans as it only recently became available. It'd give us more time to research how it would be best developed. Are you up for recruiting staff for the cafe? We'd need someone who knows what they're doing to manage it."

"I was thinking that leasing it to an existing business might be a better way to go. If we make the initial lease twelve months, that will give us enough time to get the other development finished. We might decide to keep the cafe under lease at that stage or terminate it and go our own way. It keeps our options open."

Matt sat in thought for a few moments. "I like the way you're thinking. It's smart. Let's go through the rest of the plans and timelines and see how the schedule would be impacted by doing it that way around. In theory, the rest of the lots would be finished ahead of my original schedule. Getting a tenant might be an issue."

"I've got one who'd sign a lease today if you were happy to go ahead." Zane grinned. If Matt agreed to this, Asha might change her opinion of him. See him as a good guy, a guy who cared. Not a guy who she'd believed for ten years made a bet about getting her into bed. Seeing how upset she'd been earlier that morning had affected him. He'd wanted to put his arms around her and protect her. It had shocked him when those feelings surfaced. She'd been distant and unfriendly for years, yet he still wanted her friendship, her approval.

"Perfect. As long as it isn't Asha Jones, I'm happy to consider your person."

Zane's mouth dropped open. All of this discussion had been so he could recommend Asha.

Matt stared at him. "From your face, I assume you were talking about Asha?"

Zane closed his mouth and nodded. "She'd already made plans for the cafe. I believe she has signage and menu boards ordered. She'd been led to believe she was signing a five-year lease. Why won't you consider her?"

Matt's face hardened. "I might have if she'd had a civil conversation with me this morning rather than being argumentative and downright rude. Her throwing arm's pretty impressive as you've seen by the dent in the back of my car."

"Asha did that?"

"Yep."

Zane shook his head. She was not making this easy for him. "If she paid for the repairs, would you consider her as a tenant?"

"Nope. I wouldn't want to be in business with someone who flies off the handle like that. In fact, she's not someone I'd want to be in any kind of relationship with." He raised an eyebrow. "If you're planning to start something with her, I suggest you be careful. Now, let's start looking at the plans. I'm still open to your suggestion about the cafe. Finding a tenant, however, might be the issue."

Zane took the pages Matt held out to him and did his best to push his disappointment and all thoughts of Asha from his mind and concentrate on the figures.

Asha's head was pounding by the time she let herself in through her front door around three that afternoon. It had been a long day, full of emotion, and she was exhausted.

Max came running down the hallway to meet her, and she leaned down and scooped him up. She buried her face in his fluffy tummy. He purred and snuggled into her arms. Asha smiled, how could she not with this greeting?

"Thank goodness for you, Max. Coming home to an empty house on a day like today would probably have done me in."

The cat wriggled in her arms, so she carried him through to the living area and sank into her favorite blue wingback chair. Max immediately snuggled into her lap and raised his head. Asha laughed and stroked him under the chin. "If only my life were as simple as yours."

"Knock-knock." Steph's voice traveled down the hallway.

"Come in," Asha called. "I'm in the living area, but I can't move."

Steph appeared in the doorway, a large bouquet in her arms.

"Wow, you shouldn't have," Asha said. "You can't afford those."

Steph smiled. "No, I can't. The flowers were at the front door. Didn't you see them when you came in?"

Asha shook her head. "I was in a daze. I probably wouldn't have noticed if they were on the doormat. Who are they from?"

Steph lay the flowers on the coffee table and took the card from the arrangement. She handed it to Asha and sat down on the couch across from her. Max immediately left Asha's lap and went to visit Steph. She laughed as he lay down beside her on the couch and stretched out, exposing his belly. She scratched and stroked it. "He's more like a dog than a cat. Shame I'll be sneezing any minute."

Asha smiled as she opened the envelope. "To our dearest, Ash. We're so proud of you. The new cafe will be a huge success. Love Mom and Dad." She threw the card onto the coffee table beside the flowers. "I can already see Dad's face when I have to tell him. It'll be that *you should have gone to college* look."

"Of course, it won't be. He'll be as disappointed as we all are. Did you see Zane again today?"

"Zane? No, why?"

"I was wondering, that's all."

"No, and I realize he knew nothing about my plans to lease the premises. If he wants to work with an idiot like Matt Law, that's his problem."

Steph nodded. "Is it worth looking at any of the other premises along Main Street? A couple are standing empty."

Asha shook her head. "No, it was the positioning of the Sandstone Cafe that I loved. That plus the fact it was already fitted out as a cafe. It would cost me thousands to fit out a shop not already set up for it. That would mean huge loans from the bank, which I'd prefer not to do." She sighed. "I spent the afternoon calling to cancel the tradesmen I'd hired for tomorrow and Friday, then firing the women I'd hired before they worked a shift. I'll know for another time not to be so efficient."

"How did they take the news?"

"Disappointed. Both were thrilled when I offered them jobs. I think they were looking forward to being part of the team as much as I was. I've got a wonderful sign to hang out somewhere too."

"Store it until you need it," Steph said.

There was a knock on the front door.

"It's like rush hour in here," Asha said, standing. "You keep up with your job while I answer it."

Steph smiled and continued rubbing Max's belly.

"Zane?" Asha opened the front door, surprised to see him standing there.

"Can I come in?"

"Of course, Steph's in the living room if you want to go through. First left," she said as he walked down the hallway. What was Zane doing here? She probably owed him another apology. She'd given him a bit of one that morning, but something more, now that she'd calmed down, was in order.

Steph appeared in the hallway as she walked from the door to join them. "I'd better go," Steph said. "I'm teaching again at five, and I think Zane wants to talk to you alone. I can come over later if you want? Cook you that meal I promised."

"No but thank you. I need an early night. I hardly slept last night, and then with everything that happened today, I'm exhausted. I plan to have an early night and wake up tomorrow knowing it's a new day and a new beginning."

Steph smiled. Those were her words Asha was saying. She was always going on about living in the moment and not dwelling on things we couldn't control. Asha would do her best to embrace that spirit and move forward.

"Okay, I'll drop by the food truck in the morning. See how you're feeling."

"You don't have to keep tabs on me, Steph."

Steph raised an eyebrow. "Yes, little sis, I do."

Asha hesitated for a moment outside the door of the living room and ran her hand through her wavy auburn hair. She probably should have brushed it. She shook her head. What was she thinking? This was Zane. She didn't need to do anything to impress him. She plastered a smile to her lips, entered the room, and immediately stopped. The fake smile disappeared and was replaced by a genuine one. Zane, eyes closed, was lying on the couch with Max snuggled into the crook of his arm, his head resting on Zane's chest. It was a gorgeous sight. Asha's heart contracted. Big, strong Zane with little Max. They were a perfect combination.

She shook herself and cleared her throat.

Zane's eyes immediately jolted open. He smiled. "Sorry, I found a friend who was fairly insistent I lie down."

Asha walked over and scooped Max up, much to the cat's disgust. She sat down and put Max on her lap, but he ran straight back over and jumped onto the couch next to Zane. "Sorry," she said. "He's rather forceful, runs the house."

"Don't all cats?" Zane rubbed Max around the neck and under the chin as the cat repositioned himself next to him.

Asha nodded. "I'm sorry about this morning. I should never have jumped to the conclusion that you knew about my application to lease the cafe."

"No need to apologize. I would have been upset too. I wanted to come and chat with you. I had an idea after you left about convincing Matt that we lease you the cafe for the next twelve months before we do any work on it. Leave us to concentrate on the other three lots and you to run the cafe. I was hoping that at the end of the lease term, you and he would come to an arrangement where, even if renovations were required, he would leave you in the space as a tenant."

Nausea swirled in the pit of Asha's stomach. She'd launched a rock, quite a big one, at Matt's pride and joy. Within half an hour of doing it, guilt set in. It was an expensive car and would cost a lot to get fixed. Orla had suggested she calm down and see Matt in the morning with her checkbook open. "No point making enemies of powerful people in this town." Orla was right. She was silly to get someone like Matt offside. He had a lot of influence over the town, and at some stage, she might need his support—definitely someone to be civil with.

"Did you speak to Matt about it?"

Zane nodded. "I did, but my timing was terrible."

Asha couldn't help but smile. "Let me guess; he'd recently become a victim of a stoning."

Zane laughed. "Yes, you could say that."

Asha groaned. "I plan to see him in the morning and offer to pay for the damage. I won't lie; it was so liberating hurling that rock at him. He deserved it. He was so smug, so arrogant. Part of me wanted to hit him with it. I don't imagine it's put me high up the list of tenants for the café?"

Zane shook his head. "No, I'm afraid it hasn't."

"If I pay for the damage?"

"Still, no. I asked him that myself, but he was clear that he didn't want someone who was volatile or had anger issues working with him."

"I didn't realize I was so volatile until today."

"I'd call it passionate. You were deeply disappointed, and you showed that reaction."

"And put the final nail in the coffin as far as the cafe is concerned."

"I'm happy to work on him for you," Zane said. "But I can't guarantee anything."

"No, I've made my bed as Mom would say. I'll regroup and start making another plan. I still have the food truck, so there's no urgency. I'd best take my time planning my next expansion. Hopefully, Steph's right and something better will become available."

Zane nodded, still stroking Max. "If there's anything I can do to help at any time, say the word. I feel like I have a lot to make up to you, Ash."

"You've nothing to make up to me over this. This was all my own stupid doing."

His dark eyes met hers. "Not over this. Over the prom. Steph told me what you went through."

"It's old news. Let's not rake it up. I'm happy to start again from now."

Zane shook his head. "I'd like you to hear me out. You and I have different experiences of what happened that night." He went on to tell her how excited he was when she agreed to go with him. That Jenna had finally relented and said if he liked Asha, then she was okay with it. How he'd felt ten-foot-tall walking into the prom with her. School was about to end, and he had a chance with a girl he'd had a crush on for years. "It was as if a whole new life was about to start." He went on to tell her how he came back from the bathroom planning to ask if she'd go to the movies with him that weekend on a proper date. That he was nervous. To discover she'd gone home had shocked him.

"I couldn't understand it. I thought we were having such a great time."

Asha couldn't believe what she was hearing. He *had* wanted to be at the prom with her. He *had* had feelings like she had. "What about Chippy and Jack? They had quite a bit to tell me that night."

Zane shook his head. "The first I've heard about any bet was when Steph told me on Monday. I had no idea. I would never have made that kind of bet or treated you so badly. As I said to Steph, if we'd kissed that night, I probably would have jumped out of my skin. I certainly wouldn't have expected the night to go any further than that. I'm not sure if I would have wanted it to. I liked you. We would have taken things slowly. Gone on dates, got to know each other as more than Jenna's friend and Jenna's brother."

"You honestly didn't know of the bet?"

"Not until Steph told me."

Asha let out a long breath. She'd held onto this for years.

Truly believing the boy she liked had done something so awful to her. Instead, it was his stupid friends who thought they were funny. Zane had liked her, had wanted to date her. "I feel like such an idiot."

"Don't. Of course, I wish we'd worked it out ten years ago, but we didn't, and we have now. I would never hurt you, Ash, not then and not now."

Her eyes met his. They were full of sorrow, compassion, and what? Desire? No, he couldn't like her now, not after all of this. She'd thrown a rock at his bosses' car earlier; he probably thought she was crazy.

She was at a loss for words. She should probably offer him a drink or something, but right now, she wanted him to go. She needed to be with her thoughts. Unravel what had happened today, with the cafe, with Matt and now with Zane. Tears filled her eyes, she was exhausted, and it was all too much.

"Hey," Zane said, his tone gentle. He detached Max from him, stood, and came over to stand in front of her. He crouched down and put his hands on her knees. "There's no need to be upset. What happened in the past happened, and we can move on from it on good terms, I hope." He searched her eyes, waiting for an answer.

Asha nodded.

"So, how about this. We pretend it's the night before the prom. We both have a million things running around our heads. Mine, for instance, are questions like does she like me? Is she only going with me because I'm Jenna's brother? Will she say yes if I ask her out? Whereas your thoughts," he grinned, "are more like, wow, he's so handsome. I'm so lucky to be his date. I think I'll have to ask him out after."

Asha laughed and swatted his hands off her knees. "You wish." She stood, breaking the spell that had descended on them. "Thanks, Zane. I appreciate you dropping in."

Zane nodded and walked toward the door. "I'll take that as my cue to leave. But, Ash." He turned to face her, his eyes boring into hers. "Give serious thought to that last suggestion. The one where you realize you want to ask me out."

Asha's stomach flipped. Was he serious? For the past ten years, up until a few hours ago, he'd been the enemy. Now he was suggesting that change. Her heart had been trampled once today, would she risk it being trampled again so soon?

Zane's gaze moved from Asha to where Max lay on the couch. "See you next time, Max." He gave her a wink and let himself out of the front door.

*Z*ane pulled his new black pickup into the lot outside J.R Construction. Lately, he seemed to spend more time in Drayson's Landing than Hope's Ridge. Two weeks had passed since he'd spoken with Asha, and he had to admit he was disappointed he hadn't heard from her. Ten years might have passed, but the attraction he felt to her as a teenager hadn't. He'd decided to give her some space, and coupled with a hectic work schedule, he'd hardly had time to do anything about asking her out himself.

"Zane, ol' man." Henry Busterling clapped him on the back as he entered the construction offices.

"Hey, Buster. How're the plans coming along?"

"All done for the three lots we need to provide public notification for. Still working on the existing Sandstone Cafe, but that should be finished later today. I can drop that into you myself. I've got a hot date tonight at Traders, so will be down your way."

"Hot date? Sounds promising."

Buster laughed. "I wish. Isaak owes me a couple of beers, so I said I'd stop in to collect. It's about as interesting as life gets right now."

"Really? Thought you'd have women flocking around you." Zane wasn't joking. Buster reminded him of one of those guys off an ad for aftershave. Blonde hair, deep blue eyes, clean shaven. He was probably in his mid-thirties. It was a surprise he hadn't settled down.

Buster's eyes clouded over. "Not after what happened. But that's a whole other story. One I don't want to revisit. Now, let's talk about the plans."

Buster had alluded during previous discussions to going through a difficult time about twelve months ago. The way he spoke, he seemed to assume Zane knew what had happened, but Zane didn't. Only visiting his parents a couple of times a year when he'd been living in the city meant he often missed out on important news, and if he was honest, other people's lives and problems weren't high on his list of interests.

Buster unrolled plans from one of his long tubes and spread them on the table in front of them. "I'm surprised Matt's willing to go through the public notification process. I'm not sure he needs to with what he's proposed."

"I think it's more about keeping the town on his side if he can and supportive of the project."

Buster laughed. "Operates a bit differently than his old man did."

"That's why he's ticking the box of public notification. The town meeting's on Friday afternoon."

"I'll be interested to see how that goes," Buster said. "I'm guessing there will be plenty of objections. They're probably all together somewhere now working out their line of attack before they've seen the plans."

Zane knew Buster might be right. He imagined Asha would be leading the group, but he hoped she wouldn't. It might make things awkward between them if she was. For now, however, he wanted to change the subject. "Heard of any other land becoming available in the Ridge?" he asked.

"For what purposes?"

"Commercial. Ideally, to develop for a cafe or something similar."

Buster shook his head. "No, but I can keep my ear to the ground for you. Sometimes you can make it happen yourself."

"What do you mean?"

"Like Matt did with the Sandstone Cafe. Find out who owns the property and make them an offer. You never know when the timing is right. And if it's not right when you first contact them, then at least they know you're interested if they do decide to sell."

Zane nodded. It made sense. He'd need to do some reconnaissance work in the Ridge and see if there was anywhere suitable for a cafe.

"There is a place in town here," Buster said. "The owners spoke to me about possibly developing it but since then have decided to sell and go traveling before settling down somewhere else. The for-sale boards will go up next week. It's Grayson's Eatery if you want to check it out. Down next to the mini-mart."

"Thanks, I'll take a look after we finish here." He opened his briefcase and took out a file. "I've drawn up some schedules I want you to look over. We still need to finalize things before we can make the final submission to council. Let me know what you think about these."

The two men pored over the schedule for the next half an hour, discussing the pros and cons of different approaches and whether Zane's timeline was feasible. They made some minor tweaks, and a short time later, Zane strode back down the main street. He put his briefcase back in his truck, crossed the road, and walked in the direction of the mini-mart. It was a lovely town with wide sidewalks and oak trees planted every fifty feet. While it was much larger than Hope's Ridge, it retained a laid-back, welcoming feel. Zane wondered whether Asha would consider opening a cafe here. He pushed the door open to Grayson's Eatery, surprised at how many people were seated in the cafe. It was midmorning, so he guessed people were stopping for coffee and a snack, but he hadn't expected this many. The booths that lined the far wall were full of workers who looked like they were having a meeting. Their hi-vis vests and work boots looked a little out of place among the rest of the patrons.

"Can I help you?" A middle-aged woman with a rounded face and warm smile caught his attention.

"A latte to go, please."

"Sure, take a seat while you wait." She nodded at the stools that lined the counter, and Zane sat.

His eyes traveled to the walls that displayed old street and road signs. It gave it a feel of a roadside diner.

"Nice place you've got here. Have you been here long?"

"Twenty-five years," she said as she fiddled with the coffee machine. "Got married, bought the business and have been here ever since. Raised three kids, and life seems to have disappeared."

Zane laughed. "Looks like you still have plenty of life left in you." She must be in her late forties he figured, certainly no older.

"Hope so. We're planning to sell up and go traveling now the kids are independent and able to look after themselves."

"Sounds wonderful. Where are you off to?"

She placed Zane's coffee in front of him. "Africa, I say. Tom says Australia, so I figure we'll do both."

"And have you got a buyer for the business?"

She shook her head. "Haven't put it on the market yet. I'd

prefer to lease it, but Tom wants to sell." She laughed. "We never agree on anything."

"You'd be open to leasing then?"

"Possibly. Why, are you interested?"

Zane shook his head. "Not for me, but I might know someone. I'll chat with her and tell her to get in touch."

The woman handed him a card. "The numbers are on there, or she can contact the realtor in town. We're doing everything through him."

Zane thanked her, picked up his coffee, and headed back out onto Main Street. His lips curled into a smile as he slipped the card into his pocket. If nothing else, he had an excuse to see Asha.

Asha couldn't believe she'd let her mother rope her into going to one of Steph's hot yoga classes. Her parents had returned from their trip a week earlier, and Asha had been surprised and relieved when her father had hugged her and told her another opportunity would come along.

"I thought you'd be disappointed in me."

He'd looked genuinely shocked. "Disappointed? I couldn't be prouder. You're looking to expand, grow your business, and employ people. It's a huge undertaking, Asha. Sure, these premises didn't work out, but something will. You need to practice patience."

Apparently, according to both Steph and her mother, there was no better way to do that than practice yoga. It was her second class, and she did have to admit that, other than almost dying from the heat, she was enjoying it. Steph assured her she'd get used to the heat after a few sessions, and she hoped she was right. She was a fantastic teacher. Her voice was gentle but engaging, and her demonstrations of the positions were quite phenomenal. Asha had no idea her sister was so flexible. She hadn't realized anyone could be so flexible. She said as much now as she refilled her water bottle from the filtered water stand in the reception area.

"I'm very proud of her," her mother said.

"You should be, Sue," Bodhi, the owner of the studio, said. "She's my best employee."

"And your only employee," Steph said, joining them.

Bodhi grinned. "Employee of the month every month."

Steph raised an eyebrow. "Pay rise every month, then?"

"You're teaching out of your love for yoga, Steph, not for monetary rewards." He raised his eyebrows. "You should meditate on that later. Now I'll leave you ladies to your relaxation and tidy up the studio. Are you staying for my Yin class, Steph?"

Steph nodded. "Of course. I'll take a shower and get changed. I'm dripping as usual."

"Don't you get dehydrated being in that hot room so often?" Asha asked.

"Nope, I hydrate the day before. Three to four liters at least."

"It keeps you looking gorgeous," Sue said. "Look at that healthy glowing skin, Asha, I wish I looked like that."

"Clean eating, clean living," Steph said. "Now I'd better get organized so I can enjoy Bodhi's class. Did either of you want to stay for it? It's very relaxing."

Asha couldn't help but notice the dark rings under Steph's eyes. Her skin did look hydrated and healthy, but she looked exhausted. She was surprised her mother hadn't noticed. "Not for me," she said.

"Me either," Sue said. "Your father's expecting me to cook him dinner tonight, I'd better get moving."

The three women said their goodbyes before Asha and her mother left the studio.

"I'm a bit worried about Steph," Asha said. "I think she's still having nightmares about the accident. She looked exhausted."

"Really? I thought she'd moved past all of that. Do you think I should talk to her?"

"Maybe. I might drop around tonight after dinner and see if there's anything I can do. She said that stress usually brought on the nightmares, but I'm not sure she has anything to be stressed about. If she does, it might do her good to talk about it."

Sue leaned forward and hugged Asha. "You're a good sister. Let me know what you find out, and I'll do what I can to help."

Asha drove away from the studio deep in thought. Something was bothering Steph and visiting after dinner was a good plan. She smiled at the thought. She hadn't seen Zane since they'd last spoken, and she quite liked the idea of casually bumping into him. He had hinted at her asking him out, but she wasn't sure he was serious. She'd thought he might come past Irresistables for coffee or a muffin, which would be a casual way of seeing her, but much to her disappointment, he hadn't. It surprised her how disappointed she was that he hadn't. She'd ended up calling Jenna under the guise of checking in on her friend and casually asking if she'd heard from Zane and how he was settling in. Jenna said he seemed happy with the new job and seemed to have things under control. Even better, she was coming up for the weekend to check on him in person so they would be able to have another night out. Asha hung up, smiling. In the past, Jenna had always been the block between her and Zane, now she was a handy news provider, even if she didn't realize this was the case.

Zane finished stacking the dishwasher and was wiping down the kitchen counter when he heard a gentle knock on the front door. Steph was out, still at yoga, he assumed, so it was only him at home. He tossed the cloth on to the counter and went to answer it.

His heart flipped as he came face to face with Asha. Her hair was loose around her shoulders, her eyes bright and friendly. This was a different Asha to the one he'd dealt with since arriving in Hope's Ridge. "Hey, Ash, come in." He held open the door for her, and she stepped inside. "I was about to make peppermint tea; would you like a cup?"

Asha laughed. "Steph's got you trained."

He grinned. "She's converted me, that's for sure. I used to enjoy a beer after work, and now I can't wait to see which tea she's got steeping."

"And it's peppermint tonight?"

"Will be. She's out, so I'm the tea chef. Hopefully, it'll be up to your standards."

Asha's face fell.

"Oh, sorry. Of course, you came to see Steph." What an idiot he was. Just because he'd been thinking about Asha and wanting to talk to her, didn't mean she'd given him a second thought. "She went off to yoga earlier this afternoon and hasn't come home. I'm assuming she's having a bite to eat with Bodhi."

"Bodhi? Like a date?"

Zane laughed. "You should see your face. Would it be that much of a shock if Steph went on a date?"

"Of course not, but with Bodhi, yes. She'd never date her boss."

"I don't think she is. She mentioned they were working out a new class schedule, so she might be late tonight. I don't think that counts as a date."

Asha pretended to wipe her forehead. "Phew. You had

me worried for a moment. Steph breaking her own rules. She's strict about things like that. Forbidden love and all the drama."

"Really?" Zane was surprised. "She seems like the most laid-back person I've ever met. I thought she'd be an advocate of free love and free spirits."

"There's a lot more to our Steph than you know," Asha said. She hesitated for a moment. "I will have that tea if you're planning to make it."

Zane grinned and led her through to the kitchen. "How's my friend Max?"

Asha smiled. "He's good, cuddly, as usual."

Zane set about boiling the water and getting the teapot and cups ready. He added three generous scoops of tea leaves to the infuser. "How long have you had him?"

"Right on a year. I bought him for Steph. To help her after the …" she stopped. "Sorry, she might not want me talking about her stuff. I bought Max to cheer Steph up when things were difficult for her."

"So, why do you have him?"

"Turns out she's allergic to cats."

Zane's mouth dropped open. He closed it and laughed. "Gift fail."

"Worked out well for me. I never realized how much I'd love an animal. He's gorgeous. He calls the shots, of course, like most cats, but he still surprises me the way he runs to the door when I get home and sits next to me no matter what I'm doing. Sometimes I think I should take him with me to work. I think he'd happily sit on a shelf while I serve customers."

"Might be a health regulation issue," Zane said.

"That's true. And he might notice the birds that hang around on the foreshore."

"Speaking of your work and Irresistables." Zane cleared

his throat as he poured the boiling water into the teapot. He was surprised at how nervous he was. He had planned to use this as an excuse to visit Asha, but now that she was here, he might as well tell her what he'd discovered. "I was in Drayson's Landing this morning chatting with Buster, who owns the construction company. He gave me a tip that one of the eateries in the main street is about to go on the market. It's Grayson's if you know it?"

Asha nodded. "I've been there a few times. Trish, the owner, went to school with Mom. She makes the best pecan pie you'll ever eat."

"Good to know. Although if they're closing down, I might not get to taste it."

Asha frowned. "I'm surprised they're closing, I thought the business did well."

"It does. They want to travel and possibly take early retirement. I thought you might be interested."

"Me? In the cafe?"

Zane nodded. "I know it's not Hope's Ridge, but it's not far away. It's bigger, and the cafe already has a strong customer base. I don't think you could go wrong." Zane picked up the tray on which he'd placed the teacups and pot. "Let's take this out the back. I've got the heat lamp warming, so it should be nice and cozy."

Asha followed him to the back door and out to the lovely outdoor area, made more inviting with the warmth from the lamp.

"I hadn't given thought to a cafe outside of Hope's Ridge."

"There's no rush to make a decision. When Buster mentioned it, I thought of you. I know you were disappointed to lose the Sandstone Cafe, and this would give you a fresh start."

"It would, but it's in a different town. I don't want to move."

"You wouldn't have to. Lots of people commute between here and the Landing. We used to do it every day when we were in high school, don't forget. It's less than half an hour in the car."

Asha smiled. "Which is why I could never understand how the bus took closer to forty-five. Do you know what kind of lease they'd be looking for?"

"No. I went in and spoke to Trish. She said they hadn't listed it for sale or lease as yet. That's why I wanted to mention it to you. In case you were interested."

"You did that for me?"

Zane nodded as he reached for the teapot to pour their tea. "It's no big deal. It gives you another option to consider."

Asha accepted the cup from him. "I'll give it some thought. Thank you." She smiled, and her green eyes sparkled.

Zane struggled to steady his hand as he brought his tea to his lips. If her smile could have that effect on him, he was in big trouble.

"I came over to check up on Steph," Asha said, breaking into his thoughts. "Do you know if she's been sleeping? The black rings under her eyes suggest she hasn't been."

"She's had quite a few restless nights," Zane said.

"She tells you about them?"

"I'm not the best sleeper either, so we're often out here sharing a cup of tea at three in the morning." He grinned. "As normal people do."

"Really?"

Zane nodded. "I have bad dreams, so does she. It's given us something to bond over."

"Steph doesn't normally talk to anyone about the accident."

"She hasn't given me any detail, and I haven't pushed her," Zane said. "I was hoping she might once she got to know me better, but I've only lived here a couple of weeks, so that might still be some time off."

Asha nodded. "But you told her about your situation?"

"I did, but I asked her not to talk about it."

"She hasn't," Asha said. "Neither would Jenna."

Zane smiled. "You've asked both of them? Can I ask why you'd want to know?"

Asha blushed. "No reason. Hoping you're okay, that's all."

Zane's stomach flip-flopped. It wasn't only him; she felt it too. He reached out and took her hand. "Thank you, that means a lot."

They sat in silence for a few minutes, their hands entwined. Zane was amazed Asha hadn't pulled away. He turned to face her. "Would you come out with me this weekend?"

"I'd love to, but you know Jenna's going to be in town."

"How about Sunday? She's only staying until the morning. I could pick you up at twelve. Wear clothes suitable for the lake and don't be too hungover."

Asha smiled. "Don't worry; I won't be having a repeat of last time. But the lake?"

Zane smiled. "Yep, leave it with me. You'll be blown away by how romantic the lake can be."

"Okay, but if it entails holding fishing lines and gutting fish, I guarantee you right now, it'll be our first and last date."

Zane squeezed her hand, hardly believing she'd agreed to go out with him. Three weeks earlier, when Jenna had scraped him off his living room floor and dragged him to

Hope's Ridge, he would never have believed he'd be sitting here with the prospect of a new relationship. He stopped himself. He shouldn't be thinking like that. It was early days; they hadn't even been on a first date. But it was exciting. At this stage, anything was possible.

———

Asha laughed the next morning as she passed Steph a cup of coffee.

"What's so funny?"

Asha pointed behind Steph. "I've never had so much family support in my life."

Steph turned in the direction Asha pointed. Their parents were heading toward the food truck with broad smiles on their faces.

"Coffee?" Asha asked.

"Tea for me, Ash," her mother said. "Wouldn't want Steph seeing me break away from my new clean-living policy."

"Don't ask her what's in her cup then." Asha set about making drinks for her parents.

"Steph? You're not drinking coffee, surely?"

"Just a morning pick-me-up."

"Are the dreams back, hon," her mother asked.

Asha looked up to see Steph nod.

"But don't worry. I'm off to see Dan this afternoon. I'm sure he'll work out what's going on."

"That quack! I doubt it," her father said.

"Dad!" Asha reprimanded. "That's not exactly helpful."

"Saying it like it is. Those quacks screw with your mind, that's all I'm saying. You go in there for something minor and come out depressed about your childhood and every little thing that ever went wrong in your life. Ridiculous."

"What exactly are you basing this theory on, Thomas?" their mother asked. "Last I checked, you'd never been to a psychologist."

"And never will. I was talking to Roy Larsen. He was telling me about his son, Zane. The kids had his head filled with all sorts of garbage. Won't work at the mill as a result. Says Roy controlled his childhood, and he won't let him control him now."

Asha and Steph exchanged a look.

"Zane's an adult, Dad. He wants to stand on his own two feet. That's not too hard to understand, is it?" Steph said.

"Been giving you his hard luck story too, has he? Roy said he was one of those guys who had one thing bad happen to him and would wallow in it for years."

Steph's face grew red. "One bad thing? Are you for real? Did Roy tell you what that thing was?"

"No need to get angry. Yes, he gave me a rundown on it. Boy's too soft for his own good."

Asha watched on with interest. Steph's mouth dropped open. Her usually calm sister was having difficulty controlling herself.

"If you were held up at gunpoint and watched four people being shot in front of you, you'd probably be suffering too. I doubt I'd ever recover, let alone within a few months. It's people like you and Roy that make recovery difficult. Saying we should just get over things." She picked up her coffee and stormed off, leaving Asha and her parent's staring after her.

"What's the deal with Steph and this Larsen kid?" Thomas asked, accepting his coffee from Asha. "She's mighty defensive of him. Something happening between them?"

Asha only half registered what he was saying. Zane had been through that and was able to get out of bed each day?

No wonder he had nightmares and couldn't sleep. Her heart ached just thinking of him.

"I don't think Steph's got any romantic interest in Zane, has she Ash?"

"What?" Her mother's question jolted Asha back to the present.

"Steph and Zane? She's not interested, is she?"

Asha stared at her mother. That would make things awkward if she did. "I don't think so. She hasn't mentioned anything."

"Best to keep well away from him," Thomas said. "He's damaged, and it'll spill into everything he does."

"I'm worried about Steph," Asha said, changing the subject. "She's not sleeping, and she never gets worked up like that."

"Hopefully, she'll get to the bottom of it with Dan this afternoon," Sue said.

Thomas laughed. "Not likely. It's not all that hard. Twelve months ago, Steph was involved in a horrible accident. While it wasn't her fault, she'll always blame herself. Of course, she'll be more stressed than usual right now. You don't have to be a rocket scientist to work out why."

Asha stared at her father. For as out of touch as he usually seemed, for once, he'd nailed it. Of course, the anniversary of the accident was looming. "What's the date?"

"It's the fourth," her mother responded.

"Sunday's the anniversary," her father said. "The seventh. Not lucky number seven in this instance."

"You remember?"

Thomas nodded. "Of course I do. It was both the worst and the happiest day of my life. It was the day I was told my daughter had died. Then an hour later watched her walk through the emergency room and fall into my arms. For a split second, I thought I was experiencing a miracle, rather than a case of mistaken identity. Still think we should sue the police for that mix up."

"No one's suing anyone," Sue said. "Come on, Thomas. The mood you're in suggests to me you're bored. We're going home, and you're taking your golf clubs over to Drayson's to occupy yourself for the rest of the day. I'm not putting up with you when you're like this."

Thomas smiled at Asha. "Played it perfectly. Only an hour ago, I was told there were too many jobs for me to do around the house, and golf was not on the cards. Guess those jobs will have to wait now I have my orders."

Sue threw her arms up in the air. "Monday can't come around quick enough. You need to get back to work, Thomas Jones. That energy of yours needs to be channeled for good, not evil."

Asha watched as her parents walked across to the lake trail to make their way home. Sunday. She needed to spend Sunday with Steph. Make sure she was okay. She'd call Zane and ask him if he minded postponing. But then there was Zane. Tears filled her eyes as she thought of what he'd been through. She wished he'd confided in her and she hadn't heard it somewhere else. He hadn't wanted her to know. Should she tell him she knew? She wasn't sure what the best approach was. She'd ask Jenna on Saturday. His twin knew him better than anyone and would know what to do.

Zane whistled as he sat down at his carving bench in the garage. Steph had been happy with him setting up in there. Other than a shelf housing some boxes of hers and an area for her bike, she didn't use the garage and was glad to see he was. His pickup took up half of it, and his tool bench and carving supplies the other half.

Zane picked up a piece of cedar he planned to turn into a four-leaf clover. While it was a little harder than some of the wood he'd worked with, he loved the rich, slightly sweet scent it released. A memory of Asha inspired the four-leaf clover. He vividly remembered a summer when he and Jenna were about fifteen. His sister and Asha had convinced him to join them on a hunt for the elusive four-leaf clover. They'd taken a picnic to a grassy section by the lake with a ground cover of wild clover and spent hours trying to find one. Jenna had given up after about half an hour, but he and Asha had continued until their knees were sore from so much kneeling. They hadn't found one, but it was one of those memories of growing up, of long summer days with no worries and nowhere else to be, that he loved.

As he began preparing the wood, the garage door opened, and Steph appeared, pushing her bike. She leaned it up against the side wall and removed her helmet. She smiled at him. "Creating something?"

Zane nodded. "Starting a project. It's been ages since I made anything. It's a good distraction from the day."

"How's the development?"

"Still working on plans and finance. We've got the town meeting tomorrow, so I guess that will bring with it questions and possibly extra work."

Zane noticed Steph appeared only to be half listening. He wasn't surprised, the development stuff was pretty dry, but it was unlike her. "Everything okay?"

Steph cleared her throat. "I need to apologize to you. I've done something you won't like."

Zane waited for Steph to explain.

"I'm sorry. It seems your dad's been talking to mine, and

being the opinionated jerk he is, he used you as an example of why psychologists are a waste of time."

"What?"

Steph continued. "My dad isn't a believer in emotional distress and certainly doesn't believe psychologists can help anyone. He seems to think we should all be made of steel and get on with life."

"Okay." Zane was confused. "Our dads are both living in the dark ages, but why do you need to apologize?"

Steph's face turned a deep shade of red. "I got angry and told him something along the lines that if he'd been held up at gunpoint and watched four people being shot in front of him, he'd be suffering too. I'm so sorry, Zane. I had no intention of telling anyone. It just came out."

It was nice to know Steph cared so much. "Don't worry about it. I appreciate you standing up for me. I don't care what your dad knows or thinks to be honest."

"That's the thing, it wasn't only Dad. Mom and Asha were there too."

Zane swallowed. "Asha knows?"

Steph nodded. "That you witnessed a holdup and that people were shot. I stormed off after I dropped that on them. I'm so sorry. I know you didn't want anyone knowing."

Zane ran his hand over the piece of wood he was holding and gave Steph what he hoped looked like a genuine smile. "Don't worry. People are bound to find out at some stage. This town isn't known for keeping secrets. It's not something I feel a need to hide, but I don't want to have to talk about it with people I hardly know."

"If there's anything I can do to fix the situation, I will."

"Really, Steph, don't worry. Now, I plan to turn this piece of wood into a masterpiece, and you probably need to have dinner. I made pumpkin soup earlier. There's plenty in the pot if you want to help yourself."

Steph smiled. "Turns wood into masterpieces and can cook too. I might never let you move out, Zane Larsen."

Zane's smile slipped the moment Steph walked into the house and disappeared out of sight. He closed his eyes. He'd hoped to avoid his situation becoming public gossip. He hoped it didn't freak Asha out. Lucy had deserted him within a month of the holdup. Said she couldn't handle his nightmares or depressive moods. *She* couldn't handle them. What about him? He was the one living through them. Jenna had done her best to convince him that Lucy's leaving was for the best. It was the first test of their relationship, where he needed her support, and she didn't give it to him. Did he want to be with someone who wasn't there for him when it counted? Of course not, but it was still hard. He'd loved her, or at least thought he had. He was now beginning to think he loved their lifestyle and their friends. His feelings for Lucy weren't so clear.

His phone pinged with a text as he began sanding down the wood. He smiled as he saw Asha's name pop up on the screen. He swiped to open the message.

Sorry, I need to cancel Sunday. Hope you don't mind. Asha.

He stared at the message. Within a few hours of finding out he was damaged goods, Asha canceled on him. No explanation, no suggestion of re-scheduling. He shook his head. How was it that he picked women who couldn't handle anything slightly difficult? He continued sanding the wood, disappointment building inside him. He'd been looking forward to Sunday. To spending time together and getting to know the adult versions of each other. He should probably stay away from women altogether. Coping with the nightmares and the pressures of the job with Matt were enough for now. He didn't need to get caught up with another unsupportive woman.

He placed the wood back on the workbench and stood,

dusting his hands off on his jeans. He was no longer in the mood for this. The four-leaf-clover was supposed to be a gift for Asha, to bring her luck and to bring them luck. What a joke.

He slipped back into the house to his section, glad not to be faced with Steph again. He didn't want to speak to anyone. He reached his room and saw the notebook and pen Dan had given him at their session that afternoon sitting on the bed. He picked them up as he flopped onto the bed.

Rewrite your nightmares, Dan had said. It seemed like a strange idea, but apparently, there was research behind Image Rehearsal Therapy to say it could help. It was a simple method of recalling the nightmare, writing it down, and changing the storyline to a more positive one. After doing this, Zane would need to go through the new storyline he'd created for ten to twenty minutes to trick his mind into believing the new scenario and removing the old from his thinking. For some people, if they did this enough and re-read what they'd written, over time, they could find their nightmares changing to the scenes they were describing. He put the notebook and pen on the bedside table, ready to use them if he woke from a nightmare and switched off the light. It sounded kind of crazy, but right now, he was willing to try anything if it meant he'd sleep through the night.

6

*A*sha decided to shut Irresistables early on Friday afternoon so she could attend the town meeting. She'd seen it advertised a few weeks earlier but hadn't considered going. She'd assumed she'd be flat out getting the cafe up and running, and it wouldn't be something that affected her. How wrong she'd been. While she knew she was at fault over the damage to Matt's car, the way he'd behaved about the cafe still angered her. It would have been so simple to let her know what was happening. And now, his refusal to consider her as a tenant meant she wouldn't walk away and let him develop whatever he wanted. She at least wanted to ensure it was in the town's best interest. For all she knew, he planned to set up several cafes that would be in direct competition with her.

She closed up the food truck's window and grabbed her bag. The poster she'd seen in town said drinks and afternoon tea would be provided at Traders during a discussion about an exciting new development. *Drinks*. Serving alcohol was a guaranteed way to get a good percentage of the town onboard, of which Matt would be well aware.

Ten minutes later, Asha walked into Traders. Matt had

hired the function room for the event, and it bordered on over-flowing. The noise level was as loud as any Saturday night.

"Must be at least three hundred here," Steph said, moving up beside Asha.

Asha smiled. "I didn't realize you'd be coming."

"Bodhi asked me to. He had to go over to Tall Oaks this afternoon, so he can't be here. He heard a rumor that Matt's planning to include a health retreat in the new development catering for massage and yoga. We don't have the population to sustain two yoga studios. Over summer maybe, but not full-time."

"Hopefully, it's only a rumor," Asha said. "It's good that you're here. I wanted to talk to you about Sunday. I thought we could hike up to Perrywinkle Bluff. Take a picnic and make a day of it."

Steph raised an eyebrow. "You, suggesting we go hiking? What's going on?"

Ash's face flushed. "Nothing, I thought you might like some company and the distraction, that's all?"

Steph's face drained of color. "I didn't realize you'd remember." She squeezed Asha's arm. "Let me think about it, okay? I'll let you know tomorrow."

"Okay, but you're letting me know what time to pick you up. I'm not taking no for an answer." She looked across the room to a long table that had been set up with food. "This must be costing him a fortune." In addition to the food, she'd seen three guys so far walking around with trays of alcoholic drinks. Everyone in the room seemed to have a drink in hand, and the air buzzed with chatter and laughter. It certainly didn't look like a room full of people about to start protesting. She noticed a large board tucked to one side of the room with sheets of paper pinned to it. She took Steph by the elbow and led her toward it.

"He's got his plans on display," Asha said.

Steph snorted. "I'm not sure I'd call this on display; it looks like they've deliberately hidden them down the back."

The two sisters studied the plans. There was one sheet for each of the four developments.

"They're turning the three lots next to the cafe into apartments," Steph said. "That's a relief."

Asha nodded. That was quite a surprise. She'd heard rumors about restaurants and other services opening.

"Everybody, please gather around. Matt would like to speak to all of you, and we'd love to answer any questions you may have."

Asha jumped at the sound of Zane's deep voice. He stood at the front of the room, in snug-fitting jeans and a white t-shirt, looking casual, relaxed, and approachable. Matt joined him at the front of the room, dressed similarly, but being such a big, overwhelming guy, his approachability rating was a lot lower than Zane's. Asha wondered if this was why he hired Zane. To endear him more to the town?

As everyone quietened, Matt began to talk. He thanked them all for coming, hoped they were enjoying the food and drinks, and of course, hoped they'd all had a chance to look at the plans for the new development, which he pointed out.

A murmur went around the room, suggesting, as Asha had imagined, that people's attention had been distracted by the food and drinks.

"In case you haven't had a look at the plans, I'll give you a quick run-down of what we are currently trying to achieve." He went on to say, as the plans showed, that the three vacant properties next to the Sandstone Cafe would be developed into apartments.

"We will be continuing with the gorgeous Sandstone architecture of the cafe for the apartments. We want the look and feel to be carried through as much of the development as we can. The cafe has always been a talking point with its brick and detail. We are toying with the name Sandstone Corner for the apartments."

Someone in the back of the room laughed. "Even though they're not on a corner?"

"With the cafe they are," Matt said. "But you're right. They aren't technically. We'll give that name some more thought. I do like the idea of having it include sandstone."

"They're on a corner if you include the next six properties on Lake Drive." A voice Asha immediately recognized as Charlie Li spoke up. A group of people moved aside so Charlie could approach Matt. "Your plans only show this current development, don't they, Mr. Law?"

Matt nodded. "We can only develop the area we own, Mr. Li. If we owned the other six properties, then we'd have a much bigger development on our hands and more plans to show you."

Charlie turned to the rest of the room. "Which is his plan. He's been pressuring me to sell my two properties for a long time and the same with the other four properties on the other side of me. My understanding is two have already said they will sell."

A ripple of conversation broke out in the room. Asha was almost relieved to hear the anger behind some of the comments. "Is that true?" someone called.

Matt put his hands up, indicating for the room to quieten. "Owning the other properties that Mr. Li has mentioned would be a developer's dream." He looked directly at Charlie. "Mr. Li, are you planning to sell me your two properties?"

"Never."

Laughter broke out in the room. There was no hesitation in Charlie's voice.

Matt joined in the laughter, although the tightness in his

jaw didn't go unnoticed by Asha. "Your two properties would be key to any substantial development along Lake Drive," Matt said.

"But you're still buying my neighbors' properties."

Matt nodded. "I'm happy to buy any properties that have lake frontage. They make excellent short-term accommodation. It is most likely we'll do some minor renovations to modernize the properties and then use them for vacationers."

From the way Matt was speaking, it didn't sound like there would be anything to object to in his plans.

"I heard you were talking about a new restaurant and cafe precinct," Isaak called out. "Any truth in that?"

"We heard that too," one of the women said.

"Would that be so bad?" Matt asked. "To have more choice of where you can eat? To have a variety of food to choose from and different opening times." He gave a small laugh. "We might be able to go out for dinner without having to drive to Drayson's Landing."

"Traders do fine meals," one of Isaak's loyal customers called out.

Asha looked across to Zane, who'd remained quiet throughout the exchange. He would know all of Matt's plans. She wondered how much Matt would reveal to the town. She couldn't imagine him laying down all his cards and expecting their approval.

"Traders do great meals," Matt said. "But some variety is always good, and not everyone wants the pub environment. Young families, for instance, might prefer to take their kids to a less crowded venue that's not so big on drinking, particularly on a Friday and Saturday night."

"So, you're developing restaurants and cafes?" Isaak asked.

Matt smiled. "Got a bit off track there didn't I. No, that's not in the plans. Other than the existing cafe, of course. We plan to do some renovations on that and open up with an improved menu. But, that only gives us back the one cafe that we did have in town. We are looking at options to access the roof of the cafe too. It's a flat roof and would be a wonderful spot to enjoy the lake views. We're debating at this stage whether it becomes an additional dining space for the cafe or a separate space. An afternoon and evening wine bar perhaps to watch the sunset with a beer or a glass of bubbles."

A murmur of approval whipped around the room. Asha had to hand it to Matt, his plans as he described them would create a lifestyle that many in the room would enjoy. If she weren't so annoyed with him, she'd probably think he was doing something good for the town. She didn't trust him. What he was presenting now seemed too perfect. A sudden thought occurred to her.

"How many apartments are you planning to build on the three lots next to the cafe?"

While the smile remained on his lips, Matt's eyes darkened as he turned to address Asha's question. "We are still finalizing what the land area will allow us to do. We will, of course, be keeping in line with the town's low-rise only policy."

"What exactly does that mean?" Low-rise? There were no apartment blocks in Hope's Ridge, only houses and cottages.

Matt turned to Zane, who shifted uncomfortably from side to side. "What's the height limit again?"

"Four stories," Zane answered. "That keeps the top-level apartments below the tops of the trees on the lakeside."

"Won't that cause issues for the properties behind the apartments," Asha asked. "Apart from the fact people will be able to look down into their yards, they'll also be in the shade for a good part of the day when the apartments block the sun."

"It's not Hawaii, Asha," Matt said. "Four stories won't block the sun out like the thirty story apartments they have there." He turned his attention back to the rest of the room. "And we have decided only to go three stories, not four. It will bring the top of the building in line with the height of the Sandstone Cafe. I think it's important that we keep some uniformity with what we're doing. Having the skyline of the same height will help achieve this. Now, are there any further questions? I'll call the drinks waiters back in as soon as we've wrapped up."

Asha wouldn't let him off that easily. "If you're only planning some apartments, why do we hear rumors of other developments? Apart from the restaurants, we've heard you plan to set up a health retreat with massage, yoga, and wellness solutions."

"It's a small town, Asha. Rumors fly around the whole time. In saying that, yes, I have discussed the health retreat idea many times over beers at Traders. There's no secret that I'd love to do that one day. That needs the right location, and Sandstone Corner isn't it. If anyone's selling property that's tucked away from town that would make an ideal private retreat feel free to come and see me later."

Zane stepped back up to join Matt. "We'll cut questions off now as we only have the room for another half hour, and that will give you the chance to speak to Matt or myself one-on-one with any questions you have. I'd like to remind everyone that the purpose of today's meeting is to keep you informed of what we're doing. The plans are available anytime you want to come into the offices and have a look at them. We'll be lodging them with council this week, and I believe you can request copies and lodge any concerns with them. We're not hiding anything or trying to do anything that would be detrimental to the town. In fact, I would like to say how impressed I am with Matt's vision and commitment to improving Hope's Ridge. Thank you all for coming this afternoon. Help yourself to another drink, and we'll be available to answer further questions."

A small round of applause went up around the room while the majority got back to talking and drinking.

Asha glanced over to where Matt and Zane stood. Matt clapped Zane on the back, a broad smile on his face. He looked so smug. Asha found it hard to believe he wasn't planning something devious, which the town would discover when it was too late. But then she looked at Zane. Reliable and trustworthy. He wouldn't go along with anything unscrupulous, that she was sure of.

Zane did his best to look relaxed and part of Matt's team. It was true; he had been impressed with everything Matt had shown him so far and the plans for the development. He was interested in the fact that Charlie had spoken up. Matt would love to get his hands on Charlie's properties, but the older man had made it clear that would not happen. Matt hadn't seemed overly concerned, which was a surprise considering their location. Even if Matt were able to buy up the properties on the other side of Charlie, he wouldn't be able to connect his development. He'd asked Matt about it, but Matt had simply laughed. Said it paid to be patient, and that was all.

He watched the residents enjoying the free drinks as Matt answered questions. The main ones were from residents in the streets behind the development. Zane's heart had fluttered when he'd realized Asha was here. He'd hoped she would come over and talk to him, explain that canceling their date was nothing to do with his situation, but she didn't, and as the afternoon progressed, he realized she wasn't going to. Her question had been a good one, raising plenty of concerns over what impact three stories were likely to have on them. The red, angry face of Peter McCullen interrupted his thoughts.

"Can I help you, Pete?"

"A three-story development will block my view of the lake. I went up three stories for that reason. So that it was unlikely my view would ever be taken from me."

Hearing the escalated voice, Matt came over and joined the conversation. "You'll still have your view, Peter. You're far enough back that if you look to the left or right of the apartments, you'll have a clear view of both ends of the lake."

Peter shook his head. "What good's that? I want to be able to look out the window or be grilling on the roof with the clear view I've always had."

Matt nodded. "I completely understand." He put an arm around Peter's shoulders. "Come and let me buy you a scotch. I'm sure we can come up with a solution we're both happy with."

Peter hesitated for a few seconds before allowing Matt to lead him out of the function room and into the main bar area.

Zane wondered how Matt would spin it to make Peter happy. Other than only building to two stories, Zane couldn't imagine any scenario that would work.

"So, there's no yoga center planned as part of the new development?"

Zane turned to find Steph beside him. He shook his head. "No, this phase is the cafe and the apartments. As Matt said, it isn't the right spot for a yoga or wellness center. He has mentioned to me that he'd love to do that one day, but it would need a different location. I wouldn't be surprised if he comes and talks to Bodhi at some stage. He'd probably love to go into business with him as Heat Wave is already in a great spot. It needs some modernization and expansion to allow for the summertime swell of vacationers."

"I doubt Bodhi would go for it," Steph said. "He loves what he's built up."

Zane laughed. "Well, tell him he probably doesn't need to stress about it right now. It'll be a few years before Matt's in a position to consider a project like that."

Steph smiled. "Good to know. Now, speaking of yoga, I'd better head to the studio and get ready for the five o'clock class. Hope today turned out better than you expected."

Zane grinned. "Seems to be going well so far. Like I said to you before, Matt's vision is impressive. He's not trying to do anything to hurt anyone or ruin the town, quite the opposite." Zane looked around the room. "Asha gone already?"

Steph nodded. "She had a few things to do. I'll see you at home later."

Zane watched as Steph made her way across the function room and out of the doors. Whatever her reasons for canceling, it wouldn't have killed Asha to come and speak to him in person.

As she cleaned the coffee machine close to closing time on Saturday, Asha realized she'd never received a reply from Zane about her canceling the lake trip. She'd meant to have a quick chat with him at the town meeting, but he was working, and she didn't want to interrupt him. She also didn't want to give him an explanation in front of Steph. She was expecting Jenna to arrive any minute, so would check with her whether Zane would be at Traders that night as they would no doubt bump into him if he was.

She picked up her phone to double check her messages. She was also waiting to hear back from Steph about the hike to Perrywinkle Bluff. She grinned as her phone pinged with a message from her mother's phone. *Steph said she'd love to hike with you tomorrow. She'll come by at eight, or is that too early? While you two are out, I might buy her a phone!*

Asha sent a quick message back to her mother as Jenna's white Jeep drew to a stop in the parking lot. Jenna climbed out, her black jeans clinging to her skinny frame, her golden-brown hair loose around her shoulders, and her heart shaped lips their trademark plum color.

"Hey, you," Asha called. "This is becoming a habit."

Jenna smiled as she approached the food truck. "A good habit, I hope. But," her smile turned to a frown, "I can't do a big night out tonight. Mom and Dad are insisting Zane and I come for dinner. When I dropped him here a few weeks ago, I hardly saw them and haven't heard the end of it since. I'll have to go, and Mom's talking about watching family movies afterward. Dad and Zane have called a truce after he threw Zane out. She's so excited at having us all together I can't say no."

Asha smiled. "You shouldn't say no. Family time's important. I'll be finished here in a couple of minutes. We can catch up now if you like, unless you have other things you need to do?"

Jenna sat down at one of the tables. "Nope, I'm all yours until about five."

"It's only one. Why don't we drive over to the Landing for lunch? I want to check out Grayson's Eatery."

"Fine by me, but why?"

"They're putting it on the market, and I want to check it

out. See if it inspires me to move the business to Drayson's Landing."

"But you love the lake, don't you? I thought that was the whole reason you were upset about missing out on the Sandstone Cafe with its amazing views?"

"I do love the lake, but there aren't any other lakefront options here, so a complete change might be the way to go. It was Zane's idea."

"Zane?"

Asha nodded. "It came to his attention when he was talking construction with Buster out at Drayson's."

"Okay, well, hurry up so we can get over there. I'm starving. I went to a spin class before I drove up here this morning and need to refuel."

Asha was quick to clean down the benches and lock up, and five minutes later, they were in Jenna's Jeep weaving their way around the winding mountain road that led to Drayson's Landing.

"It's down near the mini-mart," Asha said as they entered the main street. "On the left."

Jenna laughed. "Considering how often we used to go there after school, I do remember." She pulled up outside the cafe. "I hope they still do an all-day breakfast," she said. "I'm craving eggs or pancakes."

"Pancakes? I thought your body was your temple?"

Jenna grinned. "I've been eating lettuce leaves for weeks. I need some real food."

"I thought you and Brad were spending lots of time together. Surely he doesn't expect you to live on lettuce."

Jenna shrugged. "He likes my body as it is and isn't a fan of fat on women, so I'm making sure I don't have any. A meal or two, while I'm here, will be good. Brad's away until Thursday, which gives me plenty of time to burn any excess off."

"You can eat whatever you want, Jen. You've never been fat, ever. Don't let a guy control you."

Jenna laughed. "He's not. He wouldn't care if I ordered a steak or bowl of fries when we go out, but I choose not to. Now come on, all this talk about food has made me hungrier."

Asha followed her into Greyson's Eatery, which was buzzing with a Saturday afternoon trade. Zane was right in that it was surprisingly busy. She'd expect them to be closed by now, not doing a roaring trade. She took a seat across from Jenna at the only free table and glanced around. It was a nice cafe. Booths overflowed with teenagers, and with a jukebox pumping out songs, and old street signs decorating the walls, it reminded her of an all-American diner. In amongst the road signs were framed pictures of well-known destinations; the Grand Canyon, Statue of Liberty, Niagara Falls. She wondered if they were places the owners had visited or planned to visit.

"Could you see yourself here?" Jenna looked up from the menu and glanced around. "It's nice. Kind of cool, although I don't see this whole road trip theme as your thing. We would need to lose all of that and put your mark on it. Better menu boards, a glass-fronted cabinet for the cakes and desserts, and some modern signage to start with."

Asha nodded. She'd been thinking along similar lines. "If it were sitting across from the lake in Hope's Ridge, I'd probably be more excited about it."

"The food truck sits across from the lake. You don't have to move. You could wait and see what happens with this development of Matt's. He might run out of money and realize he needs a tenant after all."

Asha snorted. "I think he'd go bankrupt before leasing it to me. I didn't make the best impression on him." She went on to tell Jenna about her encounter with Matt, delighted at her friend's shocked expression.

It was close to four by the time they'd finished their late lunch. They drove back to Hope's Ridge, Asha having made the decision she didn't want to open a cafe in Drayson's Landing.

"I need to be more like Steph and practice patience," Asha said. "She believes what's meant to be is meant to be. She's convinced a better opportunity will come along. I need to be patient."

Jenna rolled her eyes. "In this day and age, patience doesn't exist. Steph should have been born in the 1890s, not the 1990s. It would have suited her a lot better. How is she anyway?"

Asha was still thinking about Steph when she let herself in through the front door after Jenna dropped her home. Jenna's eyes had filled with compassion when Asha explained it was the anniversary of Steph's accident the next day. Twelve months earlier, when it happened, Jenna was so concerned for Steph she had driven straight from the city to Hope's Ridge. While Asha and Jenna had different goals and dreams, different ideas about the ideal place to live, and the pace at which life should be lived, it was gestures like returning at the time of the accident that reminded Asha what a good friend she was. She'd do anything for Jenna, and Jenna had proven she would do the same for Asha.

Max came bounding down the hallway to greet her, bringing an instant smile to her face. She picked him up and cuddled him before taking him through to the kitchen and replenishing his empty food bowl. She changed his water and sat down with him for a few minutes and brushed him. She was rewarded with a motor-like purr. She glanced up at the kitchen clock. It was after five, and she didn't have any plans for the evening. That suited her perfectly. She'd watch something on Netflix, or possibly start a book. But first, she wanted to speak to Steph. Check they were still on for tomorrow. She wouldn't put it past Steph to take off somewhere on her own for the day and on the day that she would need company.

Asha got to her feet, gave Max a final stroke, and walked to the front door. She could call Steph, but the likelihood of her answering was slim, and anyway, if she was lucky, Zane might not have left for his parents' house yet, which would give her a chance to see him and reschedule their date. Her lips curled into a smile at the thought.

Five minutes later, when she reached Steph's, she could hear laughter coming from the backyard. Male laughter. She ran her fingers through her hair and straightened her shirt, nervous energy rippling through her. She let herself in, knowing Steph was unlikely to hear her unless she yelled out. She walked through to the back door, took a deep breath, and pulled it open. The laughter stopped immediately.

"Ash, what are you doing here?"

Asha did her best to keep the smile on her face and the surprise she was feeling off it. The male laughter she'd heard wasn't Zane; it was Bodhi.

"Hey Asha," he said, giving her a smile and a wave. "Going to join us for some tea?"

Asha hesitated. She was curious as to why Bodhi was there. Steph had always sworn that he was her boss and nothing more. They looked cozy right at this moment. "No, I'm fine, and I don't want to interrupt. I wanted a quick word with Steph to make sure we were still on for tomorrow."

"What's tomorrow?" Bodhi asked. "Anything special?"

"No," Asha immediately said, seeing Steph's face pale. "Purely a date between sisters." She looked at Steph. "How about I pick you up at eight rather than you having to walk over to mine?"

Steph twirled a strand of hair around her finger. "I think I probably need a day to myself tomorrow. I don't think I'll be the best company."

"Absolutely not," Asha said. "You don't need to be the best company, but you need company. And, I gave up a date for tomorrow, so no arguments. I'll see you here at eight."

Steph stared at her open mouthed. "A date? Since when did you go on dates?"

"Since I was asked on one. Although technically I postponed so there have been no dates as yet."

"Who is it?"

Asha blushed. "I'll tell you more tomorrow. Now I'd better go home to a night on the couch with Max." She looked from Steph to Bodhi and back to Steph, raising an eyebrow. "You enjoy yourself too. I'm sure there'll be lots to chat about tomorrow."

Asha let herself out, glad she'd made an effort to come around and confirm with Steph. She was pretty sure Steph would have canceled in the morning if she hadn't. She was also extremely curious to know what was going on with Bodhi, but she was disappointed at not having seen Zane. She would call him after dinner to make sure he'd received her message. She'd feel awful if he turned up for their date and thought she'd stood him up.

Zane realized he needed to slow down, or he'd be drunk before they started on dessert. He found having a few beers was the only way he could get through an evening with his father, so he had walked the fifteen minutes from Steph's to his childhood home to ensure he could safely enjoy a few drinks and use them to relax. There had been no discussion between him or his father about his being thrown out of the family home. They'd both agreed to put it aside and call a truce. Zane was happy to do this for his mother's sake.

Jenna had escaped into the kitchen to help their mother with the meal leaving him stuck with his father. He was doing his best to show an interest in the mill and his father's ideas for expansion without looking too interested or giving any impression he'd want to join him. He did, however, offer to look into a few of the regulations and codes that the mill would need to adhere to if they were to go ahead with some of the ideas.

"I've got my head in them all day at the moment, making sure Matt's project is ticking all of the boxes."

His father shook his head at the mention of Matt. "The town wishes Matt Law followed in his father's footsteps and left Hope's Ridge. Another guy we'll have to fight at every turn."

Zane put his drink down on the small side table his mother had placed next to him. "What do you mean?"

"These grand plans he has to transform the Lake Drive area will be met with a lot of objection."

"That wasn't the vibe at the town meeting yesterday," Zane said. "In general, it seemed that most of the town was supportive."

Roy took a large swill of his beer. "Most of the town didn't turn up from what I heard. Don't forget there are over two thousand residents in Hope's Ridge. And why would there be objections? Because he's a Law, that's why. Law unto himself, no doubt. Neither Matt nor Walter ever had the town's best interests in mind. Every project had an agenda benefiting Walt at the expense of someone else. This will be no different. You mark my words."

Zane thought for a moment. He could understand where

his dad was coming from in light of Walter's reputation, but he'd seen the plans, been involved in them. "I think you'll be surprised when you see what's planned. You might be right that Matt will benefit, but the town will also. Other than the Sandstone Cafe, that corner's needed a facelift for years. It's rundown and a bad look considering its lake frontage. A vacant lot and two houses that have been falling apart for years."

"Building three nice houses would bring that part of the street up beautifully," Roy said. "High rise apartment buildings are not in keeping with the town."

"They're not high-rise! Three levels which brings the rooftop to the same height as the Sandstone Cafe. A total of twenty-four apartments spread over the three lots."

"What about the houses on the other side? Imagine suddenly having twenty-four neighbors instead of one. It'll be a nightmare during the summer. So noisy. It'll never pass council, so I hope he has an alternative plan to fall back on."

"He does, but we'll be pushing for the larger development first."

"And what about parking? Where does he plan to park twenty-four cars? More at times, if families arrive in different vehicles. It's crazy."

Zane was saved from having to answer any more questions when Jenna popped her head around the doorway of the living room and announced that dinner was ready. Zane couldn't get into the kitchen quickly enough. They were eating outside on the back deck, but the food had to be carried out. Zane picked up a large bowl of roasted vegetables and carried them through to the outdoor area. "Looks great out here, Dad." And it did. The heat lamps had taken the chill out of the night air, making it a cozy space. Their mother's planter boxes with her favorite colossus red pansies added a colorful touch, and the star-filled night sky completed it.

They all sat down, Janet insisting they join hands while Roy said Grace. Zane closed his eyes, enjoying the ritual that took him back to his childhood. It brought him comfort. Reminded him of more relaxed times, when he felt safe and protected.

Zane wondered if Asha had spoken to Jenna about him when they'd been out earlier. Not that he cared. She was no better than Lucy and not worth thinking about. The problem was, he couldn't stop himself from thinking about her. While he'd tried to convince himself that he'd be better off without a woman in his life right at this moment, his body and the way it reacted each time he thought of her told him otherwise. He hadn't planned mentioning to Jenna that anything was going on between them, not that it was, but wondered if Asha had said anything at all. "How was your lunch?" It was as simple a question he could think of to bring Asha into the conversation.

"Good. We went to Drayson's landing. Ash wanted to check out that eatery you mentioned to her."

"Really?" Zane was surprised. "What did she think?"

"We both thought it was fantastic. Busy, great atmosphere. But, it's not on the lake, and that's what she wants."

"She'll find it difficult to get anything in Hope's Ridge on the lake, or with lake views," Zane said. "She might be better off staying with the food truck if that's what's important to her."

"For now, I think that's her plan. I suggested she wait and see what happens with the development in case Matt suddenly needed a tenant, but she suggested she was unlikely to be on the short-list."

Zane laughed. He couldn't help it. "I'd say she's correct there. She had a bit of a run-in with Matt."

Jenna laughed. "Heaved a large rock at his car from what I understand."

"Good for her," Roy said. "Someone needs to put that guy in his place."

"Roy," their mother warned. "He's Zane's employer, so let's not be too harsh on him."

His father's face grew red, and he opened his mouth but shut it again when Janet shook her head at him. It appeared she wasn't putting up with any of his nonsense tonight. Zane could imagine what he had been about to say, how Zane should be working for him, not Matt.

"Tell us more about Asha's plans, hon," their mother said.

"No real plans. She was pretty upset about missing out on the Sandstone Cafe. She had her heart set on it from the minute it came on the market."

"See," Roy interjected, "an example of Matt getting what he wants at someone's expense."

"Ash will be fine," Jenna said. "She plans to listen to Steph's advice and be patient, wait for the right opportunity. Hopefully, something will come along."

"I haven't seen Steph in ages," Janet said. "She's kept to herself after, well, you know, what happened last year."

"The accident?" Zane asked.

Janet nodded. "Sue said it really affected her. She's not sure if she'll ever get over it."

"It's the anniversary tomorrow," Jenna said. "Ash is spending the day with Steph, taking her hiking somewhere to distract her."

Zane's cutlery clattered to his plate. "Asha's spending the day with Steph?"

Jenna stared at him. "Is that a problem? She's worried about her."

Zane had to do his best to keep a smile from breaking out on his face. No, it wasn't a problem, it was fantastic. It was possible Asha hadn't canceled on him because of the nightmares and not wanting to be involved with a basket case. She'd canceled because she was a kind, caring person.

"It was an awful thing to go through," Janet said. "Did you know she won't drive now? Rides everywhere on that bike of hers."

"What exactly happened?" Zane asked.

Jenna turned to him. "I'm sure I told you last year. I came home for two weeks at the time."

"Lucy and I were in Florida on vacation. You called me and told me Steph had been in an accident, but her injuries were minor. I never realized she'd been hurt badly."

"Emotionally scarred," Janet said. "I think she still blames herself, yet she wasn't to blame at all."

"No, she wasn't," Jenna agreed. "She was driving back from Drayson's Landing right on that corner where the road begins to wind up the ridge from the lake when another car came out of nowhere. Steph swerved in an attempt to miss it, but she couldn't. She caught the front bumper causing it to spin out of control. At the time, the guard rail was broken. The other driver had no chance. The car raced down the incline into the lake in a matter of seconds. The driver got out, but the little girl was trapped. Jenna tried to get her out, but she couldn't. The car sank too quickly. She was only five. When later they tested the driver, the girl's mom, she was proven to be drunk."

Zane closed his eyes. He'd had no idea. No wonder Steph couldn't sleep and was haunted by nightmares. He wasn't sure whether he'd prefer Steph's traumatic experience to his own. Neither was good but watching a five-year-old drown and not being able to do anything about it was unfathomable.

"It was Henry Busterling's ex-wife and daughter. He was distraught as you can imagine," Roy said.

"Buster?" Zane realized this was what Buster was referring to when he'd said *not after what happened* when they'd been talking about women and dating. He hadn't realized Buster had even been married, let alone lost a child.

"Yeah, that's the one. His ex was charged with manslaughter. I don't know how long she'll end up serving. It should be a life sentence, in my opinion. She's a hundred percent responsible for the death of that little girl."

"Yet Steph blames herself." Jenna sighed. "It makes me realize I don't have any problems when I hear stories like that." She looked across to Zane. "And what you went through too."

"I don't think what I went through is comparable to Buster's situation, and regardless..." Zane put up his hand to stop Jenna from objecting, "... let's talk about something a bit more upbeat. This is getting depressing." Although he wanted to change the subject, a weight settled on Zane's shoulders. He couldn't begin to imagine what Buster must be going through.

The evening continued on a lighter note as Janet spoke about the live art class she'd enrolled in. She blushed when she confirmed that yes, the models posed naked.

"She's done paintings and some amazing clay models," Roy said. "You should see them."

Janet blushed with pleasure at his praise.

Zane smiled. It was nice to see that his father could be a decent human from time to time.

"He likes the full-length female portrait I painted last week," Janet said with a laugh. "She had rather large ... well, you know what."

A ripple of laughter went around the table.

Roy grinned and enjoyed another mouthful of beer. "It wasn't that at all. I have good taste, and you're talented. End of story."

Asha stopped and wiped the sweat from her forehead. Keeping up with Steph when Steph was on a mission was practically impossible. She'd given up an hour ago and knew her sister was probably a mile in front of her by now. They'd meet at the craggy rocks that overlooked the valley and eat their packed lunches. Asha's legs had taken a few miles to warm up and get comfortable with the gradual climb up the Lost Ghost Trail. It was a walk she and Steph had done as kids with their parents, but not one she'd done for many years. She knew her legs would ache tomorrow.

She continued walking, thinking over the chat she'd had with Steph earlier in the car. The conversation hadn't flowed. Steph was distant and quiet, which she could understand. Today brought back a flood of memories, memories that would haunt Steph for the rest of her life. She hadn't wanted to talk about it, and once they left the car, she'd taken off at such a rate that Asha was worried she'd get a stitch and have to stop if she tried to catch up. Instead, she'd dropped back and let Steph go on ahead.

The trail wound steeply up to the spot Asha assumed they'd stop for lunch. Her breath was labored by the time she spotted Steph, stretched out on a rock, her small backpack on the ground beside her.

"Thank goodness!" Asha removed her backpack and sat down beside Steph. "You're way too fit for me, Ms. Yoga queen."

Steph gave a small smile. "Not sure the yoga's the key to

my fitness, but I do a lot of cycling around town and walking."

Asha nodded. "Do you think you'll drive again?"

Steph shrugged. "I don't have any need to and certainly don't miss owning a car. Saves me a fortune."

Asha couldn't argue with that. But it was the reason Steph chose not to drive that concerned her. "How are your sessions with Dan?"

"Okay. He thinks I should consider a change of scenery. Get out of Hope's Ridge for a while and get on with life."

"Really?" Asha couldn't imagine her sister living anywhere but the Ridge. "What about your job and your life here?"

Steph gave a wry laugh. "Those were my words exactly. Dan said it didn't need to be for any length of time, maybe even to take a vacation. Focus on something other than what happened."

"That sounds sensible."

Steph turned to look at Asha. "Ash, it's in my mind all the time and wakes me most nights. I don't think it would make any difference at all where I am. The thoughts and dreams will follow me."

"Maybe you need a new interest? Something to distract you?" Asha grinned. "A man, perhaps?"

Steph didn't respond but kept her focus on a bird soaring high above them on a thermal current.

"I take it there already is a man?"

That got Steph's attention, and she turned to face Asha. "What? Who?"

"Bodhi?"

Steph's face relaxed, and she laughed. "My boss? I don't think so."

"You looked cozy last night."

"We're good friends, nothing else. And there's no way I'd

jeopardize my job at the studio. It's the one thing that keeps me sane."

Asha wasn't sure whether to believe her or not. Steph might not be interested, but she'd say Bodhi was. "Are you sure he feels the same way?"

"Of course he does. It would be a disaster for us both if something happened and then it didn't work out. And anyway, I don't think of him like that."

Asha decided not to say any more. She was sure she saw desire in Bodhi's eyes when he was around Steph, but maybe she was romanticizing the situation. Steph didn't seem interested.

"But what about you?" Steph asked. "You said you'd given up a date to come here today. Who with?"

Heat flooded Asha's cheeks.

"Oo," Steph teased. "Someone you like by the looks of it. Let me guess, tall, dark, and handsome?"

"And well built, funny, and caring."

"Zane?"

"How do you come to that from that short description?"

Steph tapped her forehead with her finger. "Intuition, that's all. That and he's the only new man in town at the moment, so unless you were recycling someone from the past, I don't think there's anyone else in Hope's Ridge you'd be interested in."

"Yes, it's Zane. But it's early days, and I don't want to talk about him yet. I'll wait and see if it goes anywhere first."

Steph opened her mouth to ask another question but then closed it again and reached for her backpack. "Let's eat." She unzipped the pack and pulled out a lunchbox jammed with cheese, nuts, and fruit."

Asha studied her sister. "That's it. No more questions? I thought you'd be dying to know more."

"No, I'll hear more when you're ready. And I figure if I

leave you alone today, you'll do the same for me. I want to hike and enjoy nature and not talk about the past."

"Okay, deal. All I wanted to do was make today more bearable, so if that's what'll do it, I'm in. There is one thing I have to ask you."

Steph raised a wary eyebrow causing Asha to laugh. "Nothing too personal, more a basic request."

"Okay, I'm listening."

"Could you slow down? I suggested the hike to distract you. I'm not convinced it's doing that, but at this pace, I am convinced it'll kill me."

Zane had spent most of the day working on the four-leaf clover. It was coming along nicely, and he hoped he'd have it finished in the next week. Steph had run out early, jumping into Asha's blue van without looking back. He hoped Asha was able to keep Steph's mind off the anniversary and the nightmares that went with it. His only interruption in the day was a quick trip into town where he had Annie, the local florist, put together a gorgeous arrangement of vibrant orange Asiatic lilies. He was looking forward to giving them to Steph. He wanted to do more but knew from his own experience that nothing helped. He hoped Steph would appreciate the flowers, but if she didn't, he'd still feel better than if he'd done nothing to acknowledge what a difficult day it was.

He had no idea what time it was when he heard a car door slam and Steph calling her thanks to Asha. He stretched, wiped his sawdust-covered hands on his shirt, and walked back into the house to greet her. He'd arranged the lilies in a glass vase he'd found in the back of one of the cupboards and had them waiting on the table.

"Wow!" Steph stopped and stared at the flowers as she entered the kitchen. "They're beautiful."

"They're for you," Zane said.

Steph's brow crinkled in confusion. "Me? Why are you giving me flowers?"

Zane almost laughed at the concern that flashed across Steph's face. She probably was worried he was trying to hit on her. But instead, he smiled. "To say I'm here if you ever need to talk. Last night at dinner, Jenna mentioned that today was a difficult day for you."

Steph's face immediately drained of color. "Did she tell you why?"

Zane nodded. "She did. I'm sorry if you wanted to keep it to yourself, but it came up at dinner, and Mom and Dad had a few things to say too. We never have to talk about it again, if that's what you choose, but I wanted you to know that while our situations are different, I do understand what it's like to be haunted by something you were unable to prevent from happening."

A single tear rolled down Steph's cheek.

Alarm flooded through Zane. He was trying to cheer Steph up, not make her sad. "Hey, sorry. I can get rid of the flowers if you like. I didn't mean to upset you."

Steph shook her head. "You haven't. You've touched me." She wiped her cheek. "It's a difficult day. Did Jenna mention that the little girl's father is Buster?"

Zane nodded. "Dad did."

"I feel like I should go over to Drayson's Landing and see how he's doing. It would be a lot worse for him. But I've managed to avoid him for the last twelve months, so turning up today wouldn't help either of us."

"I'm sure he doesn't blame you," Zane said. "From what Jenna told me, his ex-wife was the one responsible. You did everything you could."

"It wasn't enough," Steph said. "That little girl could still be alive if I was a stronger swimmer."

"Not necessarily. Getting someone out of a sinking car isn't easy. Trying to get the door open is incredibly difficult. It wasn't your fault."

Steph nodded, her gaze traveling back to the flowers. Her lips turned up in the corners, and a look Zane hadn't seen on her before crossed her features. "You know, as much as I love these flowers, they will be a constant reminder of what happened."

Zane realized he was useless when it came to understanding what women needed. He'd messed it up again. "I can get rid of them if you don't want them."

"No, don't do that. I thought Asha might like them."

"They're your flowers. You can give them to her if you like."

Steph shook her head as if she was talking to an idiot. "No dummy, I'm suggesting you take the flowers around to Asha and give them to her. She told me you were supposed to take her out today, but she canceled on you. She was a bit worried that you were upset when you never responded to her message."

Zane's face flooded with heat. He'd meant to text Asha the previous night when he'd found out she'd canceled because of Steph, not because of his situation, but it was too late by the time his mother had stopped putting on home movies. "Originally, I thought she canceled because she'd found out about my background and how I was struggling with the nightmares."

Steph's hand flew to her mouth. "Ash isn't like that. Why on earth would you have thought that?"

"The timing, I guess. You told her about what happened, and a few hours later, she messaged me and canceled without any explanation. It was the kind of thing Lucy would have done. I guess I assumed I was dealing with another woman who couldn't handle anything difficult."

"In that case, you should take them around as an apology," Steph said. "Asha's nothing like that."

"She doesn't know that's what I thought, so I'm not sure an apology is necessary."

"It is," Steph insisted. "I'll tell her otherwise. If you plan to start something with her, you need to be honest with each other. Making assumptions about what another person is thinking never works. Speaking to her is the best way to avoid misunderstandings or complications."

"Wise words," Zane said. "But the flowers are for you." He glanced at his watch. "Do you think Annie will still be working?"

"She's probably closed by now, but I wouldn't be surprised if she's still at the shop preparing for tomorrow. You could go past on your way to Asha's and see."

Zane laughed. "At least I take it from the way you're practically forcing me out the door to go and see your sister that you'd be happy if we were dating?"

"Definitely. You both have good hearts. You'd complement each other."

Steph's words stayed with Zane as he jumped in his pickup, the second bunch of flowers he'd purchased for the day sitting beside him on the passenger seat. Annie had raised her eyes when he'd said he needed more flowers. "It's a small-town, Zane. People will hear if you're giving out flowers to more than one woman."

He'd laughed. "The first bunch were for a friend. A friend who suggested I come back for another bunch for someone I'm interested in."

Annie had smiled at this. "Anyone I know?"

He hadn't told her. The last thing he or Asha needed was the town gossiping about them. He pulled up the front of

Asha's small cottage moments later. He turned off the truck and took a deep breath. He wasn't sure why he was here, other than he'd missed her and wanted to see her.

Asha opened the front door, taken aback by the beautiful bouquet that greeted her. Zane popped his head out from behind the flowers and grinned.

"Hope you don't mind me dropping around unannounced?"

Asha smiled. "Not when you arrive with a stunning flower arrangement like that. Come in."

Zane handed Asha the flowers and stepped inside. He laughed as Max ran down the hallway and launched himself onto his feet.

"He has a foot fetish," Asha said. "If you stand still for too long, he'll rest his head on your feet and go to sleep. It's annoying when I'm trying to cook."

Zane bent down and scooped Max up, causing Asha's heart to contract. The white ball of fluff looked tiny in Zane's muscular arms. Max purred and pushed his head into Zane's chest, loving the attention.

"Come through to the kitchen so I can put these in some water. Would you like a drink? I was about to make some tea, but I do have a few beers in the fridge."

"Tea would be great. Steph's got me hooked. Did you have a good day with her?"

Asha nodded. "We hiked the Lost Ghost Trail at Perrywinkle. It's gorgeous up there. I should do it more often, but the thought of aching feet never appeals."

Zane sat down on one of the stools at the kitchen counter; Max still cradled in his arms. "But you're on your feet all day. I thought you'd be used to it."

"Standing around on a flat surface is one thing; hiking up steep paths is another."

"True. I'd love to go up there one day. I haven't hiked any of those trails since we were kids. Did it work as far as distracting Steph?"

Asha looked up from the flowers she was carefully arranging in a tall vase. "Did she tell you about the accident?"

"Not directly. Jenna did at dinner last night. I spoke to Steph a bit about it this afternoon, so she knows that I know. It must have been awful for her."

"It was, still is. It completely changed her life. She'd say it changed it for the better in some ways, but I'm not sure I agree." She moved the flowers into the center of her kitchen table. "Thank you again. These are beautiful."

"You're welcome. I wanted to say sorry."

"Sorry? What for? As far as I know, you haven't done anything to be sorry for."

Zane cleared his throat. "When you canceled, I assumed it was because you didn't want to get involved with someone who was having some difficulties coping."

Asha's mouth dropped open. "You're kidding. Why would you think that?"

"When you canceled on me, you didn't give me any explanation. It was the type of thing my ex would do. She moved out of our apartment without much explanation. She couldn't handle the nightmares I was having or the dark mood I was in. I'm a lot better now, by the way. I still have nightmares, but I feel more relaxed within myself. More hopeful."

Asha moved around the kitchen counter and stood in front of him. She took his hand and interlaced her fingers through his. "I hope that's partly because of me."

Zane blushed. "It is."

She leaned forward and kissed him lightly on the lips. "Good." Her stomach fluttered as she pulled back from him. "Because I'm feeling hopeful too." She went to remove her hand from his, but instead, he gently pushed Max off his lap and took her other hand in his. He pulled her to him and kissed her, this time more firmly. When they pulled apart, he reached his hand to her face and traced a finger across her lips. "You're gorgeous, Ash, truly gorgeous."

"You're pretty gorgeous yourself." Her voice was hoarse; the kiss had unbalanced her. She wasn't expecting her body to come alive the way it had. She untangled herself from his grip and went back to making the tea. Her heart thumped. If something happened between her and Zane, it had to be serious, not a fling. She couldn't risk it coming between her and Jenna.

"Why do I suspect an image of my sister appeared in your mind?" Zane asked as she poured the boiling water into the teapot.

Asha gave a little laugh. "Because you already know how I'm thinking." She stopped pouring the water and looked at him. "I'm not looking for a fling or something meaningless, Zane. If there is a chance of something happening with us, then I need to take it slowly. Make sure we're both ready and make sure we won't cause problems with our relationships with Jenna."

"Or Max," Zane added, scooping up the cat who was doing his best to rub around Zane's feet.

Asha laughed, glad he'd lightened the conversation. It was far too early to be talking about a future, but she did want to make sure he knew she didn't do casual. "How would it affect Max?"

"He'd miss me if I weren't around," Zane said. "So, we take things slowly, get to know each other again, and make sure it's something we both want before we…" He blushed again. "… before we get too serious, I guess."

"Before we tell Jenna," Asha added, hoping her cheeks weren't as red as his.

Zane raised an eyebrow suggestively. "Is that how we gauge whether we're serious or not? When we tell my sister?"

The corner of Asha's mouth curled into a smile. "There might be other ways. I guess we'll wait and see."

7

*Z*ane hummed along to the Red Hot Chili Peppers as he drove the familiar road into Drayson's Landing. It was amazing how different he felt this morning compared to Thursday when he thought Asha was walking away from him before she'd even given him a chance. He was glad he'd listened to Steph the previous night and gone to see her. The time had disappeared. They'd talked until after eleven, partly reminiscing but also talking about what they'd done since high school. Zane found himself telling Asha in detail about the holdup and how scared he'd been. She'd snuggled closer to him on the couch, rather than pulling away, when he admitted his fear. He was glad of that. He didn't want to have to pretend that he hadn't been affected by what had happened. Both Dan and the psychologist he'd seen in the city assured him that by talking about the holdup and facing it head on, in time, he would find it a lot easier. He had taken to writing in his journal each morning and rewriting the dreams he was having.

He was quite enjoying the process, his version of events making him laugh as he re-read his fictionalized versions. The common theme running through each was that he was the hero that saved the day. If only that had been the case when it happened. The journal hadn't, however, had the effect that Dan was hoping it would. That by re-writing the dreams and visualizing new scenarios, his subconscious would take them on board, and his dreams would become the stories he'd written, rather than terrifying versions of what happened. It was early days, though, and he didn't expect changes overnight. He'd arranged to take Asha out for dinner the next evening. As they wanted to keep their relationship to themselves for the moment, he would probably be bringing her back to Drayson's Landing, where it was less likely they'd bump into anyone they knew.

He pulled up in front of J.R. Constructions and turned off the truck. He took a deep breath. He wasn't sure whether he should say something to Buster or not. He picked up his files from the front seat, climbed out of the cab, and walked through the front door of the offices.

"Hey, Zane," Jodi, the office manager, said. "Buster's finishing up on a call. Can I get you a drink? Tea, coffee?"

"No, I'm good." He hesitated. "How is he today?"

Jodi gave a sad smile. "Tad under the weather by the looks of him. He didn't say anything when he came in, but yesterday was a difficult day. He doesn't like talking about what happened."

Zane nodded. He understood that better than most.

Five minutes later, he was sitting across from Buster. Jodi was right. He looked terrible. His eyes were bloodshot, his face ashen. Zane had several things to discuss with him, but under the circumstances, he couldn't act as if it was business as usual. He cleared his throat. "Before we begin, I wanted you to know how sorry I am about what happened to your little girl. I only found out on Saturday night, and I know that yesterday would have been a hard day for you. In your position, I doubt I'd want to talk about it, but I couldn't start the day pretending I didn't know and would hate you to think I didn't care."

Buster nodded. "Thanks, I appreciate your words. But, you're right. I don't like talking about it. I can't do anything about it, no matter how many times I go back in my mind and wish I'd done things differently."

"Did you know Steph Jones relives the accident every day? Blames herself."

Buster's eyes widened. "Steph? Why would she blame herself? She was the one diving in, trying to rescue Holly. The person who should be blamed is my ex wife. I can't imagine how she lives with herself. She's sober now, at least. Not much on tap in jail for an alcoholic."

"It affected Steph pretty deeply, not being able to save Holly. She was talking about you last night, saying how hard yesterday must have been for you."

Buster sighed. "No worse than any other day since it happened." He managed a wry smile. "Today might be worse. If you could get inside my head and feel the thumping that's going on, you'd be glad you didn't live in my body. Now, I appreciate your concern, but let's get on to talking about these changes to the plans. I'm getting a bit concerned about this second set of plans Matt's had me draw up. I don't see the point of them. It's a completely different development to the existing one we've finalized plans for, and he can't demolish or build on land he doesn't own."

Zane stared at Buster. What was he talking about? "Hold on. The plans for the development were the ones we put on public display last Friday. What plans are you talking about?"

Buster pulled out a large architect's drawing and turned it so Zane could see it. "He came in late last week and asked me to draw up a new set of plans."

Zane studied the plans. "But this is a completely different

development and includes Charlie Li's properties and the other four houses on the far side of Charlie's."

Buster nodded. "Matt said he'd had verbal confirmation from the four houses that they'd sell if Charlie does. He wants to at least plan and cost this option in case Charlie's properties become available."

Zane stared at the plans. Why would Matt go to all this effort when Charlie was so adamant he wouldn't sell?

"Charlie's old," Buster said as if reading Zane's mind. "Matt thinks there's a possibility his nephew, who is his power of attorney, will suggest he either go into the long-term care facility at LakeView or move to Tall Oaks and live with him and his family."

Zane looked up at Buster. "Really? But he'd still own the properties. It wouldn't mean he'd be selling them and certainly not to Matt."

Buster shrugged. "I don't know the detail, but Matt seemed to think it was a possibility. He's still submitting the other plans for approval, so the project won't be held up if Charlie's properties aren't on the market."

Zane nodded and went back to studying the new plans. It was a much larger development spanning across nine lots. The street front was to be developed with commercial properties, with three levels of accommodation above them. This plan went against everything Matt had told the residents of Hope's Ridge on Friday. He frowned and got to his feet. "I need to speak to Matt, find out if this new plan is a possibility."

"Sure. Take these plans with you if you like. I'm dropping in to see him this afternoon, but he can study them first, see if he's happy."

Zane waited while Buster rolled the plans up and slotted them into a long tube. Anger rose in him. These plans hadn't happened overnight. Matt had been planning this for some time. What he didn't understand was why he hadn't told Zane and why he'd presented a different set of plans and lied to the townspeople on Friday.

Asha was still buzzing from the previous night as she went about her usual Monday routine. She'd been busy all morning and found herself laughing and joking with her regular customers. It was rare that any customer wasn't a regular, which was part of what she loved about running her business in a small town.

As she removed a tray of freshly baked pecan and pear muffins from the oven, she heard someone clear their throat. She looked up to see Charlie Li's eyes dancing with amusement.

"You're cheerful this morning."

Asha placed the muffins on a board to cool.

"It's a beautiful day, Charlie, so yes, I'm cheerful. What can I get you?"

Charlie tutted and shook his head. "You're wasted here, you know. You are destined for greater things."

Asha wasn't sure whether to be flattered or offended. "I'm quite happy running my own business. I have a regular stream of customers and enjoy this location."

"Yes, but the cafe would have suited you better."

Asha shrugged. "It wasn't meant to be. If I believe my sister, I need to be patient, and another opportunity will come along."

"Your sister is a wise woman," Charlie said. "She reminds me of my mother. Calm and intuitive. Women like that should be listened to." A dark shadow flashed in his eyes momentarily.

"Everything okay?" Asha asked.

Charlie sighed. "You'd better give me one of those delicious muffins I can smell, and then I'll explain more about my family and me. I need someone to listen to me today, and I think I've come to the right place."

This time Asha was flattered. For a ninety-six-year-old to believe she was the right person to confide in was very flattering. She doubted she had any wisdom to share with this man from whom it seemed to ooze, but she was happy to listen nonetheless.

"I have myself in a bind," Charlie said as he carefully cut the muffin into four smaller pieces. "My only living relative is coming to visit me, and I can't stand him."

Asha's hand flew to her mouth to stifle her laughter. Charlie always seemed so easy going and tolerant; she hadn't expected this.

His face grew serious. "It's not funny. He's my nephew and heir to my fortune, and I'm not sure how I request that he not visit."

"You could say you aren't well."

"I don't like to lie," Charlie said.

"Does he know you don't like him?"

Charlie nodded. "It's mutual. He visits once or twice a year to *check on me,* which is code for looking me over to see if I'm ready to die."

Asha gasped. "No!"

"Yes. He's asked me for money many times through his life to which I've said no. A man must learn to stand on his own feet before he is ready to take on another man's hard-earned fortune. He knows that I am likely to leave my estate to him, so has been rather put out that I've lived so long and intend to live for many more years."

"That's awful."

Charlie shrugged. "It is how it is. But that doesn't help solve my dilemma."

"You could be honest. Say you would prefer he doesn't visit. If he still comes, then you can't do a lot other than ask him to leave. Alternatively, you could say you'd like to postpone the visit to another time, and you'll be in touch. That leaves things rather vague."

"Yes, that sounds like a good approach." Charlie smiled and popped a piece of muffin in his mouth. He closed his eyes, savoring it.

Asha smiled as she watched the older man. She imagined Charlie had lived quite a life. He'd been married for many years and was well known and well liked around the town. He was always the first to help those in need and the first to object if someone in town was doing something they shouldn't.

"You need to watch out for those two property rogues," Charlie said. "That was the other thing I came to tell you. Matt Law and Zane Larsen are up to no good. They are not to be trusted."

"I agree with you about Matt," Asha said, "but Zane's a good guy."

"Anyone who associates with Matt will be caught up in his devious plans. Be careful with your associations."

Asha looked away. How did Charlie know anything was happening between her and Zane? Other than Steph, no one knew.

Charlie wiped some crumbs from the corner of his mouth and stood. "Thank you. That was delicious. Now, I'll take your advice and call my nephew and be honest. I appreciate your suggestion."

Asha watched as Charlie ambled toward the lake trail. At that pace, it would take him ages to walk back around to the other side of town where his house was. He was so wise she was surprised he needed anyone's advice on anything. She frowned. He was wise and seemed to have a good read on people. She had ignored his warnings about the cafe a few weeks ago. Should she be taking any notice of his warning about Zane? No, of course not. She was old enough to make her mind up about people, and right now, Zane was the one friendship that was giving her a lift. She was confident she had nothing to worry about.

Matt didn't seem phased at all when Zane questioned the second set of plans that he'd asked Buster to draw up. "I spoke to Buster about those ages ago," Matt said. "They're the fantasy plans versus the reality which are the ones we're ninety-nine percent more likely to build from."

"It seems strange to spend so much on plans that will never be built."

Matt laughed. "Never say never. There's the slightest glimmer of hope in the form of Charlie's nephew, Albert. I'm meeting him at Greyson's for coffee this afternoon. You should come."

"Albert?"

"Yes, he's Charlie's only living relative who is set to inherit all of Charlie's estate."

"How do you know all of this?"

"Dad's talked about him for ages. Albert visited a few times when Charlie's wife was still alive, and Dad got chatting to him at Traders. They got along quite well. Albert likes his whiskey, and over a few too many, he let on to Dad that Charlie's worth a truckload. He's got other real estate in New York, probably shares, and who knows what else. He made Albert his power of attorney after his wife died, and that's when Albert realized that one day he will be a rich man."

"And you're hoping Albert will sell you the properties?"

"Not hoping, I'm counting on it. It would be ideal if it could happen sooner rather than later, so my *fantasy* plans become a reality."

"Charlie looks like he's still got quite a few years left in him."

Matt sighed. "I know."

Zane couldn't help but smile. "I don't think you're supposed to sound so disappointed that someone's going to live."

Matt laughed. "I don't wish anything bad on Charlie; it's a frustrating situation."

"How come you're meeting with Albert today? Is he coming to see Charlie?"

"He was, but Charlie called him when he arrived in Drayson's Landing and asked if they could reschedule. Albert's not too happy. It was a four-hour drive to get to the Landing. Meeting with me at least makes it worth the drive."

"That's late notice," Zane said. "Did Charlie give him a reason?"

"No, and Albert didn't ask. They're not close."

"But close enough to leave a small fortune to?"

Matt nodded. "It keeps the fortune in the family, I guess." He glanced at his watch. "I'd better go. I said I'd meet Albert at two. Come with me and meet him. I'm hoping we'll be doing quite a lot of business with him in the future."

Less than an hour later, Zane extended his hand to Albert Li, Charlie's nephew. He looked nothing like Charlie. He was stocky, dressed in worn, untidy clothes and had an unhealthy-looking pallor. He had a cigarette in one hand and shook Zane's hand with his other.

"Let's grab a table," Matt said.

Zane and Albert followed him through to a booth in the back corner of the cafe.

"Do you visit your uncle often?" Zane asked, interested that he'd never heard of Albert before. While he'd lived away himself for the last ten years, Hope's Ridge was small enough that he was sure he would have heard of Charlie's nephew long before this. Charlie had been in the town years before Zane was born and was well known to the Larsen family. Charlie's wife had babysat Zane and Jenna when they were young and had been invited to many family events.

Albert shook his head. "We don't see eye to eye on many things. I've seen him once or twice since my aunt died. For the funeral, of course, and then to work out the power of attorney information. I'm his only family, so as much as he hates the thought of me having the power over his decisions, I was his only option."

Zane could imagine Charlie's reluctance to have this man as his power of attorney. There was something about him that didn't feel right.

They ordered coffee, and then Matt got straight down to business. "I'm looking to get your signature on some documents," he said, opening his briefcase. "While I realize that none of these plans can go ahead until you take ownership of the properties, I want to get the ball rolling with investors. They need to see the timeline for when we are likely to be able to move."

"I don't have a crystal ball," Albert said. "I can't do anything until my uncle passes, and I inherit."

"A bit premature for this discussion, isn't it?" Zane asked. Matt hadn't said a whole lot about Albert Li on the way to meet him. He'd said he liked to keep in touch with him with a hope they'd be doing business in the future. From this meeting, he was getting the feeling they'd been in discussions for many months, possibly longer, over Charlie's properties. "Charlie's as fit as you or me."

Albert shook his head. "Just my luck, of course. The rest

of my family, who had no money, die young from disease and accidents. My cashed-up uncle will probably outlive all of us."

Matt laughed. "That, I doubt. Now, take a look at the documents and check that you're happy to sign them."

Zane accepted his coffee from one of the waitstaff as Albert looked over the papers. He sipped it, wondering what agreement Matt and Albert had reached. Had they put a price on the properties already?

His phone pinged with a text message. It was Buster. *Let me know when you're in town next, have a few things to go over with you that I forgot to discuss this morning. I can come to you if you aren't coming this way.*

Matt looked over at him. "Anything important?"

"Buster wanting to go over a few things."

Matt glanced at his watch. "Why don't you meet with him now? Albert and I still have more to discuss, and then we can drive back to the Ridge."

Zane nodded and stood, once again shaking the other man's hand. "Nice to meet you, Albert. I'd like to say I look forward to doing business with you, but if it's waiting on Charlie to make his exit, I think, and hope, we'll be waiting a long time."

Albert smiled, withdrawing his hand from Zane's. "The universe works in strange ways. I think we will work together much sooner than you expect."

Zane stood, smiling as he recognized Sue, Asha and Steph's mom, enter the cafe. She waved, and he left Matt and Albert to go and say a quick hello.

"Busy with meetings?" she asked as he approached her.

"Yes, more development stuff with Matt. How about you? What brings you to the Landing today?"

"An author talk at the library. A woman from Tall Oaks is releasing her first book. I thought I'd come and find out a bit more. It sounded interesting. But," she nodded toward the coffee machine, "I need a pick me up first."

"Enjoy the talk," Zane said. "I'd better get moving. Have to meet with Buster before Matt and I head back to the Ridge."

Sue smiled, her sea green eyes dancing with mischief as her daughter's did. It was like looking at a more mature version of Asha, and Zane had to admit that the thought of Asha made his heart race.

***

Asha found it hard to believe how quickly the week was disappearing as she turned the key in the lock, looked back over her shoulder, and waved to Zane, who was watching her from this truck. They'd had dinner in Drayson's Landing, their second restaurant dinner for the week. On Tuesday night, Asha had invited Zane in for tea when he dropped her home, but tonight she'd decided she'd better not. She wanted to move slowly with him and was concerned if she did let him in that her lack of willpower would see things progress a lot quicker than she was ready for. She knew he was nothing like her ex, Dylan, had been, that she could trust Zane, but that didn't mean she would rush too quickly either. There was no hurry. This was one of the best parts of a relationship. The butterflies in her tummy each time she saw him, the anticipation of what was to come.

Also, Zane had seemed a little distracted tonight. They'd still had a great time, and he'd apologized more than once, saying a few things were going on at work that were stressing him out a little, and on top of that, he'd received a phone call before coming out that had thrown him. He didn't want to discuss it until he'd had more time to think about how to deal with it. Asha had been okay with that. She liked that he'd been open enough to tell her something was bothering him but respected that he might need time to process whatever it was without her input.

"That's right, isn't it, Maxy? No rushing any part of this relationship." She scooped up her cat and carried him through to the living room where she sank onto the blue and white couch. She rubbed him under the chin. It was hard to believe she'd only had Max for a year. She couldn't imagine life without him. He was the perfect companion. "Any man I get serious about will have to prove himself to be as perfect as you, won't he?"

Max purred in response.

Asha thought about Zane as she stroked Max. The more she got to know him, the more complex she realized he was. He was a deep thinker and curious about so many things in the world. He adored nature, which he intended to share with her this coming weekend. They were going out on the lake for a champagne cruise on Saturday after she finished work and on Sunday would hike to Humble Falls and take a picnic. She'd laughed when he explained the champagne cruise would be an exclusive event for the two of them, taking place in a canoe he was hiring from the rental place by the lake. "It'll be romantic," he'd assured her when she'd snorted with laughter, saying she wasn't sure he could use the word *cruise* and *canoe* in the same sentence. She smiled now, thinking about it.

Her phone rang as she continued to stroke Max, and she slipped it from her pocket. It was Jenna requesting they FaceTime. She hesitated momentarily. Had someone told her about her and Zane? It wouldn't be the end of the world if Jenna found out, but she would prefer it was her or Zane, preferably the two of them together, who told Jenna.

"Hey, hon," she said, answering the call. Jenna's face came into view, her eyes bright, her cheeks flushed.

"How are you, Ash?"

"Great. You?"

"Amazing! Or should I say amaze-ring!" She held up her left hand, displaying a sizeable sparkling diamond.

Asha's mouth dropped open. Engaged? Jenna and Brad had been dating for less than two months. Surely, they wouldn't be rushing to get married already?

Jenna laughed. "You should see yourself. I was expecting excited screaming, not stunned silence."

Asha forced her mouth closed. "Sorry, I wasn't expecting anything like this so soon."

Jenna pouted. "That's it? Where are the congratulations? The, tell me how he proposed; can I be your maid of honor and all that?"

Asha pulled herself together, planting a smile on her face. "Sorry! I think I'm in shock. It's amazing news, Jen. Tell me everything."

Asha tried to get her head around the fact that Jenna was talking about marriage to a guy she'd only recently met. It made no sense at all, yet she had to appear supportive and excited for her friend. Jenna was planning to tell her parents in person, so that might be an opportunity to subtly suggest it was a bit early.

"We won't get married straight away," Jenna was saying. "I think six months is probably about right to wait, what do you think?"

"I don't know. I thought it took ages to get things organized and venues hire out months in advance. Don't most people say a year between engagement and marriage?"

"Well, I'm not most people," Jenna said. "I don't have Steph's patience I'm afraid. I'd elope tomorrow and marry Brad if I didn't think it would upset too many people."

"Don't do that," Asha said. That would be a disaster. She

wouldn't have an opportunity to suggest Jenna wait if she did that.

"Of course, I won't. I can't get married without you or Zane there for that matter."

"Have you told him?"

"Not yet, I called him before I called you but decided it wasn't the right timing."

"What, you just called him?"

"Yes. He was on his way home from somewhere. Wouldn't tell me where."

Asha had to keep from smiling.

"He was a bit distracted. He had some news today that's unsettled him."

"I hope he's okay?"

"Look, I probably shouldn't say anything, but it would be great if you could keep an eye out for him over the next couple of days. Maybe drop into Steph's, check he's okay."

"Is it to do with the hold-up?"

Jenna shook her head. "No, nothing like that. It's Lucy, his ex. She's finally realized what she's lost and wants him back."

Asha sucked in a breath. "What do you mean, wants him back?"

"She called him this afternoon and apologized. Said she realizes how badly she let him down and hopes he can find it in his heart to forgive her."

Asha's stomach churned. "Do you think he will?"

"I'm not sure. He was pretty messed up when she left. They'd been together for three years, and I think he'd thought about asking her to marry him. Theirs was the most significant relationship he's had. Anyway, you can see why announcing my engagement wouldn't have been the most sensitive of timing. Don't say anything about it if you do see him. Now, I'd better go. Brad's got a bottle of champagne on ice, and after he calls his parents, we'll celebrate."

Asha forced a smile for Jenna's benefit. "Congratulations, hon. You deserve happiness." It was true, Jenna did deserve happiness, but Asha wasn't convinced she'd find it with someone she'd known for such a short space of time. As they ended the call, Asha realized it was more than that. She did believe in love at first sight, but Jenna had mentioned enough things about her relationship that unsettled Asha. Brad sounded controlling. Asha would hate to see her best friend leave Hope's Ridge, partly to get away from her controlling father, only to end up married to someone similar. Right now, however, her bigger concern was Zane. It made sense that he'd been so distracted. Would he seriously contemplate going back to his ex? She guessed there was a strong possibility he would. If he'd loved her like Jenna said he had, and she was asking forgiveness, what reason would he have to say no?

Zane took a detour away from Steph's house after ending his call with Jenna. He drove to the lake and got out of his pickup and walked toward the water. He shivered and pulled his jacket around him. He didn't want to think about his day. The phone call from Lucy had thrown him. He thought they were completely over; that he'd moved back to Hope's Ridge to start again and having connected with Asha, he thought that was what he was doing.

He ran a hand through his hair and stared out across the moonlit water. The stars were bright above him, and the moon was moving toward full. The water lapped at the shore, and he heard an owl hoot in the distance. These were the sounds of Hope's Ridge. There was no traffic or blare of sirens, no neighbors shouting, or televisions turned up too loud. It was quiet and peaceful and helped calm his mind.

He sat down on a large flat rock by the lake and tried to get his head around Lucy's words. She'd apologized for the way she'd behaved, explained that she had no idea how to handle things. That she was used to him looking after her and wasn't prepared for their roles to switch. She said that she knew she had to step up and be there for him, and more than knowing she had to do this, she wanted to do it. He could tell she was crying, even though she was doing her best to hide that from him. She'd ended by saying how much she missed him and how much she loved him. He'd been so shocked he had no idea what to say, so he had promised to call her in a few days to talk further.

Every time he thought of Lucy, an image of Asha popped into his mind; the way her sea-green eyes lit up when she saw him and her total lack of awareness of how gorgeous she was. They'd been out for dinner earlier and had a great time. He'd done his best to push Lucy's phone call from his mind, not that it had been easy. He wondered if he hadn't connected with Asha before Lucy called, whether a decision would be easier to make. He realized that that was how he needed to think. If he removed Asha from the equation, would he go back to Lucy? They'd had a great relationship up until the holdup. She was a little selfish and shallow, but he loved too many other things about her, so he could overlook that. She was funny, easygoing, enjoyed the same types of music, movies, and activities that he did, and they shared a great group of friends. But she'd let him down at the only time in their relationship where he'd ever needed her support. While she'd recognized and apologized for her behavior, it didn't change what had happened and didn't guarantee she'd be there for him another time.

Zane sighed as a frog croaked, breaking into his

thoughts. Why was life so complicated? If he did get back with Lucy, that would mean moving back to the city. He didn't want to do that. He was enjoying his job here and loved spending time with Asha, Steph, and the people he came in touch with through work. What would he do if he went back to the city? He wasn't going back into finance or banking; he would probably never walk into a bank voluntarily again.

An image of Asha re-entered his mind. Her wavy auburn hair, her dimpled cheeks, and sparkling green eyes. It was more than her looks, it was the way she threw back her head when she laughed and how she listened to him as if he was the most important person she knew. She made him feel special, loved. He shook his head. He was sure Asha didn't love him. It was far too early to be thinking of things like that, but the one thing he did know was he didn't want to lose her. Being friends would never be enough. He wanted more. He stood and slowly walked back to his pickup. The decision was easier than he thought. He wanted Asha; he was more certain of that than anything else in his life. And wanting her meant he didn't want Lucy or anything that resembled his old life.

***

Asha opened Irresistables at six the next morning. She'd been awake since two, tossing and turning. Max had got annoyed with her in the end, slinking out of the bedroom and finding himself a cozy spot on the couch. She couldn't stop thinking about Zane. The most frustrating part was she knew she had to leave him to make his decision. She couldn't influence him in any way. There was no point. If it was Lucy he wanted to be with, then a relationship between her and Zane was destined to fail from the start.

But not having any control over the situation was frustrating.

She'd begun baking at three-thirty, meaning she'd over catered for the day, but that was good. She was overdue for a visit to LakeView, so she would make sure she'd closed by two to deliver afternoon tea for some of the residents before three.

Her first customer knocked on the closed serving window at six-thirty. She rolled it up and smiled when she saw her sister.

"Early class?"

Steph shook her head. "Nope decided to go for a walk."

Asha raised an eyebrow. "It's cold, and it's still dark."

Steph laughed. "It's not dark. The sky's lightening and the sun will be up any minute. Can I get coffee to go please?"

"More coffee? Still not sleeping?"

Steph shrugged. "Seems to be a theme at our house at the moment. Zane was up half the night pacing about to."

Asha nodded and set about making the coffee. She imagined Zane was pacing about Lucy rather than the nightmares that often kept him up at night.

"How are things between you and Zane?" Steph asked. "I thought I would see more of you, not less, considering he lives at my house."

Asha blushed. "We've been out a few times, but we're taking it slowly. I'm in no rush for anything, and neither is he. Jenna doesn't know by the way; neither does anyone else. We're keeping it quiet for the moment."

"You're not doing a very good job of that," Steph said. "Bodhi asked me how you were doing."

"Bodhi?"

Steph nodded. "Kirsty Magnus asked him before a

Pilates class if he knew whether the rumors about you and Zane were true. She'd been hoping he might ask her out."

Asha shook her head. "Small towns are the pits sometimes. We've been driving to Drayson's Landing to have dinner to keep away from spying eyes and gossiping mouths."

Steph laughed. "Didn't work. You might want to let Mom and Dad know before they hear from someone else."

"Hear what? That Zane and I've been out a couple of times? I don't think they need to know that. I don't think we'll be doing it again anyway."

"Why not?"

Asha passed Steph her coffee. "Rumor has it that his ex-girlfriend wants him back. Which I guess means he might be moving back to the city."

"What? Why hasn't he said anything? That leaves me without a roommate."

Asha realized she'd spoken prematurely. "It might not be happening. That's a possibility I heard about yesterday. I think she only called him yesterday, so we shouldn't jump to conclusions that he will take her back or that he's moving."

"I thought you two had something special." Steph reached through the window and squeezed Asha's hand. "I'll be sorry if he goes back to her, Ash. He's an idiot if he does."

Asha did her best to smile as she blinked back tears. "They were together for three years; I can't ask him to give that up."

Steph sighed. "No, you can't, and as I said about the cafe, you need to be patient. See what happens. If it's meant to be, it will be."

"Unfortunately, I agree with you on this one," Asha said. "I hope he makes a decision quickly and puts me out of my misery. It's driving me mad, wondering what he's planning to do."

"You really like him, don't you?"

The tears that had been threatening spilled onto Asha's cheeks. She wiped them away quickly. "Sorry, I didn't get much sleep last night. But yes, I do like him, and I'll be disappointed if it ends before it starts." She gave a small laugh. "Seems to be the story of my life at the moment, the cafe ending before it started, and now this."

"Oh, Ash, it'll work out."

"I know," Asha said. "What's meant to be and all that, but it's hard at this point. Now, you'd better get on with your walk as it looks like my morning's about to begin." She nodded in the direction of two pickups pulling into the small parking lot. Regulars were coming to get their morning coffee and muffins.

"Give me a call if you want to chat. I'm free anytime."

Asha would usually kid around about Steph not being contactable, but she wasn't in the mood. Instead, she nodded and smiled at her sister as the workmen approached the food truck.

The orders came in thick and fast and continued to do so until around one when suddenly it quietened. Asha was glad of the break. It gave her a chance to clean the coffee machine and do an inventory of ingredients. She needed to place an order with The Bean House for delivery in the next day or two. They supplied flour and sugar as well as coffee beans, so it was often her one-stop-shop which made life easy. She checked the muffin stock, amazed to discover she only had three left. So much for taking the leftovers to the long-term care facility.

"Coffee, please, Asha." She was brought out of her thoughts by Pat, the local postal worker. Postman Pat, as many of the locals fondly referred to him. She smiled and set about making Pat's usual latte. "Busy day?"

"The usual. Although I'm a bit put out, to be honest. I delivered a large parcel to old Mrs. Parkes. Did you know she averages three letters a month and only two parcels at Christmas? That's it. Nothing else. So, as you can imagine, receiving a large parcel out of the blue had me intrigued. But she wasn't letting on. She called me nosy and shut the front door in my face!"

Asha laughed. "You are rather nosy for a government worker."

Pat put on a fake scowl. "Nosy! That's not very kind. I like to think of myself as curious. And I can tell you that I see a lot of interesting parcels arrive for the folks in this town. All sorts of things that would shock you."

"And as a *curious* government employee, I imagine what you see is confidential."

Pat laughed. "Yes, of course, it is. Although I do raise my eyes at certain residents from time to time to let them know that *I know* what they're up to."

Asha fixed a lid to his coffee and handed it to him. "I have three delicious muffins left, and one of them has your name on it, complimentary, of course."

Pat's eyes widened in delight. "Thank you. I'll tell you what, in payment, I'll deliver your mail here today rather than make you wait for it until you get home. Give me a minute." He put his coffee down on the counter and walked back to his truck.

Asha put a blueberry muffin in a bag and waited for Pat to return. They exchanged her letters for his brown paper bag.

Asha flicked through them. "Thanks, although looking at these, they probably could have waited until I got home. Bills by the looks of things."

Pat waved the coffee and bag at Asha. "Better be on my way. Thanks for this, I appreciate it."

Asha smiled as he made his way back to his truck. She flicked through the letters. Electricity, cell phone, and something from the council. She slid her finger into the back of the envelope and opened it. She scanned the letter, her heart dropping as she read the fine print.

...informing you that you are currently parked on council land without a permit. Please re-locate your vehicle within seven days of the receipt of this letter. Our office is open from 9 a.m. to 5 p.m. should you need to discuss this issue further.

Asha wasn't willing to wait another minute. She locked up Irresistables and hurried to her van. She would go straight to the council offices and work this out. She'd been in this spot for three years, and no one had ever said anything about needing a permit. Hopefully, it would be a simple case of filling out some paperwork and paying the permit fee.

Zane found it difficult to concentrate on the legal documents he was supposed to be reading through and approving for Matt. The phone call from Lucy the night before had thrown him. Not because she wanted him back, but because it made him realize how quickly he was falling for Asha. He'd been distracted on their date the previous evening and owed her an explanation. He glanced at the office clock. It was nearly four. He would take the contracts home and finish them over the weekend when he could concentrate better. Right now, he needed to call Lucy and then find Asha.

He picked up his phone and took a deep breath. He'd much prefer to send her a text, but after a three-year relationship, he was pretty sure that would make him a first-rate jerk. Although he was clear in his mind what he wanted, and Lucy had been the one to end their relationship, he was still nervous. Breaking up was never fun.

She picked up immediately. "Hey, babe." Her voice was soft, full of love and hope.

Nausea churned in the pit of Zane's stomach. He cleared his throat. "Luce, I'm sorry, but I think we made the right decision a few months back about us. I'm not interested in coming back to the city or getting back together." He was met by silence. Even to his ears, it sounded like a harsh way to start a conversation. But how else was he supposed to do it? There was no point in having a friendly conversation and then dropping it in at the end.

"Luce? You there?"

"I'm here." A much harsher tone replaced the soft, caring voice. "You're ending things?"

Zane sighed. "Look, I thought you ended it a few months ago, so I've spent the last few months grieving what we had, coming to terms with that, and I can now see it was for the best. I'm sorry if you've changed your mind, but it's too late. I'm sorry."

"I'm not sure what to say, Zane." Her voice cracked, and he knew she was crying. He ran his hand through his hair. Why was he suddenly the bad guy? Gentle sobs filtered through the phone. "I have to go," Lucy said. "I can't talk now; I'm too upset." She ended the call before he had a chance to respond.

Zane put the phone back down on the desk and let out a breath. He hoped she'd be okay. He'd loved Lucy and wouldn't wish any bad on her, but it was no longer his job to comfort her. He turned his mind to Asha. Now that he'd made the call to Lucy, he could find her and explain what had happened the day before. The one thing he knew was he wanted to be honest with Asha about everything. She wasn't likely to find out that Lucy had contacted him, but if she did, then she'd know that he'd said no.

He slipped his files into his briefcase, locked the office door behind him and strode over to the pickup. A smile formed on his lips. Hopefully, Asha would still be at Irresistables, and he could surprise her with a visit. They already had plans for both Saturday and Sunday, but if she was free, she might like to go for a drink tonight too.

Less than two minutes later, he pulled into the parking lot, next to Asha's blue van. He frowned seeing her sitting at one of the tables, her head in her hands. He climbed out of the pickup and hurried up the small walkway. "You okay, Ash?"

Her head jerked up at the sound of his voice. It appeared she hadn't heard him drive up. Her eyes were red rimmed, and she hurriedly wiped her face on her sleeve. He immediately went to her and took her in his arms. "What's happened?"

She pulled back from him and did her best to smile. "I'm not having the best day. I was given an eviction notice this morning."

"I thought you owned your cottage?"

"I do. The eviction notice was for here. For Irresistables. There's been a complaint lodged at council, and they're not willing to let me operate here without a permit."

"Okay. So, get a permit."

Asha gave a wry laugh. "I went and spoke to Lily at the council offices this afternoon, and apparently there have been changes to the permit process, and it now takes up to six weeks to get one. If I were renewing an existing permit, they'd allow me to continue to trade, but because there's been a complaint made, they can't allow that. Lily was apologetic and quite upset. As she pointed out, most of the council employees walk down here on their breaks to get coffee or something to eat. They're not happy at all but have to follow procedure."

"You can't operate for six weeks? That's crazy."

"And the food truck needs to be moved on to private land in the meantime."

Zane shook his head. "I can't believe they won't turn a blind eye while you work it out. They've allowed you to trade for three years! And who would complain anyway? It's not as if you're fighting off competition or have any enemies."

"One enemy it turns out," Asha said. "The one who told me I'd regret it the moment my rock hit the back of his car. Guess this is his payback."

Zane's mouth dropped open. "Matt's responsible?"

Asha nodded.

Zane got to his feet. "Leave it with me. I'll have a chat with him. He was taking potential investors to Traders for drinks this afternoon. I'll see if I can find him and work it out. How about I drop around to your place with a bottle of wine after I've seen him so I can let you know how I go?"

"I don't expect he will withdraw his complaint, but I appreciate you trying. And yes, the wine sounds perfect, thank you."

Zane leaned forward and gave her a quick hug before turning and hurrying back to his pickup.

The sight of Max's fluffy white face didn't do much to lift Asha's spirits when she pushed open the door of her cottage. Nothing was going right. Unless Zane could perform a miracle by turning Matt around, she was out of business for at least six weeks and would need to relocate the food truck and the chairs and tables. That wasn't a huge deal, she had enough room in her driveway to house it, but the area across from the lake she'd been operating from had been set up to look like a permanent business. The chairs and tables sat on a pebbled area that she and her dad built three years ago, and the council had built a path from the lake track to the food truck. How ironic that they'd helped make her look like a permanent tenant and now were telling her to move on. She sighed as she put her bag down on the kitchen counter and went to refresh Max's water bowl and dry food. It wasn't the council's fault; she knew that. It was Matt Law's.

Even if Zane did come back with good news, there was still the news about him and Lucy to discuss. Had he made a decision yet? Would he tell her that Lucy had called? She couldn't spend more time with him until she knew what he was thinking, but she shouldn't even know about the situation, and wouldn't if Jenna hadn't called her.

Asha leaned down and stroked Max as he rubbed around her legs. "I might be home full-time as of next week, Max." The cat purred as she stroked him under the chin. "You'll be happy, at least."

She straightened up and turned on the radio, looking for anything to distract her from her thoughts. She smiled. Taylor Swift was always the right artist to lift her mood. She took a deep breath, trying to empty her mind of everything else and opened the fridge. She had some cheeses and fruit, so would put together a snacking platter for herself and Zane, not that she could imagine eating anything right now.

An hour later, with the platter in the fridge, she sat flicking through the town's local newspaper while she waited for Zane. He'd been gone a long time. Hopefully, that was a good sign that Matt was willing to listen to him.

She dropped the newspaper on the table and jumped up to open the front door when she heard the pickup pull up out the front of her cottage. Zane's face told her immediately he'd had no luck with Matt.

He held out a bottle of wine. "You'll probably need a glass of this. Sorry, Ash, I tried to talk him around, but he won't budge. Said he wouldn't let you get the upper hand after what happened with his car."

Asha took the wine and led Zane through to the kitchen. She gave a small laugh. "Fair enough. To be honest, if our roles were reversed, I probably wouldn't be generous to him either."

"I thought he might come around." Zane placed his keys and phone on the countertop. "He wants the town on side for his developments and making any enemies isn't smart. I tried to remind him that his plans haven't been approved yet, and you could stir up a lot of trouble if you chose to."

Asha took two wine glasses from a shelf above the cooktop and placed them on the counter. "I think I'll stop the war with Matt right now. He's proven his point that he's probably got more pull and power in this town than I ever will."

"He's just proving he knows the laws. And sometimes he chooses to enforce them, that's all."

Asha smiled as she poured the wine. "Isn't he your boss?"

"You're more important to me than Matt Law."

Asha looked up to find Zane looking intently at her.

"I mean it, Ash. I'm happy to do anything you need to stay in that location or find a new one. There may be a way to fast-track your permit application. I'll do some research over the weekend and make some calls on Monday."

"You'd do that?"

"Of course, I would. I meant what I said. You're important to me."

Asha broke eye contact with him.

"What's wrong?"

"It's just, yesterday, you seemed distant. I was worried something was up, that's all."

Zane pushed his hand through his hair. "I wanted to talk to you about that."

Asha handed him a glass of wine, her heart beginning to race. Was this the point when he told her that she was important to him and wanted to remain friends, but he'd be returning to his ex? Concern was written all over his face. She took a sip of wine, her hand trembling slightly. She didn't want to hear those words.

Zane gulped his drink, then gave a small laugh. "Sorry, I'm ridiculously nervous, which is so out of character for me."

"Why are you nervous?"

"I want to be honest with you, Ash. Honesty is important to me in a relationship, so I'd prefer to be upfront than have you possibly find this out down the track from someone else."

Asha bit the inside of her lip. If only he knew his sister had unintentionally shared his news.

"Lucy, my ex-girlfriend called me yesterday. She was apologetic about the way she'd handled our situation after the bank incident. She acknowledged how badly she'd let me down and wanted me to know that she was regretful." He smiled. "It was quite nice as the way she behaved at the time was a side of her I'd never seen before. Hopefully, she'll learn from this experience and won't display that side of herself again."

Asha forced a smile. "I'm glad you've worked things out. You look a lot happier than you did yesterday."

"I am. But there was more than the apology."

As much as she didn't want to hear the next bit, Asha wanted it over with.

"She asked me if we could start again. Put what's happened behind us and get back together."

Asha didn't say anything, just waited.

Zane cleared his throat. "I told her I needed some time to think, but if I'm honest, I knew the minute she asked what my response would be." He placed his wine glass on the counter and did the same with hers before taking her hands in his. "I love what we have. I know it's new, but there's no way I would give you up and go back to Lucy."

Asha stared at him. Did he really say that? "But…" she wasn't sure what she was going to say.

Zane laughed. "There are no buts. I want to explore what you and I have. Lucy's call made me realize that even more. And, if you and I weren't together, I still would have said no. Lucy and I are finished. I could never be with someone so unsupportive. The holdup tested our relationship and proved we weren't right for each other. It's probably the one good thing to come out of it. At least I knew earlier rather than later that we weren't meant to be."

"Have you told Lucy?"

Zane nodded. "I called her before I came to the food truck to see you this afternoon. She got a bit upset, which I feel bad about. I probably wasn't as sensitive as I could have been. It's never easy breaking up with someone. Hopefully, I won't hear from her again. She took most of our belongings when she moved out, so there's no reason to contact me."

"There's you."

Zane pulled her toward him and kissed her. "Yes, but I'm taken."

Asha melted into the gentle kiss, hardly believing that the day had turned out this way. She pulled away laughing as Zane's stomach rumbled. "Why don't you take the drinks through to the living room, and I'll bring in the platter of food."

Zane grinned and picked up their wine glasses. "Sounds like a good idea, and it will give me a chance to bond a bit more with Max, won't it, boy?" Max was rubbing around Zane's legs.

Asha smiled and took the platter from the fridge, loving that Zane was still talking to Max as the cat bounded alongside him to the living area. Zane's phone pinged with a message as she was about to walk through to join him. She picked the phone up, planning to take it to him when the message caught her eye. It was from Lucy.

I'm pregnant. We need to talk.

She stared at it, her stomach churning. This couldn't be happening. Not now, not after Zane told her how much she meant to him. *Pregnant.*

"Ash, do you need a hand?"

Asha closed her eyes momentarily, summoning her internal strength. She wouldn't cry. She needed to believe Steph that things happened for a reason, and her path would fall into place as it was supposed to. It appeared that it was a path that did not include Zane. She put the platter on the counter and carried the phone through to the living room.

She hesitated in the doorway, watching Zane stroke Max's head. They were so beautiful together. But that was no longer relevant.

Zane looked up; his smile replaced with a frown. "I thought you were getting the platter?"

Asha shook her head and walked across to him, his phone in her outstretched hand. "You got a message while I was in the kitchen. Sorry, I didn't mean to read it. I picked the phone up and saw it."

Zane took the phone and opened the message. His face drained of color. He looked up at Asha. "No. This can't be happening."

Asha folded her arms in front of her chest. "Apparently it

is. Now, can you leave? I'm planning an early night, and I'd say you've got a phone call to make."

"It won't change anything, Ash. I promise."

Asha gave a wry laugh. "Your pregnant girlfriend might have something to say about that. Please leave. I've had an awful day and don't need this on top of it."

"And you think I do?"

Asha didn't answer. This wasn't her problem. She had enough of her own to contend with and didn't need Zane's too. She didn't walk him to the front door, just waited until she heard his pickup start up before sinking onto the couch and bursting into tears.

8

---

*I*f Zane weren't living at Steph's house, Asha would have gone straight around to see her sister the previous night. But he was, so she hadn't. She didn't want to risk calling the house and having Zane answer. She'd drunk most of the bottle of wine herself after he'd left, drowning her sorrows after a horrible day. It was unlike her to drink so much, but the one benefit was that it put her into a deep sleep. She woke at six and had to hurry to get to Irresistables. Her first customers would be disappointed if they wanted anything more than coffee as her first batches of muffins were still in the oven at seven.

She had to control herself when midmorning Matt Law turned up. He parked further away from the food truck than he needed and walked over, a self-satisfied smirk on his face.

"What do you want, Matt?"

"An explanation. It's my understanding you're not supposed to be operating from here until you have a permit."

Asha clenched her fists, anger welling inside her. "I have seven days to move from this location."

"That's true, but if you read the letter you were sent, you'll find you shouldn't be operating."

Asha glared at him. "Why do you care so much? I'm happy to pay for your car if that's the issue."

"It's not. I like to ensure all businesses are run legally, that's all. I'm spending a lot of money improving this town, and illegal businesses like yours bring it down."

Asha snorted. "Yet you've bought your coffee here for years. It didn't seem to be letting the town down then."

"I'd suggest you close up shop now. I'll be stopping by to see the sheriff when I leave here so if you don't want a visit from him, or a fine, it's probably in your best interests." His smug smile returned. "You can't say I'm not looking out for you. I didn't need to give you a heads up."

A red Audi A3 pulled into the parking lot, and a tall blonde woman climbed out. If it wasn't for her, Asha was pretty sure she would have launched into a tirade of insults at Matt. Instead, she bit her tongue. She had to admit, she was tempted to hurl another rock in his direction and might have if the woman hadn't reached her.

"Problem customer?" the woman asked.

"Sorry, what?"

The woman smiled. "You look angry, that's all. I wondered if that guy was hassling you."

Asha forced a smile. "I have a few things going on. What can I get you?"

"A decaf cappuccino would be great. I've just arrived from the city and need something to perk me up."

"Coming right up." Asha walked back to the food truck and mounted the steps. "I've got muffins if you're hungry?"

"No, the coffee will be fine, thanks. It's a magnificent location you've got here."

"It is," Asha said. "Unfortunately, I have to move within

the next few days. I didn't realize I needed a permit and now I need to move until one's granted."

"On no. Can't the council make an exception or at least speed up the permit process?"

"Hopefully. A friend was finding out for me." She frowned. It was unlikely Zane would do this for her now. "Or I will on Monday. There's a developer in town who's decided he doesn't want me in this spot, so I'm guessing he'll do everything he can to slow down the permit process."

"Well, I hope he doesn't, and I hope you can keep trading from here."

Asha passed her the cappuccino. "Thanks, me too."

The woman handed her a twenty-dollar bill. "Keep the change. Put it toward that permit."

Asha's face flooded with heat. "Don't be silly. That's way too much. Let me give you some muffins or something, at least."

She shook her head. "There's a strong possibility I'll be driving back past here in the next few hours needing another coffee. If I am, and you're still open, then the twenty will cover another one. How's that?"

"I'll be open until at least two," Asha said. "Make sure you do come back."

The woman smiled. "I'm hoping I'll be so caught up with my friend that I won't have time to come back, but you never know." She glanced at her watch. "I'd better get going. If things don't go to plan, it's a long drive home."

Asha's spirit lifted as she watched the woman walk back to her car. She was upbeat and positive. That was the type of energy she needed in her life right now. That was the demeanor she needed to adopt. Even a slight change in her mindset gave her a lift. It was amazing what the power of positive thinking could do. Steph was always talking about it, and Asha knew she was guilty of dwelling too much on the negative at times. She smiled to herself. She would turn her mindset and the day around.

Zane continually pushed his hand through his hair, pacing to and fro as he waited for Lucy to arrive. He was glad when Steph left to take a yoga class a few minutes earlier, that he would have the house to himself. He didn't want to meet with her in a public location in town as he wasn't sure how the conversation would go, but he also wanted his privacy when he did speak to her.

Right on eleven, her red Audi came to a stop outside the house. Zane shook his hands and arms, trying to rid himself of the nervousness that had built all morning. This was Lucy. Lucy, who he'd known for three years and had loved deeply. Why was he so nervous?

He opened the door, smiling in a way he hoped exuded friendliness but not too friendly. Lucy looked as nervous as he was. They hugged awkwardly, and Zane invited her in.

"Would you like tea or coffee?"

Lucy shook her head. "Had a coffee at the food truck by the lake. Nice woman who runs it."

Zane swallowed. "Did you tell her you were coming to meet with me?"

Surprise flickered in Lucy's eyes. "Why would I do that? Some guy was hassling her when I arrived, and she looked a bit agitated. He left, so we had a bit of a chat. Do you know her?"

Zane nodded. "That's Asha. She's my roommate, Steph's, sister."

"Roommate?"

"Yes, a roommate, that's all. Steph's not my type.

Anyway, that's not why you're here, so you'd better come and sit down. We've got a lot to talk about."

———

Asha's decision to change her mindset worked wonders. She'd headed back into the food truck and started baking. The residents at the long-term care facility would probably love a Saturday afternoon treat. Often she only had enough left over for one wing of the facility, but today she would bake at least five dozen so that each resident could enjoy one if they chose to. She'd go to the extra effort of making two batches of her to-die-for brownies.

An hour into her baking, she'd served a handful of customers when the sheriff's vehicle pulled into a parking space. She sighed. This was all she needed. So much for her positive outlook. When Matt Law was around, she might as well not bother. Even as she had the thought, she changed her mind. Technically she wasn't doing anything wrong. She was baking muffins, and Sheriff Aaron Hammond might enjoy one. She took a freshly baked one from a tray and put it into a bag before plastering a massive smile on her face.

"Afternoon, Sheriff Hammond." She handed the bag out to him when he was in reach. "You can let me know what you think before I take them up to LakeView."

The sheriff raised an eyebrow. "You're baking for the seniors?"

Asha nodded. "I often take them any leftovers from the day, but as I'm not allowed to trade at the moment, I thought I'd put my time to good use. I'm waiting on one more tray to finish baking, and then I'll be ready to pack up and head up there."

The sheriff's lips curled up at the edges. "I'm glad to hear you're not trading. I had a report this morning that you might be."

"Matt Law, I assume?"

He nodded.

"Did he also mention that he threatened to attach the food truck to his vehicle and back it into the lake?" Okay, so she was stretching the truth about as far as it would go, but he wouldn't know that.

"Would you like to file a report? A restraining order, perhaps?"

"Not officially, but I hope that if it does happen, I'll be able to rely on you as a witness?"

"I didn't witness him saying it, but you've told me before the event, so, yes. I'll have a word to him when I next see him as well. We don't want to waste time and money having to haul a ruined food truck out of the lake."

The red Audi from earlier that morning pulled into the parking lot as they were talking. Her positive woman. She hoped she wouldn't say anything about paying for her coffee.

"I'm sorry about what's happened, Asha, but I do have to follow up on complaints. I hope you understand. I believe you need to have the van moved within seven days. If you have any problem finding somewhere for it, drop in and see me. I've got room at the back of my place as I'm sure a lot of the townsfolk do."

A lump formed in Asha's throat. Aaron was supposed to be here threatening to fine her. Instead, he was offering her a place to store Irresistables. *This* was why she loved Hope's Ridge. Matt Law was a jerk, but he was one of a kind in this town. Most people were like family. They looked out for each other. "Thanks, Aaron, that means a lot. I have room at my place if I can't find somewhere else where I can trade from."

The woman approached them, a tentative smile on her lips. She didn't look as happy or as upbeat as she had that morning.

"Hey," Asha said before she had a chance to speak. "I'm closed down at the moment due to some permit issues, but I'd love to make you a cup of coffee and entice you with a muffin if you're game?"

The woman frowned, looked from Asha to the sheriff, and then replied. "That would be great. I'll make a donation in your name to your favorite charity instead of payment."

Asha laughed. She was good! "No need. Today I'm in a charitable mood. Paying forward all the good deeds people have done for me."

The sheriff joined in her laughter. "Ash, I won't fine you if you're trading. I had to turn up to tick all the right boxes after Matt complained. But you know that you can legally trade from someone's property, don't you? You've got your food permit, haven't you?"

"Of course. It's the permit to be on the lakeshore that's the issue."

"Okay, well, find someone with a property in a prominent position and see if you can set up shop there." He held up the paper bag. "Thanks for the muffin. Josie won't be pleased." He laughed, patting his protruding stomach. "But she doesn't need to know."

Asha smiled as he returned to his patrol car.

"He seems like a nice guy," the woman said. "I take it he was told to come and close you down?"

Asha nodded. "He'd have to do his job if it came to it, but I'll make sure I've complied before the cutoff next week. Now, it was a de-caf cappuccino, wasn't it?"

The woman nodded.

"I wasn't expecting to see you back today." Asha looked

up from the machine as she tamped the coffee. "Thought you were visiting someone special?"

The woman sighed. "I hoped I was, turns out I wasn't." She blushed. "Sorry, you don't need to know about this. I'll grab my coffee and head back to the city."

"Don't be silly. I've had my share of trouble in the last few days. Why don't I make myself a cup too and join you? If you need to unload, I'm the perfect person to do that to. A stranger with no preconceived opinions on whatever it is you're going through."

The woman smiled. "That would be great, thank you."

Asha continued making the coffee then made another for herself. She added two apple and walnut muffins to plates and joined the woman at the table she'd chosen closest to the food truck.

The woman picked up a muffin. "Perfect comfort food."

"Bad day?"

"The worst. I ended a relationship a couple of months back and have since discovered I'm pregnant."

Asha dropped her muffin back onto her plate. This was too surreal to be a coincidence. "That sounds difficult," was all she could think to say. She was sitting across from Zane's ex. She'd obviously spent the last few hours with him, and from the look on Lucy's face, it hadn't gone well. That had to be good for Asha, didn't it? For a split second, she wondered if she should tell her who she was. But then what would that achieve? Zane probably hadn't mentioned her, and if he'd ended his relationship for good, it might, as her grandmother would say, rub salt in her wounds.

"It is. I'll be honest and say that I should never have ended the relationship. My ex went through a horrible experience that damaged him. He was depressed and a nightmare to live with. Snapping at me every minute of the day, refusing to see a psychologist and refusing to leave the house. He was in a dark place, which I can see more clearly now, but at the time it was hard to live with. My friends kept making suggestions, and I even went and saw a psychologist for advice on what I should do to help him. But nothing worked. It was as if overnight I went from being the most important person in his life to the enemy."

Asha swallowed. Steph always harped on about how there were two sides to every story, and this was a great example of that. If she hadn't met Lucy, she would have believed her to be cold and uncaring, not this woman who'd tried to help Zane.

"Does your ex know you went to these extents to help him?"

Lucy shook her head. "No. He thinks I'm selfish, cold, and uncaring. He pretty much told me that when I went to see him."

Asha sucked in a breath. "Even though you're pregnant?"

Lucy nodded. "I think he's seeing someone else. I asked him, and he responded that it was complicated, whatever that means. But ultimately, he was clear that he doesn't want a relationship with me."

"What about the baby?"

"He said he'll support me if he has to, but he needs to get his head around it all before he makes any commitments."

"If he *has* too? That's a disgraceful attitude."

Tears filled Lucy's eyes. "He was so cold. I know I hurt him, but I apologized so many times. I told him that I know I made a mistake and would do anything to fix things. I thought the baby would mean something to him. We'd talked about having a family, not this soon, but one day. It would give him something new to focus on, to help forget what happened and move forward."

Asha nodded. Lucy was right. A baby would change Zane's focus and give him someone else to prioritize.

"When did you tell him about the pregnancy?" Asha asked although she knew the answer to her question already.

"Yesterday."

"He hasn't had much time to process it then. Maybe you should give him some space. Get back in touch later in the week if you haven't heard from him. You might find that when the news sinks in, he has a change of heart. You were together for three years and were obviously in love. He might need a reminder of that."

Lucy's forehead creased in confusion. "Did I tell you we'd been together for three years?"

Heat rose in Asha's cheeks. "You said something about three years when you were talking about him. I assumed that's what you meant."

Lucy gave a small laugh. "You're paying more attention than I am." She took another bite of her muffin and sipped her coffee. "This muffin is to die for by the way."

"Take some extras with you for the road," Asha said. "If you're driving back to the city, that is?"

"I am. There's no point hanging around here tonight. I should go."

"I'm sorry that things turned out the way they did for you today. It's a long way to come for that outcome."

Lucy gave a sad smile. "I had to give it a go. This is my baby. Our baby." She blinked back tears. "I still can't believe he was so cold, to be honest. It wasn't the man I know."

Asha stepped toward Lucy and hugged her. "Drive safely, and I hope all goes well for you and bub. Hopefully, he'll have a change of heart, and you'll hear from him soon."

Lucy stepped back. "Hopefully." She gave her one last smile, turned, and walked back to her car.

Asha watched her drive off, wondering what kind of tricks the universe thought it was playing on her? Did she need to meet Zane's ex and realize not only what a strong, wonderful woman she was, but that Zane had responsibilities he needed to step up for? It was a catch twenty-two. If Zane stepped up, there was no possibility of a relationship between them, but if he didn't and shirked his responsibilities, then there was no possibility of a relationship between them either. Whichever way she looked at it, Asha realized they were over before they'd had a chance to begin.

After Lucy left, Zane lit one of Steph's incense candles and lay down in the half light of her meditation room. He turned the relaxation music on and closed his eyes. He needed to calm his mind and get his head around the things she'd said. He wanted to see Asha but was far too worked up to lay all of this on her. Although he wasn't convinced she would want anything more to do with him, he wanted to see her. Explain what Lucy had told him and ask her advice on his options. His ex had a nerve, that much he knew.

It was ages before his body unwound, and he relaxed. The tension drained from his body as he took long deep breaths as Steph had taught him. The incense and music provided an atmosphere that helped him leave behind his thoughts and hover in a different part of his consciousness. Savasana, according to Steph. The real reason for doing yoga in her opinion. When he finally opened his eyes, he realized an hour had passed. He sat up relaxed and clear headed. He needed to speak to Asha and clear things up.

He walked the short distance from Steph's to the lake trail and followed it around to Irresistables. The chairs had been packed up out the front, but Asha's van was still there, so he assumed she would be too. He was surprised she had worked today, he was pretty sure the letter regarding her permit forbade her to trade. He wondered if she'd ignore that or hadn't realized. It reminded him that he'd promised to look into permit short cuts this weekend but hadn't had the opportunity as yet.

He approached the food truck, a ball of nerves uncurling in his stomach.

Asha looked up as he approached, her face immediately clouding.

He wasn't expecting a hugely warm welcome, but he wasn't expecting her to look so cold toward him either.

"Hey."

She stood at the serving window, arms crossed, mouth downturned. "What do you want, Zane?"

"I wanted to talk to you. I saw Lucy today, and there's a lot to this whole situation that I didn't know yesterday."

"Like what?"

Zane shifted uncomfortably from foot to foot. Her standing above him, looking down on him was unnerving. He imagined this conversation with them sitting across from each other, not like this. "Any chance we could go for a walk or sit down and chat?"

"I'm closing up and about to go to LakeView to drop off muffins. If you've got something to tell me, say it."

She wasn't making this easy. "Okay, well, I've told Lucy that there's no chance we're getting back together. She wasn't completely upfront about the baby on the phone."

"I met Lucy today," Asha said. "She dropped in here before she came and saw you, although I didn't know who she was then. But she came back again for coffee before she drove back to the city. She had some interesting things to say about you?"

Zane raised an eyebrow. "Like what?"

"Let's see. There was the bit about you deciding whether

or not you'd support her depending on whether you believed you *had* to, for a start."

"That's not exactly what I said?"

"Well, what did you say? She was upset, Zane. Said you were incredibly cold toward her and not taking responsibility. I was shocked."

"Did Lucy mention to you that she wants to get back with me because she thinks I'll make a great father?"

"She didn't use those exact words, but I gathered that was the case."

"And when she said that, did she mention that although she *thinks* I'd make a great father, there's a high probability I'm not this baby's father?"

Zane resisted the temptation to smirk when Asha's eyes widened in surprise. "That's right. After she left me, she had a series of one-night stands. So not only does she not know if this baby's mine or not, she has no idea whose it is. It could be one of four or five random guys who she saw once and never again. She doesn't know how to contact two of them."

Asha's hand flew to her mouth. "I'm so sorry, Zane. I had no idea. She didn't mention any of that."

"I'm sure she didn't. And yes, I did tell her I needed to get my head around all of this. I want to look into DNA testing and whether that can be done safely while she's pregnant or whether we'd be best to wait until the baby's born. If this baby is mine, I'll support him or her a hundred percent and be in its life as much as possible. But if it's not mine, I'm not getting trapped by Lucy into co-parenting because she decided to be reckless in her sex life."

"I'm glad she was honest with you," Asha said. "Some women would lie from the start and pretend it was yours."

A smile played on Zane's lips. "I'd like to think Lucy wouldn't have done that, but the fact that two of her one-night affairs were African American and one from Malaysia, there's a high probability that if the baby isn't mine, it will be of mixed race. I'd like to think I would have noticed when it was born if that was the case."

Asha sucked in a breath. "Wow, I wasn't expecting that."

"Neither was I. Look, Ash, like I said yesterday. I don't want this coming between us. We're great together, and I know there'll need to be some changes if this baby is mine, but my gut tells me it's not. Lucy had a stomach bug the week before the holdup, and we hadn't," he blushed, "we hadn't been together for a couple of weeks. After the holdup, we weren't together at all. For this baby to be mine, she'd have to be at least five months pregnant by my calculations, and she's only four. I don't think we have anything to worry about. What do you say? Can we give it another go?"

Asha shook her head without seeming to give it another second's thought. "Not now, Zane. There's too much happening. I appreciate that you're being honest with me about all of this, but there's only so much I can handle at one time. Right now, my priority is sorting out Irresistables and what I'll do for work. I don't want the distraction of a relationship, particularly not when you have so much on your plate."

The air whooshed from Zane's lungs. She might as well have punched him. He'd laid his heart on the line for Asha, been completely honest with her, and explained what he wanted. And what had she done? Similar to Lucy four months ago. When things got tough, she got going. He didn't bother to respond. Instead turned and walked back toward the lake trail. He wasn't about to waste another second on her.

Asha did her best to block all thoughts of Zane and the wounded look he'd given her when she'd said he had too much happening to get involved with him. She still had a job to do that afternoon, and with over seventy muffins to deliver, she needed to get them packed into the large boxes she kept especially for deliveries and get moving.

By the time she reached LakeView she had a smile on her face and was ready to face the residents. They didn't need to know anything about her day other than she'd been thinking of them and wanted to make it enjoyable.

Greta, one of the long-standing staff members, greeted her warmly as she walked through the front doors.

"Please tell me those boxes are full of afternoon treats?"

Asha grinned. "Sure are. There's enough for all of the residents and the staff too. Do you want first pick?"

Greta's eyes widened. "Yes, please!" She helped herself to one of the double chocolate mint muffins. "I think you'll have some happy customers today!"

"Hope so. Is it okay for me to do the rounds?"

Greta nodded, her mouthful of muffin, and Ash took off down the east wing corridor. LakeView was split into four different modules, with fifteen residents in each. Each module varied according to the required care level. She entered the high care module and was greeted by Tim, a male nurse in his fifties.

"You picked a good day to come, Asha, nice and quiet for a change. We might stick to muffins with fruit only if that's okay. Chocolate makes Bert crazy, and Doris might go on a rampage trying to steal everyone else's."

Asha laughed, knowing he was only half joking. She handed over a box of raspberry and apple muffins. "Hopefully, they'll enjoy these." She continued into the next two modules, speaking to each resident and offering them their choice of muffins. Her face glowed with the praise the older people lavished on her. If she couldn't work over the next six weeks, she'd make sure she visited here a couple of times a week with baked goods. She'd planned to expand beyond muffins and brownies, and they would be a good audience on whom to experiment with some new recipes.

As she moved into the final module, she did a quick check of the muffins. She still had twenty left, which should be enough. She hadn't allowed for visitors but had given out three extra in the third module to visiting family.

As she entered, Verna, the nurse in charge of the module, rubbed her hands together as she greeted her. "I hope you have something chocolatey left."

Asha opened the box of double chocolate fudge brownies. "You have a choice of these or an orange and chocolate muffin."

"Brownie, for sure, thank you! A few of the residents have gone out in the mini-bus, so I think you'll find there are only ten in here this afternoon."

"Eleven, if you're counting me?" Charlie Li appeared in front of Asha. "My friend George would love a muffin, and if you have an extra, I'd enjoy one too." He reached into his pocket for his wallet.

"They're not for sale, Charlie. They're to be enjoyed," Asha said. "And yes, there's enough for the two of you."

Charlie lowered his eyes. "Oh no, I couldn't expect you to give me one, Asha. It's your business. Please let me pay. In fact, let me pay for all of the goodies you delivered today. You have been too generous."

Asha laughed. "Now *you're* being too generous. This is my gift to the residents. If you want to be generous, then I'm sure they'd love you to come back and visit or to bring them a little treat another time." Asha smiled at the older man. He was probably older than all of the residents in LakeView, and here he was visiting them. She bet many of them would trade ages with Charlie if they could trade lives with him too. He was fit, active, and intelligent. Strangers would believe he was in his sixties or seventies, not his nineties.

"You are too kind." He selected a muffin, for himself, and one for his friend then gave a little bow. "May you have an abundant source of income, wealth, and fortune, Asha." He winked. "Old Chinese saying."

"After the week I'm having, I could use all three of those, Charlie."

He frowned. "Anything I can help with?"

"Not unless you happen to work in the permit department at council?" She explained what had happened with Matt Law and Irresistables.

Charlie shook his head the moment Matt's name was mentioned. "That boy needs to be taught a lesson. Trying to steal our properties and turn the town into a tourist mecca. I will not have it."

"Steal your properties?"

Charlie nodded. "He has been back to see me since the town meeting, putting pressure on me to sell my houses so he can develop a tourist precinct of apartments, shops, and restaurants. The rest of the town will suffer if it goes ahead. He needs to be watched carefully. He and that Zane Larsen. Both of them are up to no good."

"Zane? I don't think he'd do anything to hurt the town."

Charlie watched her for a moment then tapped his nose with his finger. "Ah, that is right. You two are an item, I believe."

Asha coughed. "What? No, we're not. I believe he's an honest person, that's all. I don't think he'd do anything underhanded." She wondered what information Charlie had and why Zane hadn't said anything if Matt was trying to develop the entire strip of Lake Drive.

"You move your food truck," Charlie said. "Tomorrow,

bring it to my house. I have a location that will suit your business."

Asha touched his arm. "That's so kind of you, but I can't do that. Your house is lovely but operating from a front yard isn't viable."

Charlie laughed. "That is not what I'm offering. Bring the food truck at eleven o'clock. You will be surprised."

"Do you own the location you're thinking of?"

Charlie nodded. "I do. I'll draw up a lease tonight, and if you're happy with the conditions, then you can begin trading on Monday." He clapped his hands together as if it were all finalized. "My neighbors will be happy."

Asha watched him as he took the muffins and shuffled down the corridor, disappearing into George's room. It would be too good to be true to find a suitable venue so quickly. But if it wasn't at his house, where was this fantastic location? She hadn't heard that Charlie owned anything in Hope's Ridge other than his houses. Surely she'd be aware of it if he did? But she had nothing to lose. She could hitch the food truck to the back of her van, and if Charlie's location was no good, then she'd take it home and park it in her driveway until she came up with a better solution.

Asha spent another ten minutes visiting the remaining residents and chatting while they chose their muffins. She walked out of LakeView much lighter than when she'd walked in. Not only had she offloaded all the muffins, but she'd also unloaded some of the tension she'd been carrying around too. Her awful day hadn't turned out so badly, after all. She might have a place to operate from, and she'd made a lot of elderly people happy. If she continued to block out all thoughts of Zane, she could almost say she was happy.

Zane nursed his third beer and stared at the flames dancing in the fire pit. A dark cloud had settled over him after walking away from Asha, and while he knew drinking was probably the worst thing he could do right now, he didn't care. Only a few days ago, he'd begun to move beyond the fear and depression he'd arrived in Hope's Ridge with, but now it was once again breathing down his neck. Perhaps he hadn't outrun it after all.

He gave himself a mental shake. He was being melodramatic. It was just women. He couldn't count on them for anything, and moving forward, he wouldn't. He wasn't going near another woman for a long time, possibly ever.

"Zane?"

Steph stood at the back door, dressed in her yoga clothes. She'd taken the Saturday evening class.

"Hey, Steph." Zane swigged his beer. So much for staying away from women, although he didn't count Steph in the same category as Lucy or Asha. They were friends, good friends, and neither wanted any more than that.

"Can I join you?"

"Of course. There are more beers in the fridge if you want one. I'll have another, too, thanks."

Zane leaned back and continued to watch the fire as Steph disappeared back into the house. It was close to five minutes before she reappeared. She'd changed into sweats and carried two steaming mugs.

Zane raised an eyebrow. "That doesn't look like beer."

Steph passed him a mug. "It's not. Looking at the empties on the counter, I figured you'd had enough."

Zane laughed. "Three beers are hardly excessive."

"It is for someone who has trouble sleeping and suffers from nightmares. Want to talk about it?"

Zane ran his hand through his hair. "I'm not sure where to begin."

Steph sipped her tea. "The start's always a good place."

"Lucy came to visit me today." He went on to tell her what had happened that morning and that there was a slight possibility he was going to be a father.

"You know, there are non-invasive paternity tests now," Steph said. "A friend of mine organized one when she wasn't sure who the father was. They take blood from the mother's arm or something. I have no idea how it works, but the baby's DNA finds its way into the mother's blood, so if they have a sample of Lucy's blood and DNA from you, they can check it."

"Can they? Lucy thought the test that was done during pregnancy had a risk to the baby."

"The old way used to, but this has no risk at all."

Zane sipped his tea, deep in thought. As much as he wanted to get the results as soon as possible, he wasn't sure if he was ready to learn he would be a father if that were the outcome.

"I guess the thought of becoming a dad is pretty scary," Steph said. "It explains the beers."

Zane smiled. "Yeah, it is, although I'm fairly confident it's not mine. Based on how far along in the pregnancy she is and when we were last together. Unfortunately for Lucy, she went on a bit of a bender after she left me. She isn't sure how to contact a couple of the guys she slept with."

"Oh no, the poor thing," Steph said.

Zane looked at her. "Poor thing? It's pretty irresponsible."

"I'm sure she didn't set out to get pregnant. If she was acting recklessly, it was probably an indication that your breakup affected her more than you realize."

Zane thought about that. It was a possibility. "I honestly

don't know what to think. But I'll call her in the morning and mention the paternity test. It has to be stressful for her, not knowing who the father is, and she probably should minimize stress while she's pregnant."

Steph smiled. "It's nice to know you still care about her."

"Of course I do. We had three amazing years together. It's the way it ended that I don't want to revisit in any relationship. I'm not going near another woman as anything but friends for a long time."

Concern filled Steph's eyes. "Did something happen today, with you and Ash?"

Zane nodded. "There's no *me and Ash* anymore."

"You don't have to tell me if you don't want to, but I'm a good listener. I hope she didn't do anything stupid?"

Zane sighed. "No. She's got a lot on at the moment." He went on to tell Steph about the eviction letter Asha had received and that she might not be able to trade until a location permit came through."

"That's awful, but why would that end your relationship?"

"Asha's got a lot on her plate, and she doesn't want to take on my baggage as well."

"You should give her a chance, at least, Zane. Just because Lucy let you down doesn't mean Ash would."

"She already has, Steph. She told me straight out that she didn't want the distraction of a relationship with someone who had so much to deal with."

Steph fell silent for a moment. "That's unlike Asha. I'm sorry, Zane. Do you want me to talk to her?"

"No, definitely don't discuss it with her. She's right in that we both have a lot to handle at the moment, and we're better off moving on, each sorting out our own problems." He stood. "Thanks for the drink. I'm going to bed."

Steph smiled at him. "Might see you back out here around three."

Zane laughed. "I hope not, but if you do, it's my turn to make the tea."

Zane dropped his empty beer bottle into the trash and washed out his mug before heading to bed. It had been a long day, and he was emotionally, if not physically, exhausted. Instead of the usual tossing and turning for ages, he fell into a fitful sleep immediately. At two, he sat bolt upright in bed, gasping for breath. His heart thumped and sweat covered his body. He got out of bed and paced the room. He'd relived the holdup again, but this time one of the gunmen had shot the teller in the head, not the leg, and proceeded to shoot the customers one by one before turning the gun and pointing it between Zane's eyes. Zane had squeezed his eyes shut, hardly able to breathe, while another of the gunmen screamed for him to be killed. He'd woken as an explosion reverberated around him.

Zane calmed himself. *It was only a dream, a stupid dream.* He pulled off his soaked tee and grabbed a fresh one from his drawer. His journal sat on top of the drawer, so he picked it up, grabbed a pen, and sat back down on the bed to write. He lost himself in his story. No one was shot in this version. He smiled as he wrote a description of himself overcoming two of the gunmen. The third lay down his gun, a quivering mess after witnessing Zane's incredible kung fu moves. Actually, he wasn't sure if the action he was writing was kung fu, but whatever it was, it was impressive.

An hour later, he sat back and read through the pages he'd scribed. Did it matter he was always making himself the hero? He grinned. No, it didn't. After all, he was the only one reading it.

He decided to go back before the actual hold up, to write a scene from the perspective of one of the gunmen.

Maybe he had a good reason for holding up the bank. A sick child perhaps and he couldn't afford to pay medical bills to help him. Zane imagined he'd do anything if he had a child in need of help. He paused for a moment. He could imagine himself as a dad. A son he could take out on the lake, teach to fish and swim and camp. Or a daughter. If Lucy's child was his, all of these things would be possible, even if he were only a weekend and vacation dad. He shook himself. Where had all that come from? He'd only allow himself to think about those things once he knew for sure he was the child's father. For now, he wanted to keep writing.

A few pages later, he jumped at the sound of breaking glass. He hurried from his room, stopping when he reached the kitchen. Steph was crouched down, picking up shards of glass. She glanced up apologetically when she heard him.

"Sorry. Hope I didn't wake you?"

"No, I've been up for ages. I'll get a broom and help you."

"Could you throw me my flip-flops too? I don't dare move in case I cut my feet."

Zane moved swiftly into action. Getting both his and Steph's flip flops and the broom. They had the kitchen cleaned up within a few minutes.

"Now," Zane put a pot on the stove to boil. "My turn to make tea. What do you feel like?"

Steph laughed. "I love how it is completely normal for us to be hanging out at three in the morning." She glanced at the clock. "Closer to four, I should say."

"I know. Imagine how lonely we'll get when one of us starts sleeping properly."

"We'll have to catch up during normal hours, like regular people who sleep."

Zane smiled as he prepared the tea. "Shall we take it outside?"

"It's too cold," Steph said. "I've been sitting in the living room for a while. I lit the fire, so it's quite cozy."

Zane handed her a mug and followed her into the living room. The lights were dim, and Steph had soft music playing. "Wow, this is beautiful," Zane said. He sat on one of the chairs near the fire, noticing Steph had an open notebook on the side table next to the other.

She picked it up and closed it, her cheeks flushing. "I decided to try that technique you mentioned, of re-writing my dreams."

Zane smiled. "I was doing the same when the glass smashed. Are you finding it useful?"

Steph nodded. "My dreams are changing slightly. I nearly saved her tonight. I guess I need to keep doing it, keep re-reading and visualizing the new version."

"I had one of the worst nightmares I've had in ages tonight," Zane admitted. "Writing the journal did seem to be helping, but after tonight I'm beginning to wonder."

"But you still got up to write?"

Zane blushed. "I'm enjoying it. I've always read quite a lot, mostly thrillers and crime books, so I've been expanding what happened, turning it into a story." He laughed. "Tonight, I wrote from the perspective of one of the gunmen. Gave him a motivation for what he was doing."

"What was his motivation?"

"A sick child, and he can't afford medical treatment."

"Interesting. Kind of turns it on its head, doesn't it? Suddenly we might feel sympathy for the gunman rather than fear or hate. Maybe that was what he was like in real life?"

"The one who shot both the teller and the security guard wasn't doing it for a reason like that."

"No, you're probably right." Steph thought for a minute, then grinned. "We could combine our stories. His motive was that his daughter was badly hurt in a car accident, and the other driver managed to save her from drowning, but she's in a coma. He needs the money for the medical bills."

"Which means we don't want him to get caught," Zane added. "Maybe he's the one that got away, and the money he took was used for his daughter who survives."

"He then turns religious, vows never to do anything like that again, pays back the money to the bank through hard work and…"

"…and they all live happily ever after."

They both laughed.

"It'd be nice to write our own stories, wouldn't it," Steph said.

Zane nodded, sipping his tea. "It would make life a lot easier, although it could get complicated if we're writing different endings that affect other people."

"Like if you wrote your ending where Asha wanted to be with you to support you and become part of your life, rather than you wanting to be independent or go back to Lucy."

Zane raised an eyebrow. "Is this hypothetical still, or did you want to say something?"

"Got me," Steph said. "I know Asha well, and the last thing she is is selfish. She's an incredibly caring person and rarely puts herself first. She was burnt badly in her last relationship, so she's more likely walking away because she has strong feelings for you and is scared of what they might mean."

"Really?"

Steph nodded. "Her ex was a taker. It was always about him and his problems. I think he was attracted to Ash because she put him first and was always there to help solve his problems. But he was one of those guys who was quite insecure, and that showed by him putting her down all the time. She'd go out of her way to do nice things for him or to make his life easier, and he'd tell her she'd done it wrong or hadn't done enough. She couldn't win. And then when she needed him, forget it. She got pneumonia, and he went on vacation with a friend rather than looking after her. Said he couldn't risk catching it. If he were going to catch it, he probably would have had it before she'd been diagnosed, and the doctor said that once she started antibiotics, she was less contagious within forty-eight hours. Mom and I were with her a lot of the time, and we never caught it. For him, it wasn't about catching it; he didn't want to have to look after someone else."

"What a jerk."

"He was. The only good thing about the pneumonia episode was that it highlighted that to Ash. She ended it before he returned from his vacation."

"Is he still in town?"

Steph smiled. "Why? Think you might have reason to be jealous?"

Zane shook his head. "No, although I might want to flatten him if I saw him."

"See, that's because you care about my sister. Now, go and tell her that and stop messing about feeling sorry for yourself."

Zane laughed. "I'm not sure she'd appreciate a pre-sunrise visit. Maybe I'll think about it and, if I decide I agree with you, I'll visit her later in the day."

───────

After cooking a batch of pistachio-chai muffins, Asha left them on the counter to cool. It took her two hours to pack up the food truck and hitch it to the back of her vehicle ready to transport home, via Charlie's. She'd cooked the muffins partly for sentimental reasons, they were the first recipe she'd ever baked in this oven, and partly so she'd have a gift to give Charlie to thank him for his generosity. She'd been tempted to drop in to see him, thank him for his kind offer, and tell him she'd decided to take the food truck home. But she'd realized that would be rude, especially after the text message she'd received from him querying the dimensions of the food truck and the area outside she'd require for the tables and chairs. She'd sent back an estimate, as, without a tape measure, she had no idea.

What she wasn't able to transport were the bench tables that she had out the front of Irresistables for customers. She needed a pickup or a trailer of some kind. She'd rung her father, but he was out playing golf, so her mother promised he'd help her in the afternoon once he returned. She could stack them in her small garage until she was able to trade again.

Asha blinked back tears as she slowly maneuvered the food truck past the tables and out through the parking lot onto the road. If all had gone to plan, she would have been feeling sentimental as she watched someone else drive away with the food truck while she moved into the Sandstone Cafe. She breathed deeply as she slowly drove around to Lake Drive toward Charlie's. She pulled up opposite his house. He had a prime position directly across from the lake with nothing to block his view. It was obvious to see why Matt would want this property and those next to it. She smiled. Good for Charlie, sticking to his guns and refusing to sell.

She took the box of muffins off the front passenger seat and climbed out of the car. Charlie had mentioned his neighbors, so she knew he could share them around or freeze what he didn't eat today. She walked the cobbled pathway that wound from Charlie's front gate past a host of bushy plants and two bird feeders to his front door.

"Asha!"

Charlie opened the front door, his arms wide open.

She smiled, surprised by the warm welcome and hug. She pulled back and held out the muffins. "I came to thank you for being so generous. There's a little something in here for you. They'll freeze well if you don't have friends around to share them with today."

"You didn't need to do that."

"I wanted to. And it was nice of you to offer to help, so although I won't take you up on the offer, I did want to thank you."

Charlie frowned. "What do you mean, you won't take me up on the offer? Of course, you will. I've drawn up the lease already. Come in, and we'll get it, and then I can show you the site. I've marked out with spray paint the boundaries under our lease agreement."

Asha bit the inside of her lip. He was so serious. It was generous of him, but unless he somehow owned the lakefront, she couldn't imagine anywhere that would work for her. Still, she didn't want to be rude, so followed him inside. She was surprised by how modern the house was. Charlie had lived there for a large part of his life and appeared to have kept up to date with current trends. The hallway opened into a large open plan kitchen, dining, and living area. An island with two bar stools separated the kitchen from the dining area. Asha couldn't help but notice the Miele appliances and Krupp coffee machine.

"Your house is lovely, Charlie."

He nodded. "My gorgeous wife, Ying Yue, is responsible for this. She had a wonderful eye for design." He bowed his head momentarily before pointing at a document file on the dining table. "This is what we need." He picked it up and ushered her back to the front door. "We can sign this on location."

Asha allowed him to direct her out into the street. "Did you want to ride in my van?"

Charlie laughed. "No. It's not far. We walk." He linked his arm in hers, looked both ways and crossed the road back toward the spot she'd parked the food truck. He continued past it on to the vast expanse of grass between the road and lakeshore. Asha assumed he was heading to the lake trail, and they would walk from there. She hoped it wasn't too far. He was in his nineties, and while he was fit, she wasn't sure exactly how fit.

Before they reached the trail, Charlie dropped her arm and spread his arms out wide. "What do you think?"

Asha frowned. "I think we're on the lakefront, Charlie. The council-owned lakefront. I can't operate here; it's no different than where I was."

Charlie tapped his nose. "Ah, but it is." He pointed to spray-painted lines on the grass. "I took your measurements and then added some extra space for expansion and improvements. You will draw a bigger crowd here than in your previous location, so you might need more tables, for instance."

Asha stared at him. She wasn't sure how to handle this. She couldn't set up here. Matt Law would be on her back immediately as would the sheriff.

Charlie smiled. "You pleased?" He didn't wait for a response, just passed her the file containing the lease.

She began to read. The agreement between them was for a term of one hundred years. She stifled a laugh. "Charlie, I don't think a hundred years is realistic, do you?"

"Why? Because I might be dead next week?" He rolled his eyes, this time making her laugh.

"No, I'm sure you'll live for many years, but probably not a hundred, and I probably won't either."

"Asha, I own this land." He gestured in a grand

sweeping motion with his hands. "To the end of the lake in that direction and the other side of Main Street in this direction. I have no intention of allowing it to be sold or developed."

Asha's mouth dropped open. "You own it?"

Charlie nodded.

"But how? I thought it was all owned by the state?"

"No. This land has been in my family for a hundred and fifty years. I may look Chinese, but I am as American as you and your family. My great-grandfather emigrated from China in 1850, hoping to strike it rich in the Californian gold rush. In 1853 he did. The gold he found allowed him to buy up property both here and in New York. New York because he knew the investment would be worth a lot one day, and Hope's Ridge for his family and lifestyle. The land has passed down to my Grandfather, my father, then to me." Sadness crossed his face. "Unfortunately, Ying Yue and I were not blessed with children, so I do not have a direct heir to pass the land to. There is only my nephew." His face darkened as he referred to him.

"However, it would give me great pleasure to watch your business thrive in this location."

Asha couldn't believe her ears. This was crazy. There was no better location in Hope's Ridge. She continued to read through the lease. It was unlikely she could afford such prime real estate. She reached that section and looked up. "Charlie, the payment won't work I'm afraid. I can't accept these terms?"

"Too much? Okay, halve it."

Asha laughed. "No, I mean, it's not enough. You're asking for four muffins every second day and unlimited tea and coffee. I need to pay you money as well."

"Why? I don't want money. A muffin every second day will be quite a treat. The other three are for my neighbors;

you know the Smythe's. Their son Barnaby is living with them, as you probably know. They struggle on welfare, so I like to help out where I can."

Asha nodded; she did. Barnaby had been involved in a road accident ten years earlier, which left him with quadriplegia. He'd moved back in with his parents so they could look after him. From what Asha understood, they lived in the second property Charlie owned. "Perhaps you could use my rent money to help them?"

Charlie shook his head. "They are quite comfortable now; I've made sure of that, and they are very proud. They'll accept baked goods but no money. Now, sign on the last page, and I'll send it all to my solicitor so that if I'm hit by a bus tomorrow, you'll know that it is all legal."

Asha hesitated. This didn't feel right. It was too much.

Charlie took her hand. "Asha, you're a good person. You bring much joy and happiness to this town with your friendly smile and your delicious food and coffee. You give your time and baked goodies to those in LakeView and don't ask for anything in return. The universe has come to me and told me to pay my good fortune forward to someone who deserves it. I feel lucky to have found someone deserving."

Asha blinked back tears. She was overwhelmed by his kindness and generosity. She turned to the last page of the contract and signed, slipped the papers back into the file, and handed them to Charlie before flinging her arms around him.

Eventually, he pulled away, a smile dancing in his eyes. "You be careful, Asha Jones, if the townsfolk see you and me like this, there will be rumors flying about." He winked suggestively, causing Asha to laugh. "Now, drive that van of yours up here, and we'll work out the perfect angle for you to give yourself and your customers great lake views.

9

*I*t was after lunch by the time Zane decided to find Asha. He could feel Steph's eyes boring into him for most of the morning, but he wanted to be clear in his mind about what he wanted to say before he went rushing off. He pulled on his running shoes, deciding he'd go for a run along the lake trail before doubling back to Irresistables.

"I hope you're going to see my sister," Steph said as he stretched on the driveway.

"Going for a run," Zane said. "If I happen to run past the food truck, then I might drop in on her."

Steph raised her eyebrows and continued pulling weeds from the flower bed bordering the house.

Zane laughed and took off at a medium pace. He loved running. It was something he'd done since he was a teenager. It was great for clearing his head or tuning out, and of course, the rush of endorphins when he finished was the whole point.

He decided to wind through the back streets before joining the lake trail on the south side of town. He'd then run to the furthest point, where he'd bumped into Steph that day, before turning and running the whole way back to the food truck. By the time he reached it, he should have run off enough energy to justify a muffin, assuming Asha would sell him one. He reached the lake trail within a few minutes and increased his speed. Twenty minutes later, when he arrived at the turn around point, he was panting. He didn't slow or stop. He turned and took the pace up another notch as he headed back to town. His mind clear, he enjoyed the rhythmic thud of his shoes on the path, doing his best not to think of anything beyond the moment. He rounded a bend running parallel to Lake Drive and many of the houses. He'd soon see Matt's development. He did his best not to think about that. There were too many things stacking up at the moment to make that a truly enjoyable experience. He had concerns he needed to explore further before he voiced them.

He pushed the pace up another notch, loving that although the air was crisp, he'd worked up a sweat. He had the trail to himself, and there was one lone boat out on the lake. It was hard to imagine that summer wasn't far away when the lake would be crowded with vacationers.

He turned the corner, and the main section of Lake Drive and the Sandstone Cafe came into view. He moved his focus to the track ahead and pulled to a stop. With his hands on his hips, he tried to catch his breath. The food truck sat near the foreshore. What on earth was Asha doing?

He walked slowly toward the van, conscious that he needed to breathe normally to be able to talk to her. He stopped when he heard raised voices. One Asha's, the other angry male voice, sounded liked Matt's. He quickened his pace, straining to listen to what they were saying.

"Lodge a complaint for all I care," Asha was yelling at him. "I have a lease that gives me one hundred years tenancy on this spot. There's nothing you can do about it."

"A hundred years?" Matt laughed. "You've got to be

stupid if you believe that. This is council land, Asha. The same council land you were evicted from earlier today. I suggest you move on, or I'll be speaking to our friend, the sheriff, again."

Zane could see Asha now. She had her arms folded across her chest and a smirk on her face. "Good idea. Get him, and we can sort this out. Now, if you don't mind, I'd like you to leave. You're not a paying customer, so I'd like you off my premises."

Zane waited while Matt stormed off toward his car, climbed in, and drove off at top speed. He didn't want to deal with him today.

"Hey," he called out to Asha. "Great spot!"

Asha turned to him, her smile tentative. "Seems like my luck turned around earlier today."

"You can operate from here?"

"For the next hundred years."

Zane raised an eyebrow. "That you'll have to explain."

Asha laughed. "Take a seat, and I'll fill you in."

Zane sat down on the narrow bench Asha had put next to the food truck.

"Let me get this straight," Zane said after listening to Asha relate what had transpired since she'd bumped into Charlie the previous day. "Charlie owns a huge chunk of the lakefront?"

Asha nodded. "Apparently. And he doesn't want it developed or ending up in the hands of someone like Matt, so he's created an ironclad lease for me, and his will is quite specific."

"Does he own the Lake House too? I've always wondered who owned that."

"I'm not sure, you'd have to ask him. I'd say anything's possible."

Zane smiled. "Matt will have a fit when he realizes this land is privately owned."

"He already has." Asha laughed, pink spots appearing on her cheeks. "Would you like coffee? I haven't had a chance to bake today. I assumed I was closing shop, not moving to a better location than the last."

"How did you get it here?" Zane asked.

"I towed the food truck this morning and bought this one bench. I planned to ask Dad to bring the table and chairs over later. If Charlie agrees, we'll move the rocks and sleepers from the previous location to go under the tables to make it a little nicer."

"Sounds great." Zane was still trying to wrap his head around the fact that Charlie owned such prime real estate. "And yes to the coffee, thanks. I wanted to chat with you."

Asha opened her mouth then shut it again, shaking her head. She nodded in the direction behind Zane. "Looks like you'll have to take a number."

Matt's BMW pulled up with a patrol car behind him.

Zane turned and looked. Great, just what he needed. A showdown between Asha and his boss.

"I have a lease, Sheriff Hammond," Asha said before the sheriff reached them. "This is private land, and I have every right to be here."

"Who owns the land?" Matt asked.

"Charlie Li," Asha replied.

The sheriff smiled and turned to Matt. "You can stop wasting my time now. If you weren't already aware of the facts, Charlie owns half of Hope's Ridge. He also operates under the company name of Yin and Yang. Look it up some time. It might surprise you."

"You're not going to do anything about *her*?" Matt gestured wildly at Asha. "She can't set up business there. It blocks the view from the new development for a start."

The sheriff nodded at Asha and turned to leave. "She's on private land, Matt, and she has a permit to operate her food truck. There's nothing for me to do here."

"No way." Matt hurried after the sheriff as he walked back to his patrol car.

Zane turned to Asha. "I think that's the biggest smile I've ever seen on your face. It suits you."

Asha laughed. "Shows me I should listen to Steph more. She told me to be patient and that something better than the Sandstone Cafe would eventuate. I'm not sure this is better than the cafe, but it's certainly a prime location in town."

"Steph's a wise woman," Zane said.

"Zane!" Matt's voice was practically a scream.

Asha raised an eyebrow. "Sounds like someone wants you."

Matt was already storming back toward them. "We need to work this Charlie Li stuff out. Whether he owns the land or not, there have to be restrictions on something that's been considered public access for this long. I want to get as many complaints lodged as quickly as possible."

"Matt, it's Sunday," Zane said. "I know you're not happy, but there's probably not a lot we can do today. Why don't we meet in the morning and discuss it then?"

"If you want to have a job in the morning, I suggest you come with me now."

Zane glanced at Asha, whose face was unreadable. He'd come to find Asha to talk to her. Find out whether Steph was right about him misunderstanding why she didn't want anything to do with him. Going off with Matt to destroy Charlie Li, and he assumed getting Asha removed from the lakeshore, would hardly earn him brownie points. But then again, maybe he should go. Calm Matt down, make him realize how unreasonable he was being, and talk him out of doing anything. Yes, that was probably the best plan of attack for now. Who knew what Matt would do on his own otherwise?

Matt had already started walking toward his car.

"I'll catch up with you later, Ash." Zane flinched as he saw the hurt flash in Asha's eyes. "I'm not siding with Matt," he added. "But I'll keep an eye on him, make sure he doesn't do anything stupid."

"Do whatever you need. It makes no difference to me."

Zane was torn. He wanted to explain to Asha, make sure she realized what he was doing was for her, not against her, but he didn't have time. Matt wouldn't wait. "I'll catch up with you later," he restated. He turned and jogged after Matt wishing things with Asha could be easy for once.

Asha wasn't sure whether to laugh at what had unfolded with Matt and Zane or to be upset that Zane had gone off with Matt so quickly. One minute he'd wanted to talk to her, and the next, he was trotting after Matt to find out a way they could shut her down. She shook her head, deciding the best thing, for now, was to push Matt and Zane out of her mind and get Irresistables set up ready for trading the next morning.

She still needed to relocate the tables and chairs and set them up. She would need to speak to Charlie, ask whether he'd be open to her removing some of the grass and bringing in some stones or wood chips to give the seated area a nicer feel to it and to eliminate the need to mow. She'd done that in the previous location. Used wooden sleepers to mark out the area she needed, then had one of the council's diggers remove the top layer of dirt and grass for her, which she replaced with small stones. She wondered if she could reuse the materials from the previous site?

206

There was no reason not to, other than the logistics of moving it all.

"Hey, Asha," Bill Sorensen, the Mayor of Hope's Ridge, waved from the walking track. His wife held the other end of the lead attached to Murphy, their Irish wolfhound. "Found a new location?"

Asha smiled as they walked over to her, willing her heart to stop racing. She was doing nothing wrong, so why did it feel like she was? Matt Law had stirred her up. "Yes, Charlie Li owns the land and has leased me this spot."

Bill rolled his eyes. "For one hundred years, I imagine."

Asha laughed and leaned down to pat Murphy. "How did you know?"

"I didn't, but Charlie has been talking about getting tenants on the land to ensure development can't go ahead here. He's within his rights to do that, of course, although I'm not sure it will hold up for the entire one hundred years."

"That's fine. I don't expect to need it for that long."

"Will you move the chairs over from the other spot?" Kelly, his wife, asked. "I did love sitting by the food truck and having a muffin and coffee from time to time. It's a better view here if you're able to move them."

"I was about to call Dad," Asha said. "See if he can help me move them with his pickup later today. I'll need to ask Charlie whether I can take up some of the grass and make an area similar to the one I had over at the other spot."

"Let me know if he agrees," Bill said. "The maintenance boys can come and give you a hand tomorrow or Tuesday."

"Really?"

"Of course they can," Bill said. "You've been providing this community with a wonderful service for years now. It can be Hope's Ridge's way of saying thank you. It'll only take them a couple of hours. They've got the equipment.

They can also scoop up the rocks from the other site and bring them over. It seems mad to waste them, and that way, we can replant the other site with grass and get it all uniform."

Asha wasn't sure what to say. She was overwhelmed by such a generous offer. "Thank you," was what she managed.

Kelly reached for her husband's hand and squeezed it. "It's moments like these when I realize why this town should keep you as Mayor, and," she grinned at Asha, "why I should keep you as a husband."

Bill laughed. "Don't be silly. It's what anyone would do. The quicker we get Irresistables back up and running, the quicker we can resume our morning coffee rituals."

"I'll be operating as of tomorrow," Asha said. "There's not too much to set up as I run off gas, and that's all connected. I might need to put a sign up at the other spot with a big arrow pointing this way."

Both Bill and Kelly laughed. "I think word of mouth will travel quickly. Now we'd better get back to our walk and let you finish setting up. Drop into the council offices tomorrow, as soon as you've cleared it with Charlie, and we'll get the boys out to help you move the rocks and the tables and chairs if you haven't done those already."

"Thanks, Bill, I appreciate it."

Bill gave a mock salute. "At your service, my lady."

Asha was still smiling as Bill, Kelly, and Murphy made their way back to the lake trail. Bill Sorensen had been mayor for the last six years, and she wasn't sure she'd ever heard a bad word against him. Although she imagined Matt Law probably wasn't his biggest fan. She could only imagine Matt's anger if she did receive council help to move the rocks, wooden sleepers and chairs, and tables from the other location. In fact, she couldn't wait to see his face.

"You need to calm down," Zane said as Matt kicked open the front door to his office on Main Street.

"Don't tell me to calm down. I'm trying to improve this town, and every time I turn around, there's something more stupid happening than the last time." He turned and stared at Zane. "Do you understand why I'm angry?"

"I get that you're not Asha's biggest fan, but she has a right to operate her business."

Matt took a deep breath. "It's no longer about Asha; that location is incredible. We don't want anyone there, other than us." He shook his head. "Imagine what we could do if we had access to that lakefront. We could develop the entire area into an amazing restaurant precinct. Put in an open-air bar looking out across the lake. It would be pure gold."

Zane frowned. "How did you not know the land was privately owned? I thought you were on top of everything like that in town."

"I thought I was too. I can't believe it to be honest. Dad mentioned something to me once about Charlie being worth a fortune, but I had no idea that he owned so much. I can't imagine Dad knew, or he would have mentioned it. And then there's Albert; he definitely would have told me if he knew."

"From what you said after we met with Albert at the cafe in Drayson's Landing, he's not close to Charlie. Charlie might own lots of other investments Albert's not aware of."

Matt nodded. "It's possible." He sat down at the meeting room table and fell silent. Zane sat watching him, half expecting him to jump up any minute to work out ways of evicting Asha. But he didn't. His face grew more thoughtful as he sat there.

"You know, I'm beginning to think I've been tackling this Asha situation the wrong way."

Zane sat straighter in his chair. "What do you mean?"

"Well, you have a strong connection with her." Matt waited for Zane's reaction.

He ended up nodding, aware that his face had flushed with heat.

"And she's got something going on with Charlie, or he wouldn't have invited her to use his land."

"So?"

"So, I've turned her into the enemy when I should probably be doing exactly the opposite. Give her the cafe if she wants it and see if we can work together."

"That's a bit of a turnaround."

Matt nodded. "I know. But it ticks a lot of boxes. It gives us a tenant now, which I'm beginning to think is a good idea rather than waiting until we've renovated. It gives her the dream of her own cafe, and it removes the food truck from the eye line of the development. Win-win."

A flutter of excitement built in Zane's stomach. Asha was incredibly upset to have missed out on the cafe, and he could only imagine her delight if it was offered to her. "What's the catch?"

"Nothing. I'd offer the same lease terms as she was offered previously. We would need a condition that we could renovate within reason around her."

"Okay." Zane continued to stare at Matt. This seemed too good to be true.

"You look skeptical."

"You don't usually do anything without careful consideration, and you ensure that you're rewarded," Zane said. "I'm trying to work out what's really in this for you."

"Look, getting her off the lakefront is a huge bonus. The other thing would be showing Charlie we can work together.

If Asha's on our side, she might be able to convince him that development's the way to go."

"That's a bit of a long shot."

"I know, and it's not my main motivation, but a bonus if it happened to work." Matt took his car key from his pocket. "I'll see her now. No point her getting all set up on the foreshore if she wants the cafe after all. I'll go alone for this one, make it look like it's coming from me, and you haven't put me up to it."

Zane followed Matt out of the cafe. Part of him wished he could see Asha's face when she realized she was getting the cafe after all, but another part of him was left feeling uneasy. Matt's sudden turn about didn't ring true. He was up to something; Zane just wasn't sure what.

Asha braced herself as she saw Matt's flashy car pull off Lake Drive and park opposite Irresistables. What was his plan of attack this time? She was interested that Zane wasn't with him. Did he have him working back at the office, trying to find ways to close her down? She wasn't sure if she was angrier with Matt, Zane, or herself for thinking Zane was a good guy. He was no different to her ex, out for himself, not caring who he trampled along the way.

She folded her arms across her chest and watched from the serving window as he walked toward her. His smile threw her immediately. It wasn't his smug, *I'm about to get you evicted*, smile, it was a genuine smile which unnerved her.

He pulled a white hankie from his pocket and waved it as he walked toward her. He looked so silly she couldn't help but smile. He used the hankie to mock-wipe his forehead and grinned.

"My lame attempt at calling a truce."

Asha's body relaxed at his words. Had Zane turned him around?

"Actually," Matt continued, "not only a truce, but I owe you an apology. I've behaved like a spoilt brat for the last few weeks." He looked her directly in the eye as he spoke. "Ash, I'm sorry about how I handled the Sandstone Cafe. You're right. I should have come to speak with you the moment I knew it was for sale. And to be honest, part of me didn't because I didn't want anyone else knowing it was on the market. I should have spoken with you when the deal closed, and I hope you'll accept my apology."

Asha was too stunned to speak. Matt Law apologizing? Either Zane was a miracle worker, or there was something up.

"I'm also sorry I got you thrown off your other location." He had the good grace to blush. "That backfired on me, which serves me right."

"So, you're not planning to get me removed from Charlie's land?"

Matt shook his head. "I'm beginning to realize that you and I should be working together, not against each other. We both want the same thing; better facilities and services for the town. It's taken me longer than it should have to realize this."

"Okay." Asha still couldn't see where this was heading.

"I was talking to Zane," Matt said, "and he made me realize that working out a lease with you for the Sandstone Cafe would be beneficial for all of us."

Asha's eyes widened. "You'd lease me the cafe to get me off the land here? What's the catch?"

Matt smiled. "No catch. We have two different development ideas for this strip of Lake Drive. The one you saw which is for the residential development, and then we have another set of plans to develop the same area and the next six properties if we were able to acquire them."

"Charlie's houses and the four next to them?"

Matt nodded. "We have verbal agreements with the four next to Charlie, but of course, his properties are rather key to the new plans."

Asha frowned. She couldn't see where she came into any of this.

"We may have to wait until Charlie dies or is no longer capable of making his own decisions to go ahead with that plan unless there's a way to convince him to do it earlier."

"Charlie won't move," Asha said. "He loves the house he's in and is helping out the family who he lets live in the house next door."

Matt nodded. "That's okay. It's probably only a matter of time in that case. He's ninety-six, he can't live forever. I'm happy to wait him out."

"That doesn't guarantee you'll get the properties. I imagine he's got an ironclad will."

"True. I'll need to keep my fingers crossed that whoever inherits is more open to progress than Charlie."

Asha stared at him. From anyone else that would sound like a reasonable comment. From Matt, it didn't. Knowing him, he knew who would inherit and had the contracts of sale drawn up. Regardless, she didn't understand where she fit into all of this. "I appreciate the offer of the Sandstone Cafe, but I'm a bit surprised, to be honest. Do you want me off the lakeshore that badly?"

"That's one part of my plan, but I'll lay it on the line, Asha. You have a great connection with Charlie, and I think that could help me down the track. If he sees us working together and likes the improvements we make on the Sandstone Cafe, he might reconsider his position on his two houses and also on the foreshore."

"That's it? You only want him to see us working together."

Matt nodded. "He sees me as the enemy, and that's not the case. I'd like to win his trust if nothing else. I'd even like his input on some of the developments I'm doing. Did you know he's an architect by trade?"

"Really?"

Matt nodded. "My dad told me that. It always surprised him that Charlie was so against development when he'd done such amazing designs. I'd love to get him involved. Even if he doesn't change his mind about these properties, having him on side would make it easier for the rest of the town. They all love and trust Charlie."

Asha stared at Matt. This was a completely different side to him. "But what if he disagrees with your ideas."

Matt laughed. "I'd say that's likely. If he's coming from an architectural point of view, then I'm open to listening. I wouldn't be bothering otherwise."

Asha found her lips curling into a smile. The day was turning out far removed from what she'd imagined.

Matt held out his hand. "So, what do you say? Truce and we put a lease together for the cafe?"

Asha hesitated before taking his hand. "A big yes to the truce and a most likely for the cafe. I'll get back to you tomorrow if that's okay?"

Surprise flickered across Matt's face. "I thought you'd be throwing your arms around me and jumping up and down."

Asha took her hand back and laughed. "That's happening on the inside, but I want to give it a bit more thought. When the lease fell through, I considered all of the reasons why that was a good thing. I need to reconsider and check whether that is what I want now."

"Sensible approach. I tend to jump into things and backpedal later. I thought you and I were the same in that respect. It's good to know if we're going to work together that you're not as reckless as I thought you were."

"Reckless?" Asha grinned. "What on earth would ever make you think I was that?"

Matt leaned down and picked up a large rock. He handed it to Asha. "I'll leave this with you, and you can ponder the answer to that question and the more important one of whether you would like the Sandstone Cafe or not."

He grinned again before turning to walk back toward his car.

The next afternoon, Asha smiled to herself as she cleared empty coffee cups and plates from the tables in front of the food truck. Her discussion with Matt had played in the back of her mind since the previous afternoon. The sudden turnaround had surprised her, but the more she thought about it, the more she realized that he was probably right. If they worked together, both they and the town would benefit. It also gave her back her dream of running a proper cafe. The only thing that might make her say no would be the lease term. If it were only twelve months, then it would be too big a risk. If Matt would extend to three or five years on the same terms as the original lease, then she couldn't see any reason why she wouldn't go ahead. She wasn't sure that the food truck on the lakefront was his real motivation for making the offer, it wasn't that big an eyesore, but whatever his reasons, there seemed no downside for her.

"You look deep in thought."

Asha looked up and smiled at Steph. "Sorry, I was miles away. Here for coffee?"

"No, tea. Heard about your big move, so I wanted to

come and see for myself." Steph looked out to the lake. "It's a great location, better than before."

"I know." Asha took the dirty dishes up into the food truck and set about making Steph's tea. "I couldn't believe it when Charlie offered it, but it seems to be my week for good luck. Coming off the previous few weeks, I guess it was owed. Now, what tea would you like?"

"Surprise me. But, I'm so pleased for you, Ash. I know it isn't the cafe, but it's the next best thing for now."

Asha put a green tea and peppermint tea bag into Steph's cup and filled it with boiling water. She attached the lid and handed it through the serving window. "There's been a development on the cafe front."

Steph raised an eyebrow. "What kind of development?"

Asha made herself a tea and filled Steph in on her discussion with Matt. "Let's sit on the bench," she suggested. "I was planning to close up soon as it's not busy."

The two sisters sat down at a table that had a clear view of the lake.

"This is beautiful," Steph said. "What will you do about the cafe?"

Asha was about to speak when she saw Charlie waving at her from outside his property. He shuffled across the road and continued in the direction of Asha and Steph. "Don't say anything for the moment," Asha said. "Charlie's been so lovely, and if I accept Matt's offer, I'll need to let him know I'm moving on already."

Steph nodded and sipped her tea as they waited for Charlie to reach them.

"Here for your rental payment?" Asha asked with a smile. "Let me guess, cappuccino with half a sugar."

Charlie shook his head, his eyes darting from Steph to Asha. He looked utterly unnerved.

Asha took him by the arm. "Come and sit down, Charlie. Is everything okay?"

The older man shook his head, and Asha could feel his body trembling. "I've had quite a shock," he said.

Asha looked across the top of Charlie's head to Steph, who raised her eyebrows. "Can I get you some sweet tea or something to calm your nerves?"

"No, but I need to speak to someone, and I saw you here. I hope you don't mind?"

"Of course not."

"I had a visit today from social services. Someone's reported me as unfit to be living on my own. They came to assess me. There was talk of me needing to go into a home. Into LakeView I guess."

"What?" Asha couldn't believe it. Charlie was more capable than many of the seventy-year-old residents of the town. "Who reported you?"

"They wouldn't tell me, but I'm pretty sure I know who. The assessor said that because of my age, they are taking the report seriously and think I may not be capable of making my own decisions. She asked who my power of attorney is."

"This is ridiculous," Asha said. "You're of perfectly sound mind. They'll be able to see that, Charlie. I wouldn't get too worried."

"And we can vouch for you if necessary," Steph added. "I think the whole town would get behind you if you needed it. We all see you daily, and you're more with it than half of the people who live here."

"The person who reported me gave several examples of why I'm no longer capable of living independently," Charlie said. "They were all made up, which makes me believe it's someone who wants to get rid of me. Social Services have contacted my next of kin wanting to meet with them to discuss their opinion."

"The nephew you mentioned?"

"Yes, the nephew I have nothing to do with and haven't seen for a long time. A nephew who'd be happy to get his hands on my fortune."

Knowing Charlie owned half of the foreshore made Asha better realize how much of a fortune was at stake. "Do you think he's the one who spoke with social services?"

"Possibly, although my suspicions are closer to home. I think Matt Law is behind this. He wants my properties, and he'll do anything to get them."

Asha's mouth dropped open. "No way! Matt wouldn't go that low, surely?"

"He's been threatening me for years with this exact scenario," Charlie said.

"But if everything goes to your nephew, how does that benefit him? Does he think your nephew will sell?"

Charlie nodded.

"Charlie," Steph said. "This nephew of yours. What does he look like?"

"He's in his sixties, dark hair, short, stocky, dresses poorly. Why?"

"I assume he's also of Asian descent?"

Charlie nodded.

"I was talking to Mom this morning, and she mentioned she bumped into Zane at Grayson's Cafe. He was there with Matt and an Asian gentleman. She only commented as she said he looked familiar, but she couldn't place him. You know what Mom's like, into everyone's business."

"She met Albert many years ago when Ying Yue was still alive," Charlie said. "It would have been him. I had no idea that dirty dog Matt Law was in touch with Albert. I wonder how long that's been going on?"

"Long enough to plan this," Asha said. Anger bubbled inside her. The fact that Zane would go along with something so underhanded spoke volumes about his character.

Steph slammed her hand down on the table. "I'll go home right now and evict Zane. The fact that he could be part of this is unbelievable. He's not the person I thought he was at all."

"He works with Matt Law," Charlie said. "That should have told you what he was like from the start. They are bad, bad people."

"He was acting strangely last night," Steph said. "Now, I know why." She turned to Charlie. "Before I go, what can I do to help? I can get the town to rally around and present evidence to social services that you're of sound mind."

"They will have a medical team do that," Charlie said. "I have to hope they don't decide I'm senile or can't care for myself."

Asha put a hand on his. "Charlie, if for any reason social services say you can't look after yourself, I'd be happy to move in with you, so they leave you alone. It doesn't have to be permanent. I can keep my place and come and go as we need to satisfy their checks. Don't you worry, there's no way we'll let anyone put you away, especially if it's a result of Matt being after your land."

A lump formed in Asha's throat as tears filled the older man's eyes.

"I could never ask you to do that."

"You aren't asking, I'm telling you. You've looked out for me with Irresistables, and it will be my way of looking out for you if we need to."

Charlie nodded, unable to speak.

Steph squeezed Asha's shoulder, signaling her approval. "I'll see you both later."

Asha nodded. Her usually calm sister's eyes were blazing. She was as angry as Asha was. That Matt and Zane would put Charlie through something like this was unthinkable.

———

Zane was so deep in thought about Matt and what he might be up to, that he didn't register the anger flashing in Steph's eyes until it was too late. She was yelling at him before he had time to work out what was happening.

"Get your stuff and go. I'm not living with a liar and a cheat."

Zane had stared at her, stunned into silence. He had no idea what she was talking about.

"Don't look all innocent," Steph said, her voice still raised. "What you and Matt have been scheming with Charlie's nephew is appalling. I'm ashamed of both of you."

"Steph…" Zane had begun, but she'd held her hands up.

"Don't bother. I know for a fact you met with Charlie's nephew and that Matt will pull out any dirty trick he can to get hold of Charlie's properties. You can't deny any of that, can you?"

Zane shook his head. No, he couldn't. But he couldn't see how any of this made him a liar or a cheat. "I'm not Matt, Steph. Whatever you think I've done, you've made a mistake."

Steph laughed. "There's no mistake. You're supporting Matt's despicable plans, which puts you in the same category as him. Reporting Charlie to social services is disgraceful. Now, get your stuff and get out. I'll refund your unused rent so that you won't be out of pocket."

Zane tried to argue. He tried to explain to Steph that he would never be involved with something like that, but she wouldn't listen. "You're making the situation even worse. While you're working with Matt, no one is going to believe you don't know what's going on, so I'd suggest you stop lying right and start packing."

Zane had moved through the house in a daze shoving his belongings into the large duffle he'd brought with him. He honestly had no idea what had happened for Steph to act so crazy. Sure, he'd met with Albert, and yes, he worked for Matt, and while he had a niggling suspicion that Matt was up to no good, he had no concrete evidence, and Steph certainly couldn't. And Charlie? What was that about?

He froze as he emptied the contents of the laundry hamper into his bag. If Steph were acting this way, she'd most likely spoken to Asha. A heavy weight settled in the pit of his stomach. If this was Steph's reaction, what would Asha's be like?

Zane knocked on Asha's front door only minutes after leaving Steph's. Steph wouldn't listen to him, but he hoped Asha would. He'd had no idea Matt would go to the extreme of calling social services over Charlie. While he realized his part in all this could look bad to an outsider, part of him was angry with Steph for not believing him. He thought she knew him better.

Asha's door opened, and she stood hands on hips, a scowl on her face. He wasn't expecting an invitation inside the house.

"I need to explain, Ash. You and Steph have got it all wrong."

"I only need to know one thing," Asha said. "Did you know that Matt was trying to do a deal to buy Charlie's properties through his nephew?"

"I did, but it was my understanding that this was something that would only be broached after Charlie died."

"So, there was no talk at all about getting Charlie declared unfit to be able to care for himself?"

The vein in Zane's forehead began to pulse. "Not serious talk."

Asha threw her hands up. "How can that not be serious? Tell me this then, are you aware Matt already has the plans drawn up for the other development?"

Zane nodded.

Asha shook her head in disgust. "You knew about the nephew, you knew about the other plans, and you knew there was talk about getting Charlie put in a home. You're as bad as Matt is, an absolute disgrace. Now please leave."

Zane stared at Asha. Her face was red, her fists clenched at her sides. "Hold on. You need to listen to me. Matt's plans are exactly that, his plans. They are nothing to do with me."

"Are you for real? He's your boss. You work for his company. A company that presented one set of plans to the town and went behind everyone's back to develop a second set of plans, which include having an elderly gentleman thrown out of his home. You might be able to live with that, but I certainly can't, and I don't want anything to do with you or Matt. As I said, you're as bad as he is."

Zane bit the inside of his lip. His anger matched Asha's now. She wouldn't listen to him. She'd made up her mind that he was a bad guy and that was it. He turned away from her and walked back toward his pickup, not turning when he heard the door click shut behind him.

He climbed into the truck and turned it on. He had two options. A room above the pub at Traders, or his parents' house. He sighed. Neither was particularly appealing right now, but of the two, home called to him. After the day he'd had, he needed the comfort of his mom. She was the one person, other than Jenna, who gave him a soft place to fall.

He was relieved when he knocked on the front door that it was his mother who answered. He didn't let on that he needed a place to stay. He said he wanted to pop in and see her. Janet immediately pulled him into a hug and asked what was wrong.

A lump filled Zane's throat, and tears pricked the back of his eyes at his mother's intuitive concern. "Just a bad day, Mom."

She led him inside and into the kitchen. "Your father's out at his Probus meeting. He'll be home any minute."

Zane nodded and accepted the beer his mother took from the fridge.

"You look like you could use that. Now, what's happened? Are you suffering over the holdup again?"

"No, for once, it's something else." He went on to tell her about Matt and the situation with Charlie.

"That's awful," Janet said. "How could he do that to an old man?"

"He's like his dad," Roy said, entering the kitchen. "Those Laws are a law unto themselves." He smiled at the pun on words and clapped Zane on the back. "Good to see you, son." He opened the fridge and helped himself to a beer. "Now, I heard part of what you were saying as I came in, but not all of it. I take it there are problems with young Matt?"

Zane nodded. "He's been planning a few things I was unaware of until today with the Lake Drive development. He has much bigger plans than what he showed the town or even me. Some of it feels a little underhanded."

Roy sat down on the stool next to Zane. "What will you do about it?"

"I'm not sure at this stage, but it's causing me a few problems." He went on to tell them how Steph had thrown him out.

Roy laughed. "Good on her, standing up for Charlie. That's the type of town spirit we want around here."

"Asha was as bad," Zane said. "It's all well and good that they're sticking up for Charlie, but neither of them will listen to me when I say I didn't know what was happening."

Roy frowned. "It's never a great excuse when things are going wrong." He held up his hand as Zane was about to object. "Don't get me wrong. I'm not saying I don't believe you; I'm saying it sounds like a weak excuse. Sometimes people would rather hear that yes, you knew about the situation and were hoping to change the outcome or something along those lines."

Zane nodded. He wished he'd thought to take that tack with Asha. "I'll see Matt tomorrow. Make sure he knows that I won't work with him if he continues to pursue the development and Charlie in the way he's currently doing."

Roy clapped him on the back again. "Good, you let Matt Law know that his behavior is not acceptable." He got up from the stool. "Now, I've got a game to watch. You're welcome to join me if you like."

Zane shook his head. "No, I need to think about a few things, thanks, though."

"No problem." He turned to walk toward the living room, then stopped and faced Zane. "And son, you can move back if you need to and the job at the mill's there waiting. As soon as you're rid of Matt, let me know, and you can start."

A weight settled in the pit of Zane's stomach. For a short moment, he'd thought he and his father were connecting, but no, it always came back to him working at the mill. He would have to go through the whole conversation with him again and be on the receiving end of his anger. He closed his eyes at the thought.

"Why don't you head up to bed, love," his mother said.

"Bring your things in and settle into your old room. We can chat more in the morning."

Zane hugged his mother and went out to the pickup to collect his bag. He'd have to go back to Steph's to get his carving tools and workbench, but there was no hurry. He threw the duffle on the floor at the foot of his bed before falling on top of the blankets.

Ever since he'd arrived back in Hope's Ridge, he'd been riding a roller coaster. He'd left the city to get away from the memories of the holdup and start again. Now, in addition to the nightmares he was still having, he had made enemies of Steph and Asha and would probably need to quit his job. On top of that, there was a possibility he might be about to become a father.

He stopped as he thought about the last *problem* on his list. Would that be such a problem? Maybe a baby would be the change he needed. A chance to focus on someone other than himself. He wasn't interested in getting back together with Lucy, but that didn't mean they couldn't co-parent together and make it work. The more he thought about it, the more it seemed like something he would like. Imagine if it was a boy. That would be pretty awesome. A small smile played on his lips as he pictured himself out in a boat on the lake, teaching a little boy to fish. Next to the boy sat Asha, her green eyes dancing, the wind blowing through her hair. He sat up and shook himself. Where had that come from? He doubted Asha would ever trust or talk to him again, and that suited him fine. He was done with women; they were all too hard. Moving forward, it would be him and his son, and maybe they'd get a dog. He lay back down, allowing the fantasy to play out in his head a little further. Fishing; beach holidays. They'd take a trip to Iceland one day and explore the volcanoes the land of ice and fire was so famous for.

His phone pinged with a message drawing him out of his fantasy.

You're off the hook. A DNA test confirmed Shamus is the father. He's really happy, and we're going to make a go of it. Good luck. x

Zane stared at the phone, his chest tightening. This was what he wanted, wasn't it? He was free of Lucy and not about to become a father after all. But where did that leave him? Quite likely unemployed after he spoke with Matt, no friends now that Steph had thrown him out, and no Asha. The first two he could handle, but the third was a problem. No matter how much he tried to convince himself that he didn't want or need Asha, his heart denied it. He needed her to believe he wasn't part of Matt's plan to take over Charlie's land, and he needed her to know that...that he what? That he loved her? He turned over and buried his face in his pillow. He couldn't have thoughts like that; they would lead to one place only. To hurt. And right now, on top of everything else, that was not something he could handle.

Asha sat on her blue and white striped couch with Max on her lap. The rhythmic stroking of his back calmed her as much as it calmed him. She'd needed something to relax her when she'd got home and had settled for peppermint tea and Max. She'd considered pouring herself a large vodka but had decided against it. She had some decisions to make tonight and needed a clear head.

"Not that I have to think about it, do I, Max?" She sighed. How was she back here again? When Matt had come to see her and called a truce, she'd allowed herself to get excited again. All her plans for the Sandstone Cafe had come rushing back, wrapped up in the excitement she'd previously had. Although she had to admit that something hadn't sat quite right, which was why she'd hesitated over accepting his offer. At the time, she wasn't sure what it was, but now she knew exactly why she'd been hesitating. She was a better judge of character than she'd given herself credit for. There was no way she could go into business with someone like Matt. Even if it was strictly a lease agreement with nothing more to do with him, she didn't trust him. It seemed he had hidden agendas for everything he did, so who knew what his real motivation was in offering her the cafe.

She smiled, thinking of his horror when he realized she wasn't moving the food truck; that it would be visible to his new development. The one thing she was glad that had come out of today was that Charlie had confided what was going on to her and Steph. She'd been serious when she'd said she'd move in with him if it meant keeping his houses. She'd walked him home after Steph left and promised to drop in the next day to see him. She'd suggested that it would be a good time for him to see a lawyer and find out what his rights were. She'd also offered to set up a meeting and go with him if he thought that would be helpful. He had been incredibly grateful.

Asha had allowed herself to think about Charlie since she got home but had done her best to push all thoughts of Zane from her mind. She didn't want to dwell on him or what he'd done, but more and more thoughts of him crept into her head. It was hard to believe that he'd gone along with Matt on this. Lucy had said how harsh he could be, that he was only out for what he could get, but she'd dismissed it at the time, figured that was how girls talked about their ex's. Now she saw this first hand. She took a deep breath. What would she say to Jenna when she spoke to her next? Your brother is a complete jerk? She probably couldn't say anything. Jenna had tried to keep them apart since they were teenagers, and she was now seeing why that would have been a good idea. She sighed. There might be no reason to speak to her friend about it at all.

She continued to stroke Max. "So, we're back at this point, Maxy boy. No cafe and no relationship." She rubbed him under the chin. "But, we have each other, and I still have Irresistables." Max meowed, making her laugh. "Yes, and we have a new location, even if it isn't the cafe. And it's a better location, so I should be happy, shouldn't I?"

Tears filled her eyes as the words came out. Happy was not an emotion she was experiencing. She was so angry with Zane that it hurt. Angry that he'd betrayed her trust, angry that he'd lied to her and most of all angry that he'd given her hope that a relationship was possible. He'd stirred up emotions in her she hadn't experienced before. He'd made her push past the reservations her last relationship had left her with, made her make the conscious decision to trust him, and to believe he was a good guy. And look what he'd done. Let her down exactly as Dylan had. But this time it was worse, so much worse. Not because they'd been together for long, but because her feelings for Zane were so much stronger than they had been for her ex. A tear rolled down her cheek as she came to this realization. He'd taken her heart and crushed it, and she would never forgive him.

10

*H*aving hardly slept, Zane went for another run early the next morning, deliberately avoiding passing Irresistables or Asha's house. After a quick shower, toast, and coffee, he was in his pickup on the way to see Matt at the Main Street office. He'd been reviewing in his mind most of the night why he hadn't picked up on Matt being so calculating. Matt had presented himself as a good guy with some great business ideas. That he would go to such extremes with Albert over Charlie's fortune was unimaginable and certainly not something Zane wanted to be associated with. He wanted it stopped altogether.

By the time he pushed open Matt's office door, he was clenching his fists in anger.

"Hey," Matt looked up from his desk. "Something up? You're looking pretty worked up."

Zane let out a long breath, willing himself to remain calm. "It's the Charlie Li situation. I'm not comfortable with the way you're handling it."

Matt raised an eyebrow. "Handling what?"

"Trying to acquire his land pretty much any way you can."

"It's business, Zane. Nothing more. If Charlie chooses not to sell, that's his prerogative."

Zane shook his head. "I'm talking about you contacting social services and trying to get him declared incompetent to look after himself. That's underhanded."

Matt's laugh didn't reach his eyes. "I'm a concerned member of the community looking out for my elders. He's done enough things to make me worry for his safety, that's all."

"Oh, come off it. Charlie's more with it than half of the sixty-year-olds in this town."

"His nephew, who is both his next of kin and power of attorney, seems to think otherwise too. I think you'll find he's sent a report to social services."

"Did he mention when he last saw his uncle to make these accusations? He and Charlie don't have a relationship."

"It's none of our business," Matt said. "If he's fine to be at home and make his own decisions, then I can continue to make offers to him for his land. If he is declared unfit and Albert takes over, then we have something to work with. For now, it's business as usual, so how about you get on and do what I'm paying you for. Buster's expecting you at ten."

"To go over which plans? The ones you showed the town or the ones you plan to have developed?"

Matt sighed. "As we both know, both plans need to be worked on until I have a firm decision either way as to whether I can acquire any of Charlie's land. In addition to that, there's the land he owns on the lakefront to explore too. We have a lot to juggle at the moment before we go ahead with anything. I've also got meetings at the bank tomorrow to discuss business loans. I'm hoping if I can put enough together, I might be able to make Charlie an attractive offer that will give him the chance to sell on his terms before his hand is perhaps forced in other ways."

Zane stared at Matt. He spoke as if this was the usual way to operate. To mislead the town about his project and to manipulate an old man out of his property. "Sorry, Matt, I can't work for you anymore. We don't share the same business or personal ethics."

Matt's mouth dropped open. "You're quitting over this?"

Zane nodded. "And I plan to ensure you don't rip Charlie off." As the words left Zane's mouth, he knew that was what he needed to do. He didn't wait for Matt's response. Instead, he turned and walked out of the office and out on to Main Street. A lightness settled on him. He'd thought Matt was a good guy, but now and then, an unease had come over him. Something hadn't sat quite right in his gut. He should have trusted and explored that feeling earlier. As he had the thought, an image of Asha entered his mind, causing a stab of pain in his chest. He did his best to push all thoughts of her aside. He needed to trust his gut there too, but right now, he had something important he needed to do.

Asha did her best to keep herself occupied by cooking seven different muffin varieties. She'd already dropped into the council offices and requested help from the council workers to move the tables, sleepers, and rocks over to transform an area in front of the food truck, which would overlook the lake.

Bill Sorensen had seen her come into the offices and organized a team himself to help her after lunch. Asha was still amazed by his generous offer but knew that was how Bill worked and why Hope's Ridge thrived with such a good Mayor leading them.

The morning had been busy. Word had spread that she'd been moved on from the other location because of Matt's complaint, and she was now situated in a better location for most of the town. Coffee and muffins were in huge demand as a result.

There was a lull around eleven, and as she wiped down the counter, Asha realized how quickly the morning was flying. That was good as she was doing her best to not think about Matt or, more importantly, Zane. Although one thought kept coming back to her. She assumed it was Zane who convinced Matt to lease her the cafe, but why? Did he think she could persuade Charlie to sell them his land or get involved with the developments? Was he planning to use her to do that? She dislodged the thought. It made no real difference now what his intentions may or may not have been. She could never trust him again.

The slam of a car door had her look up. She gritted her teeth. Matt Law. If he knew what was good for him, he'd stay a long way away from her.

He approached her with an uncertain smile on his lips.

Asha remained in the food truck, her hands on her hips. This ought to be good.

"Hi," Matt said. "I need to talk to you."

Asha didn't respond.

"There's been a misunderstanding somewhere which I need to clear up. I was speaking truthfully to you the other day when I said we should be working together. I meant that then and I mean it now." He put the envelope he was carrying on the counter. "This is the lease for the cafe. I spoke to Andy this morning, and he was happy to let me know the original terms you'd been planning to sign. This one's the same. Five years, same rent, and the rest is fairly standard."

He hesitated before taking a step back from the food

truck. "Look, I'll leave it with you to review. If you have any questions drop in and see me or give me a call."

Asha picked up the envelope as Matt turned to leave. "Hold on. You can take this with you now." She held it out to him, unopened. "I'm no longer interested."

Matt didn't reach for it. "You're kidding. Whatever Charlie or anyone else has told you isn't true."

"How do you know what Charlie's said to me?"

"Zane threw a fit this morning. Quit his job. I assume he'll move back to the city as a result."

Asha's stomach churned. "He quit?"

Matt nodded. "Yes, same as you. Assumes I've done something terrible to Charlie and wants no part in it."

"But you have, and you know it. Reporting him to social services."

Matt shrugged. "Like I told Zane, I'm a concerned citizen. If he's fit and well enough to look after himself, then good for him, but if he's not, he should be helped. We don't want him getting sick or having a fall and not having anyone to look after him."

Anger rose in Asha. "From anyone else, I'd think they were caring words. From you, I know you're full of it. Get out of here, Matt. I have the council guys coming over soon to put down rocks for me to get my tables and chairs operating again."

Red splotches appeared on Matt's cheeks. "What? You're saying no to the cafe?"

"I wouldn't work with you in a million years." Asha threw the envelope in his direction. "Take this with you when you leave. I'll be enjoying the next hundred years or so right here thank you very much."

Matt picked up the envelope that had fallen at his feet and shook his head. "You know, I knew you were dumb, but this proves to me that you're dumber than I thought."

"That's enough of that, young man."

Asha almost laughed as the color drained from Matt's face. He'd spoken only a day ago about wanting Charlie to see him as a good guy, a team player. He certainly wasn't getting that from him today.

"Mr. Li," Matt said. "I was only having a bit of fun with Asha. And how are you today? How's that hip holding out?"

Charlie stared at Matt. "There's nothing wrong with my hip, and there's nothing wrong with my brain. Now, you may not be aware, but you're standing on my property, and I'd like you to leave."

"Look…" Matt cleared his throat. "I wasn't trying to interfere with social services; I was concerned, nothing more. I'm happy to talk to them if you like, tell them I might have been mistaken."

Charlie shook his head. "No need. Someone else is already doing that on your behalf."

"Who?"

Charlie checked his watch. "Zane Larsen should be in a meeting with my caseworker as we speak. He came to see me this morning and explained his role in all of this and yours too. I'm disappointed in you, Matt. A small part of me hoped you were your own person and not a carbon copy of your father. His interests were never the town's, and I see that yours aren't either."

"I think there's been a bit of a misunderstanding," Matt said. "Everything I'm doing is in the best interests of the town."

"Kicking an old man out of his home and doing deals behind his back with his nephew? That might be in the best interests of the town, in your opinion, but it's not in mine."

"Why don't you do what Charlie asked, Matt, and leave," Asha said. She'd listened with interest mainly to the part where Zane had gone to see Charlie and now was at social services.

Matt looked from Asha to Charlie and threw his hands in the air in frustration. "Fine. Hopefully, at some stage, you'll realize that my plans would be a huge improvement to the town and bring in a lot more money and tourism for everyone. I'll be in touch, Charlie. I was planning to meet with the bank first and then come and see you. See if there's a price that you would be interested in selling at."

Charlie smiled. "Don't waste your time. No amount will ever have me sell my properties to you."

Matt nodded and began walking back toward his car. Asha was surprised that he'd gone quietly. Usually, he had to have the last word if things weren't going his way. She was about to say as much to Charlie when Matt turned around. "I won't bother you again, Charlie. I'll keep my dealings strictly between Albert and me moving forward." He grinned. "Whether you're alive to see it or not, those properties will become mine. I can be patient, but if you were to exit this world sooner rather than later, it would be appreciated."

Asha gasped at Matt's words before turning to Charlie. "I'm so sorry. He's a disgrace."

Charlie laughed. "He's said a lot worse to me previously, Asha."

"I should have listened when you said how awful he and Zane were."

Charlie's laughter died, and his face turned serious. "No, for once I was wrong. Zane came and saw me this morning. He was upset. Said he knew Matt wanted my houses but had not been aware of the unscrupulous way he was handling it."

"But Zane met with your nephew."

"He was there for part of the meeting but not when

anything underhanded was discussed. Matt sent him off to complete some work with Buster, and Zane assumes this was when those discussions took place."

"So, Zane wasn't part of it?"

Charlie shook his head. "No, and he's doing everything he can to help me now. As I mentioned, he's off to see the social services caseworker who assessed me. He intends to tell her what Matt was planning and that I was set up. He's also organizing a new lawyer to come and talk to me tomorrow about my power of attorney and my will. I would like to make some changes."

"That sounds like a good idea," Asha said. "If you need help with any of that, please ask, won't you?"

"Thank you. Zane believes I'll need a formal assessment to be declared of sound mind so I can make those changes, but again, he's offered to help me do all of this."

"He must feel bad to be offering to do so much."

"He is. Says he had a gut feel about Matt a while back, which he should have listened to. But he needed a job, and Matt's looked like it would suit him perfectly. I'm not sure what he'll do now for work, but he's promised he'll help me before he moves back to the city, if that's what he has to do."

The city?

Charlie rubbed his hands together. "Now, in all this excitement, I forgot what I came here for in the first place. My rent."

Asha did her best to smile. Charlie's words weighed heavily on her mind as she directed him toward the waiting bench. "Tea or coffee?"

"Tea please and a muffin with chocolate if you have one."

Asha set about organizing Charlie's rent payment, her mind whirling. Not only had Zane apologized to Charlie, but he was also sorting out the issues Matt had caused. She thought back to the words she'd spat at him. *You're as bad as*

Matt is, an absolute disgrace. It appeared she'd been wrong. He hadn't knowingly set out to manipulate Charlie after all.

Warmth spread through her as she had this realization. Zane wasn't the bad guy she'd painted him as. The warmth disappeared as quickly as it had appeared, replaced by a dull ache. He might not be the bad guy, but he was moving back to the city. So regardless of what type of guy he was, the one thing he wouldn't be was *her guy.*

Although he had no idea what his long-term prospects were, Zane left the office of social services lighter and happier than he had been in months. If the only good thing that came out of him moving back to Hope's Ridge was stopping Matt from forcing Charlie off his land, then it was worth coming back. He knew Charlie would be happy with what he had to tell him. The caseworker who'd assessed Charlie didn't need any convincing that Charlie was of sound mind and was perfectly capable of looking after himself.

"The call we got about him raised suspicions straight away," she'd said. "Anonymous calls are pretty rare with what we do and are usually a sign that someone's out to get someone. And the guy who called," she flipped through her file, "a Matthew Law, was outed by Mr. Li's next of kin anyway."

"Albert told you it was Matt?"

She'd nodded. "He was speaking in support of Mr. Law but hadn't realized it had been an anonymous complaint to begin with. It appears both men are working together to remove Mr. Li from his home."

Zane nodded. "They're after his property for development."

They'd gone on to discuss Charlie's file a little further.

That while they were declaring him fit to be on his own, an annual check would be carried out to make sure this stayed the case.

The good news for Charlie was it was unlikely he needed another check to declare him of sound mind if he did want to change his power of attorney. The government already had it on file.

He was deep in thought during his thirty-minute drive back to Hope's Ridge. He needed to find a good lawyer for Charlie to talk to and assumed his dad would have someone in mind. He considered calling him but then decided against it. He'd drop in at the mill and ask him in person.

Time disappeared as he wound down the ridge, into town, and along the back road to the mill. He'd deliberately avoided driving along Lake Drive. He wanted to sort everything out for Charlie before he gave any thought to the fact Asha's face kept flooding his thoughts.

He pulled into a parking space outside the mill and jumped out of the pickup and hurried into the front office. His mother was sitting behind a computer screen, tapping away on the keyboard. She looked up as he approached.

"Zane. Is everything okay?"

Zane smiled as she got to her feet. "Yes, it's good. Is Dad around? I wanted to ask him if he has a good recommendation for a lawyer."

"You're not in trouble, are you?"

"No, it's for Charlie Li. I'm helping him out with a few things."

"He's out in the warehouse chatting with the new manager." She rolled her eyes. "Between you and me, I don't think he's working out all that well. Isaak complained that he thought we were trying to rip him off, and Dad's realized it was Jim, the manager's fault. He was asked to select some timber for a new tabletop for Isaak at Traders and gave him a damaged piece of maple. Dad's not happy."

"Okay, thanks. I'll find him." Zane gave his mother another smile and headed through the office area to a door that led into the warehouse. Timber was stacked in piles according to the wood species, and the smell of sawdust permeated the air. Zane took in a deep breath. It was the smell of his childhood, a comforting scent that he was surprised to realize he missed.

His father was in a heated discussion with a man Zane hadn't met before but assumed was Jim, the new manager. Jim was gesticulating with his hands wildly, and Zane's father's face was getting redder and redder. He waved to Zane as he approached, a look of relief crossing his face.

"Zane, come and meet Jim," he called, looking like he was doing the best to calm himself down.

Jim turned to look at Zane as he approached. "Ah, the child prodigy, I assume."

Zane stopped, taken aback by the venom on the other man's voice. He was in his forties and had dark eyes and an impressive scowl. "Sorry?"

Jim spat on the ground near Zane. "You, the wonder child who could run this place standing on your head." He removed the hard hat he was wearing and thrust it into Zane's chest as he pushed past him. He turned briefly. "I suggest you get yourself another manager. I can't work for a pathetic little man like you."

"Hey," Zane said. "There's no need for that."

Roy placed a calming hand on Zane's shoulder. "Ignore him, son. The man's a fool."

Jim took a step toward them and then changed his mind and turned and stormed out of the warehouse.

Zane turned to his father. "What was all that about?"

Roy shook his head. "He wasn't up to the job and didn't

like me pointing out where he needed to improve. I know from what you said that I need to be open to other people's ideas but not a guy who wants to operate as he does." He gave a wry smile. "He's probably related to your friend Matt the way he goes about things. I found out he was overcharging customers for some goods and using some of the imperfect pieces among the orders for others."

"Why would he do that? What's in it for him?"

"With the seconds or imperfect pieces, I allow the staff to take what they can use. We don't get much for it, so I consider it a small bonus for them if they can use it. He was slipping pieces into orders and helping himself to the good quality pieces."

"You caught him doing that?"

"Not exactly, but I know he was. I was in the process of getting cameras set up to catch him, but it looks like I don't need to now. Good riddance to him."

He clapped Zane on the back. "Now, what are you here for? Not to work at the mill, I assume?"

Zane shook his head. "No, some advice." He went on to explain what had happened with Matt and Charlie and his visit to social services.

"Good for you, son," Roy said. "I'm proud of you putting Charlie before yourself and telling that Matt Law off. Hang on, and I'll get you a number for a lawyer I recommend. He helped us with that situation of the employee trying to claim he was injured here when he had a car accident on a weekend."

Zane remembered how stressed his parents had been at the time.

He took the number his father handed him.

"You quit your job?"

Zane nodded.

"Could I ask you to consider something?"

The muscles in Zane's neck immediately tightened. He didn't want to have another discussion about him working at the mill.

"Your mom and I had a chat last night. It made me realize that you working at the mill wouldn't happen. She made me understand how suffocating it would be to have your old man calling the shots the whole time on your career and not having the freedom to build a business how you want to."

"I never said it would be suffocating," Zane said.

"No, you didn't, but I get that that's what you might be feeling. And you know, you're right. I took over from my old man, and until he died had to do everything his way. It used to drive me mad. He had some good processes, of course, and the mill was doing well, but I had visions for bigger and better things. I had to wait thirty years before I got the opportunity to have a proper say in anything, and he had to die of a heart attack from all of the stress he was under for me to have that opportunity. That's not something I'd want for you."

"So, you understand."

Roy nodded. "Finally, I do. But I wanted to ask you something. Would you consider doing a month's work for me? It would be a contract position while I replace Jim. Take on some of his responsibilities but also to help me on the finance side. I think you're right that we could run some things in the business better."

Zane's mouth dropped open. Was his father really asking for his help?

Roy laughed. "No need to look so shocked. Your mom mentioned how some of the accounting tasks, for instance, are being done on archaic software. I need someone who knows what they're doing to upgrade us and bring us into the twenty-first century and train the office staff. I also need someone I trust to do it. Some of the financial information is quite sensitive."

"And it's only for a month?"

Roy nodded. "It might not take you that long, but that would also give me enough time to replace Jim."

Zane stared at his father. "Hold on. Jim only quit moments ago, yet this sounds like something you've given thought too."

"I was about to fire Jim, which I think he realized," Roy said. "Quitting allowed him to save face. Look, give it some thought. Unless you've got plans to hurry back to the city, I'd love your help. Mom would love you to stay too. And you can stay with us until you find somewhere else. There's no rush to make any changes."

Zane left the mill in a state of shock. Who was the man he'd spoken to? His father could be a good guy, he knew that, but he could honestly say it was the first time in his life his father had treated him as somewhat like an equal. He'd promised to think about the job and let him know that evening. He sat in his pickup for a few minutes, trying to get his head around it and work out whether he'd be willing to do the job. He had no real reason to say no. He had no current job and no plans for what he would do next. Although for now, his priority was still Charlie. He would revisit the older man with the lawyer's details and suggest they call him together to make an appointment. He wanted to make sure Charlie knew he was working for him now, not against him.

Asha pushed open the door to Steph's house, calling out to her sister.

Steph appeared in a long sleeve shirt and floaty pair of

yoga pants, looking as if she'd stepped out of a health magazine. She was holding a glass of water with fresh lime in it.

"Other than the occasional coffee, do you ever drink anything bad for you?" Asha asked. "You're beginning to annoy me with your glowing good health look."

Steph laughed. "Switch the coffee for tea and water and start serving chia balls rather than muffins, and you too can look as tired as I do."

Asha moved closer, realizing that while Steph's cheeks glowed, her eyes had dark rings under them. "Still not sleeping?"

Steph shook her head. "I was pretty rattled after last night. Throwing Zane out was horrible. He looked so shocked. I still find it hard to believe he's such a low-life."

"Turns out, he's not." Asha followed Steph through to the kitchen, where Steph poured her a glass of water and listened as Asha explained what had happened.

"So, Zane not only quit his job, but he's got things worked out for Charlie with social services?"

"Sounds like it. He's also organizing a lawyer to help him change his power of attorney. He doesn't want his nephew having any say in what happens to him or his estate either when he can't manage it himself or when he dies."

"Good," Steph said. "That means Matt can't get his hands on it." Her face paled. "I feel terrible. I shouldn't have thrown Zane out."

"I feel terrible, too," Asha said. "I've been awful toward him. I haven't trusted him at all, which isn't fair."

Steph raised an eyebrow. "I think you have your ex to thank for that."

"And what I thought he did to me at the prom," Asha said. "Even though I now know he didn't do anything wrong, it got things off to a rocky start."

"What will you do now?"

"I don't know. Charlie said Zane's returning to the city." Tears welled in Asha's eyes. She blinked furiously to keep them from escaping. "I messed it up with him, Steph."

Steph leaned forward and drew Asha into a hug. "And you *really* like him, don't you?"

Asha nodded, her face buried in the comfort of her sister's shoulder.

"It's not that hard, Ash, you need to tell him."

Asha pulled back. "I don't think he'll listen."

Steph smiled. "Well, I think he will, and to be honest, what do you have to lose?"

Asha stared at Steph for a moment. Her sister was right. If she didn't speak to Zane, she'd lose him for sure. If she did, she might still lose him, but at least she'd given it a shot.

"Where do you think he went after you threw him out?"

"His parents, I imagine, but you could always call Jenna, she'll probably know what he's doing."

Asha slipped her phone from her pocket and pulled up Jenna's details. Her friend answered her Facetime call immediately.

"I was about to call you. What's happened? I spoke to Mom. She said Steph threw Zane out."

Asha couldn't help but smile. Jenna looked furious on behalf of her brother.

"Why are you smiling?"

"Because of how defensive you are of Zane. Yes, Steph threw him out, but it turns out to be a misunderstanding. I need to speak to him, so I thought I'd check with you if you know where he is."

"He's at Mom and Dad's. He quit his job, and he's a mess."

A lump caught in Asha's throat. "A mess?"

"Ash, I brought him back to Hope's Ridge to help him, not fill his life with drama. Do you have any idea what's going on? Mom said there was a girl, someone he'd fallen for too, but she's worried he's about to have his heart broken on top of all of this."

"He cares for her?"

"That's what Mom said. Look, I have to go. Brad needs me to run some errands for his mom. If you do see Zane tonight, can you message me, let me know how he is and who this woman is. If she hurts him, she'll have me to deal with."

Nervous energy coursed through Asha as she ended the call. Zane had told his mother he'd fallen for someone. He wouldn't have done that if he weren't still interested, would he?

"Find out," Steph said.

Asha spun around. She'd forgotten her sister was in the room listening to her conversation.

Steph shooed her with her hands. "Find him. Tell him I plan to apologize too, and his room is here waiting for him if he's willing to forgive me."

Asha nodded, every fiber of her body tingling with nervous energy. Her emotions had been on a roller coaster for weeks now, would this conversation enable her to step off and start enjoying life without all of the drama?

A weight lifted from Zane's shoulders the moment Charlie opened his door. The older man was full of gratitude, having already had a phone call from social services to assure him that he was not considered at any risk, and they had no plans to assess him again for twelve months, which was the normal timeframe at his age.

"I got the name of a lawyer from Dad too," Zane said, holding out the paper for Charlie.

"Ted Baker, he's got an office in Tall Oaks," Charlie said. "I've heard good things about him."

Zane called Ted and explained Charlie's situation over the phone to him while he was with Charlie. They scheduled a meeting for the next week when Ted would be in town. Ted assured him he could work out all of the power of attorney issues and that yes, he could act in this position if that was what Charlie wanted. Charlie had shaken Zane's hand about five times before he'd been able to leave. "I have a lot to thank you for, Zane. You are a good man, and I owe you an apology." Charlie bowed his head. "I told Asha you and Matt were rogues or something similar."

Zane laughed. "Working alongside Matt, you had every right to call me that, Charlie. No apology is necessary. I'm glad we've been able to work together now and right all of this."

"That Asha, she's a good girl," Charlie said. "You make sure you look after her, okay?"

Zane nodded. He didn't intend to question the older man's words. The knowing look in his eyes said everything. He needed to find Asha and talk to her. Make her understand that in all the turmoil that had been going on, the one person he couldn't get out of his head was her.

As Charlie let him out of the front door, Zane hesitated. Asha's blue van pulled up across the road, and she climbed out and hurried in the direction of the food truck.

"Now's your chance," Charlie said, digging his fingers into Zane's back and giving him a gentle push in Asha's direction. "Good luck."

Zane's heart rate increased as he walked the short distance from Charlie's across the road toward the food truck. Asha had disappeared inside, and with the front serving window closed, he couldn't see her. He reached the van and hesitated. Should he call out to her or wait for her to come out?

The door to the van flew open, deciding for him. Asha hurried down the two small stairs that led into the van and stopped as soon as she saw Zane. "Oh!" Her hand flew to her mouth in surprise. "I wasn't expecting to see you here."

Zane took a deep breath. "I need to talk to you."

"I need to talk to you too. I was picking up a couple of things before coming to find you. I'll lock up, and then let's take a walk along the lake trail. I've got some things I need to say, and I think they'll come out easier if I'm walking rather than sitting directly opposite you."

Zane's heart sank at her words. Whatever she had to say couldn't be good. As much as he wasn't sure exactly what he wanted to tell her, he knew part of it was that he needed her in his life, wanted her in his life. But not as a friend, as much more than a friend. He was pretty sure she wasn't about to say anything similar to him.

He waited for Asha to lock up, and then they walked across the grass to the lake trail. They walked for a few minutes before she finally spoke.

"Steph asked me to apologize for the way she treated you last night," she said. "Charlie explained to us this morning what you did, quitting your job, and then helping him. He also made us realize you weren't part of Matt's scheme to get his properties through the nephew or another underhanded motive."

Zane nodded. Asha wasn't apologizing for herself but for Steph.

"She said if you want to move back in, you may."

"That's what you wanted to talk to me about?" Disappointment was an understatement for how Zane was feeling. Asha wanted to speak to him to pass on a message.

"I'm sure Steph will come and see you too, but when I said I was coming to find you, she asked me to pass on the message."

Zane walked alongside Asha in silence, playing her words over in his mind. He suddenly stopped. "Hold on. You said you were coming to find me, and she asked you to pass on the message?"

Asha stopped and faced him, her face flushed as she nodded. "Yes, I was coming to apologize too for the way I've been treating you. How I haven't trusted you when I should have. The one thing I've realized from all of the ups and downs of the last few weeks is that only one thing matters to me. It's not the Sandstone Cafe or even Irresistables." She hesitated momentarily. "It's you."

Zane couldn't believe what he was hearing. "You mean that?"

Asha nodded, her eyes filling with tears. "Charlie said you might be moving back to the city, and I realized that I want you in my life. I've never felt like this before."

Zane stepped closer to Asha and took her trembling hand in his. "I came here to tell you the same thing. I've had feelings for you since I was a teenager, Ash, and they haven't changed. If anything, they're got a lot stronger." He wiped a tear from her cheek. "You're so feisty and beautiful. I'm falling in love with you."

Asha's eyes widened.

"Sorry, I shouldn't have said the L word. I know it's too early."

Asha shook her head. "No, it's not." She reached up and kissed Zane on the lips before pulling away. "I feel the same, but I wasn't expecting you to say it."

Zane pulled her to him. "Well, I am. I love you, Asha Jones, and I want us to be together."

"But aren't you returning to the city? Charlie said he thought you were, and Jenna did too."

"Jenna?"

Asha blushed. "I called her to see if she knew where you were as I knew you wouldn't be at Steph's."

"Right now, the only place I want to be is where you are. I also think I need to stay here to protect Charlie and make sure Matt doesn't work out some other way to get to him."

"You'd do that for Charlie?"

Zane nodded. "Of course I would, and I know you would too."

Asha grinned. "I should warn you, Jenna's threatening to kill whoever this woman is your mom told her is about to break your heart."

Zane cupped her face in his hands. "Are you planning to break my heart?"

Asha shook her head. "I'm planning to love you with every piece of mine."

Zane's body tingled with pleasure at Asha's words. He pulled her closer, knowing that he'd found the safe place he was looking for. It wasn't Hope's Ridge, as Jenna had thought, it was in the arms of the woman he knew he could love and who would love him back. He'd definitely come home.

11

-----

*A*sha sang along to Gloria Gaynor's 'I will Survive' as she prepared Irresistables for the morning trade. It was hard to believe a week had passed since she and Zane had finally come together and revealed their feelings. They'd spent every minute possible together since. Zane had spent many nights at her house, making Steph question whether he'd moved back in with her or not.

"You sound happy," Charlie called to her as he approached the food truck. "Must be a man, I think."

Heat rose up the back of Asha's neck. "Might be."

Charlie tapped his nose. "A wise old man believes he is the right man for you, Asha. Love him as you wish to be loved, and you will be happy."

Asha thought about Charlie's words. They were so true. "Now wise old man, what can I get you? I assume you're here to collect your rent?"

Charlie's eyes sparkled. It had been an ongoing joke since Irresistables had moved onto Charlie's lakefront property. Most days, he came for his rent, but he rarely took muffins for himself, only for his neighbors. Asha, of course, tried to insist he take more, but he always patted his flat stomach and said that Ying Yue would not like him eating so many treats.

"No, but I would like to add another clause to the lease if you will allow me to?"

"Oh?" Asha was surprised. Charlie's lease had been quite specific. She couldn't imagine he'd ask for money now after saying no to it since day one, although she'd be quite happy if he did.

"It's not something that needs to go on the lease, but a separate agreement between you and me," Charlie said. "As you know, I no longer wish Albert to be my power of attorney. I'd like to ask you to take on that job."

"What? No, surely there's someone better equipped?"

Charlie shook his head. "I have no other family, and most of my friends in Hope's Ridge are quite old. They might not outlive me, so there's no point asking them. I trust you, Asha. I would like to go through my wishes with you if something was to happen to me or if I was unable to make decisions for myself. I would be honored if you'd say yes."

Asha wasn't sure what to say. There was no reason to say no, she just hadn't expected to be asked to do something so important for someone she didn't know well.

"It's not about how well you know me," Charlie said, seemingly reading her mind, "it's about how well I know you. I knew from when you were little that you were an honest and caring child. I've seen you grow into a woman who shares my values, sense of fairness, and respect for others. I trust you implicitly, which is why I would like to ask for your help with this."

A lump lodged in Asha's throat. Charlie's words were so kind. "Of course, I'd like to help you. You let me know what I need to do."

Charlie's face broke into a wide smile. "We have a meeting with my lawyer on Friday to go through the details and sign the official forms. I've told him to meet us here at two. Will that suit you? I thought we could celebrate with tea and muffins after the signing."

"Of course," Asha said, "that would be fine."

Charlie reached for her arm and squeezed it. "You're a good girl. You and I must talk through the details before Friday. Are you free tonight? I am cooking a banquet in your honor."

"Really?"

Charlie laughed. "No, but I am making Ying Yu's famous Kung Pao chicken. It will be ready at six."

"Then I'll arrive before six," Asha said. These decisions were important to Charlie, and she needed to treat them as a priority.

"In the meantime, I'll be talking to Zane Larsen. He'll be answering to me if he doesn't treat you right."

Asha laughed. "I'll make sure to warn him."

Charlie clapped his hands together. "Now that that's all finalized, we should discuss today's rent payment. I think a chai latte would be perfect."

Asha grinned as she went to prepare Charlie's latte. It would be wonderful to be able to do something for a man who'd been so kind to her. She hoped it was many years before the power of attorney was needed if it was needed at all.

———

Zane was jolted out of his thoughts when the back door swung open, and Steph stepped out.

Her eyes widened. "Oh, sorry, didn't realize you were here, let alone up at this time."

Zane smiled. "It's three o'clock in the morning, where else would I be but outside looking at the stars?"

Steph came and sat across from him. "You okay?"

Zane nodded. "Couldn't be better. I woke by habit rather than a nightmare. I couldn't get back to sleep, so I decided to sit out and enjoy the night sky."

"Thought you'd be at Asha's tonight?"

"She was invited to Charlie's for dinner. He's asked her to be his power of attorney and wants to go through the details with her." Zane laughed, remembering the look in Charlie's eyes as he told him in no uncertain words that Asha was a precious jewel and needed to be treated accordingly. He'd agreed with Charlie, promising he would do everything in his power to make her feel loved and important.

"That's great," Steph said. "Once that's done, he shouldn't have to worry about Matt anymore. I heard he's having some trouble with the planning office. Bodhi's sister works there and mentioned they weren't approving some of the plans for the new development."

"Serves him right. Now, why are you out here?"

Steph sighed. "More nightmares."

"You look exhausted. I thought they were getting better?"

"They were, but the last three nights they've been full-on. Back to the original versions, or probably worse. The journal writing isn't working."

"There must be something triggering them."

Steph was quiet for a moment before she started to speak. "I saw Buster in the street the other day. I wanted to talk to him but ended up running in the opposite direction. I couldn't face him."

"Buster doesn't blame you," Zane said. "It was an accident for which you're in no way responsible."

Steph shrugged. "I know, but I'll always wish I'd been able to do more, and I'm sure Buster does too."

"Buster might wish for a lot of things, but I can tell you that he doesn't blame you."

"You've spoken to him about it? About me?"

Zane hesitated. He didn't want Steph to think he'd been talking out of turn, but he also needed to be honest. "Around the time of the anniversary of his daughter's accident, I was working with him. I told him that I wanted him to know how sorry I was. I mentioned you were having a hard time with the anniversary and he was surprised. Said you shouldn't be concerned, that you'd done all you could for Holly. The only person he holds any anger toward is his ex-wife."

Steph nodded. "That's good to hear."

"You don't look convinced?"

"I'm not sure what to think. If I was in Buster's shoes, I'm not sure how I'd feel."

"Can I make a suggestion?"

Steph shrugged.

"I'll take that as a yes. My suggestion is that you see him, talk to him. If you've avoided him ever since it happened, it's probably contributing to your anxiety and your dreams. Get it over with. I think you'll be surprised by his reaction."

Steph remained silent, not committing to anything.

"You can't go on like this forever, Steph."

"No, I can't, and neither can you." Steph smiled, and Zane knew the subject was closed. "So, what are your plans now that you're happily in love, Zane Larsen? I heard a rumor you were working at the mill. I found it hard to believe after everything you've said about your parent's business."

"Only for a month to help Dad out," Zane said. "I'm unemployed, he needs someone, so it's a perfect arrangement. Perfect if you're happy for me to continue sharing that is."

"Of course, I am. Well, at least until you and Asha do something more official."

"Speaking of official," Zane did his best to change the subject before Steph started questioning his intentions. "I heard from Jenna yesterday. She's trying to work out a date to come up and discuss the wedding with all of us. Apparently, we'll all have a million jobs to do, and she wants to put a schedule in place. She also wants help organizing an engagement party."

Zane watched Steph's reaction. She was nodding, but the smile on her lips didn't reach her eyes. The nightmares and memories of the accident were spooking her. Zane wished there was something he could do to make it all go away.

Late the next afternoon, Asha intertwined her fingers with Zane's as they walked hand-in-hand along the lake trail as the sun set over Hope's Ridge. Shadows cast across the lake by the red maples that lined the shoreline. Asha shivered, and Zane immediately pulled her close to him, dropping her hand and placing his arm around her shoulder.

"You and Charlie are official, then?" Zane asked.

Asha laughed. "Yes, why, are you jealous?"

Zane joined her laughter. "I probably should be. He's got you wrapped around his little finger."

"No, he hasn't, but I do love him. He's such a character and such a decent human."

Zane's arm slipped from her shoulder down around her waist. "As are you, Ms. Jones. Not only are you a decent and gorgeous human, but you're also doing a good thing for an old man. Are you completely clear on all of his wishes if you did have to enact the power of attorney?"

Asha nodded. "Yes, he went through them at dinner the

other night and then again this afternoon with the attorney. Like I said to Charlie, I hope I don't ever have to be the one to do any of this, but if I do, I'll definitely do what he's asking."

"Fingers crossed you won't have to," Zane said. "Now, I heard a rumor that Matt Law was seen running from the food truck today."

Asha laughed. "Where did you hear that?"

"Isaak witnessed you yelling at Matt and him eventually running away. What did you threaten him with this time? Another rock?"

"He came by to tell me he'd got a tenant for the Sandstone Cafe, and I could expect the competition to kill my business. I suggested he get off my property before I killed him. I believe there are rumors that I was holding a rather large kitchen knife up and waving it around in the air when I kindly asked him to leave."

Zane's laugh faded, and he became serious again. "Do you think the competition will be a problem?"

"Possibly, but we'll have to wait and see. I'd imagine a cafe would sell a range of food and people will want full meals. Hopefully, they won't be doing too much in the way of cakes and muffins. I have a lot of loyal customers, so I'm sure I'll be fine. Knowing Charlie, he will probably run all of Matt's customers out of the cafe."

They continued around the lake, the sun dropping further behind the ridge and the temperature plummeting.

"I think we need to head back," Zane said. "You're shivering."

"Did you want to come back to mine?" Asha asked, "or shall we go to Steph's?"

Zane hesitated. "I'd love to come back to your place, but I'm worried about Steph. She's struggling with the accident still. I think she needs to talk to Buster, but she won't do it."

"We might need to force the issue," Asha said. "Get him over to see her. He doesn't blame her, and she needs to know that."

"I was thinking the same, but I know she'll hate me if I do it behind her back."

"Hey, you love birds!"

Both Asha and Zane froze as the familiar voice cut across the grassland. Asha turned to Zane as he dropped his arm away from her. "Have you told her?"

He shook his head. "I thought we should do it in person."

"I guess that's now then."

They walked toward Jenna, keeping a distance between them.

Jenna stood on the track, hands on hips, a huge smile on her face. "You both look so guilty."

"I'm sorry, Jen," Asha said. "We planned to tell you, but there's been a lot going on, and we knew you were busy planning the engagement party, so we didn't want to worry you."

"Worry me? Why would it worry me if my best friend and brother got together?"

"Because you always told us we weren't allowed to," Zane answered.

"I said that when we were fourteen," Jenna said. "Now you can do whatever you want, and to be honest, I couldn't be happier. I won't have to listen to either of you talk about your nonexistent love lives anymore. Which means you have to stay together."

Zane put his arm back around Asha's shoulders and pulled her to him. "Don't worry. We intend to. Now, how come you're here, unannounced? Did Mom know you were coming?"

"I called her on the way. I wanted to go through the list

for the engagement party, everyone's jobs, and discuss the logistics of having people from here come to the city for the night. I also heard a rumor about you two, so I wanted to see if it was true."

"A rumor?"

Jenna nodded. "I bumped into Matt Law. It turns out he knows Brad. They worked together years ago and have kept in touch. They catch up occasionally. I was having a drink with Brad when Matt arrived to meet with him. He wasn't all that happy to see me, which surprised me. We've always got along okay before, although I always thought he was too arrogant and full of himself."

"I imagine I'm the reason he wasn't happy to see you," Zane said. "I'm not his favorite person right now."

Jenna laughed. "Neither of you are. I ended up leaving them to their drinks after he spewed out what an awful person you are, and that Asha's been out to bring him down for a long time. It was pretty funny. The other thing he mentioned was that you were perfectly suited, and he pitied me having someone like Asha joining the family." She raised an eyebrow. "Is it that serious already?"

Asha looked at Zane. Of course, they weren't ready to make a commitment, but she thought they were serious. She expected him to brush Jenna off. His answer, therefore, sent tingles down her spine.

"We couldn't be more serious," Zane said, squeezing her hand. "But we have no reason to rush into anything and certainly wouldn't want to upstage a certain sister of mine who's planning the engagement party of the decade."

"Perfect answer," Jenna said, her white teeth flashing. "Now, I've got to get over to Mom and Dad's for dinner. Let's catch up tomorrow, Ash, and go through your list of duties as my maid of honor. Will I see you at Mom and Dad's, Zane?"

Zane shook his head. "Not tonight. Asha and I have plans. I'll see you tomorrow, and you can give me my list of instructions then."

"My only instruction is to look after my best friend and no breaking any hearts." She looked from Zane to Asha. "That goes for both of you."

Zane saluted. "Yes, ma'am." He laughed as Jenna rolled her eyes and turned to walk back to her Jeep.

Asha looked at Zane. "She's right, you know. It's probably the only advice either of us needs right now. To look after each other and not break any hearts."

Zane pulled her close and kissed the top of her forehead. "I couldn't agree more. And I can tell you right now; I intend to spend the rest of my life loving you with so much passion a broken heart is something you'll never think about again. Jenna thought bringing me home was about me finding Hope's Ridge again and falling back in love with it. It wasn't at all. It was about me finding you, and falling in love with you, which is exactly what I've done."

Asha's heart swelled with love for this strong, decent man. She thought back to Charlie's words, *love him as you wish to be loved, and you will be happy.* She knew in that moment exactly what her future held.

The End

FREE BONUS SCENES

Would you like to read more about our friends in Hope's Ridge? Sign up to my mailing list at www.silvermckenzie.com.au for exclusive access to bonus scenes featuring our Hope's Ridge family.

These aren't deleted scenes, they are bonus scenes written exclusively for my mailing list subscribers and new scenes are added each month. You'll also have opportunities to win free books and Amazon gift cards.

Their heartbreak was absolute. Can they help each other move forward?

Twelve months ago, Steph Jones's easy-going outlook was destroyed when she was involved in a motor vehicle accident that claimed the life of a five-year-old. Plagued with the horror and memories of that day, Steph cannot forgive herself and is unable to move on.

In the nearby town of Drayson's Landing, Henry Busterling is mourning the first anniversary of his daughter's death. How can Buster move forward when he blames himself for the accident? With his ex-wife serving a prison sentence, Buster's empty home is a constant reminder of all that he's lost.

For Steph, confronting the past is the only way to move

forward. But that's easier said than done when she can't look Buster in the eye, let alone be in the same room as him. Immersing herself in her yoga is much more attractive than facing the man she's been avoiding for the past year.

When circumstances force Buster and Steph together, Steph has an opportunity to admit her guilt and ask for forgiveness. But with Buster planning to move beyond Hope's Ridge and its devastating memories, has Steph left her chance to make peace with the tragedy too late?

Available now from Amazon or
www.silvermckenzie.com.au

RETURN TO HOPE'S RIDGE
Book 3 in the Hope's Ridge Series

Dream wedding—or nightmare?

When Jenna Larsen dreamed of her wedding day, she never visualized it being the most humiliating day of her life. But it was.

Devastated and mortified by the turn of events, Jenna returns to Hope's Ridge single and seeking solace in the comfort of her parents' home.

Matt Law has spent the last six months proving to the residents of Hope's Ridge that he's changed. He wants to be part of the town and part of the community, but one act undoes all of his hard work and makes him an enemy—Roy Larsen: the influential owner of the town's mill; a major supplier to Matt's businesses; and furious father of the bride.

While Matt does his best to tame Jenna and her father's

fury, there are bigger issues brewing. His father, the majority owner of his businesses, is persuaded by an outsider to move his investments from Hope's Ridge. But who exactly is venture capitalist Susan Lewis, and why does she have so much influence and power over his father?

As Jenna does her best to move on from the wreckage of her wedding day, an opportunity arises for her to work with Susan. Their business collaboration could ultimately destroy Matt's businesses. Matt ruined Jenna's life—she's single, unemployed, and without a home because of him—and now she has the opportunity to ruin his. But will she?

Available now from Amazon or
www.silvermckenzie.com.au

ABOUT THE AUTHOR

SILVER MCKENZIE is a pen name of women's fiction and domestic thriller author, Louise Guy.

Louise decided to write the Hope's Ridge series under a pen name as while the series sits nicely in the women's fiction category, the books have a stronger romantic story line than her other women's fiction titles which tend to have more intrigue and suspense. The Hope's Ridge series is also set in a fictional US town so the books are written in US English compared to Louise's other books that are set in Australia and use Australian English. She also decided Silver was a pretty cool name and it might be the only chance she has to name herself!

Silver has lived in the UK, New Zealand and Australia as well as having traveled to over thirty countries. Today, Silver and her husband are permitted to share a home in Queensland, Australia, with their two sons and a rather bossy, but beautiful cat named Pud.

If you are interested in checking out books written by Louise Guy, go to: www.louiseguy.com

Both Silver and Louise are easy to find on Facebook.